THE LATE SOONER

SALLY JADLOW

Roots & Branches
Denton, Texas

Published by Roots and Branches, an imprint of AWOC.COM Publishing, P.O. Box 2819, Denton, TX 76202, USA.

ISBN-13: 978-0-937660-32-4
ISBN-10: 0-937660-32-9

Visit the the author’s website: http://www.sallyjadlow.com

Introduction

I set about to clean out Mother's house. In the spare bedroom, I opened the antique cabinet and drew out a stack of memorabilia. Halfway down the pile of old newspapers, I discovered a speckled brown ledger book with ragged edges. It crackled as I opened the yellowed pages. Each line contained a date and a comment on life in the 1880's. It was my great-grandfather Sanford's diary.

The more I read, the more I wanted to share Sanford's story, rather than bury it in some safe place for another 119 years.

The basic story line is true and the historical facts, carefully researched. Where he left gaps, I filled in the blanks. I hope you derive as much pleasure from this book as much as I enjoyed writing it.

Come now with me to the year 1887.

CHAPTER 1

January 30, 1887 - Made an ax handle today.

Frozen gusts blitzed across the western Missouri landscape at dusk as Sanford leaned against the door to latch it behind him. He took off his gloves and rubbed his hands together over the wood stove in the kitchen.

"Lordy! It's cold out there. Saw your dad in town today. He thinks the government's going to open the Oklahoma Territory soon. Think maybe we ought to homestead down there."

Placing her mending on the kitchen table, Lucy stared at him. "Have you gone daft? You figure on pulling up stakes here to move down to that wild place?"

He plopped his hat on the ladder-back chair and shoved his hands in his pockets. "We gotta do something, my doe. Ran into Mr. Dawson today. His family's coming from back east in the next month or two."

She placed her hands on the table and leaned toward Sanford. "Mr. Dawson isn't the only landlord around, you know."

"There *is* no land for rent."

Lucy's gaze could have stared down a diamond-backed rattler. "Did you even look?"

Sanford sank into a kitchen chair, raked one hand through his dark hair, and sighed. "Lucy, I've looked high and low. There's no land to rent or to buy around Winston, even if we had the mon..."

"And a move to Oklahoma Territory's going to make things better?" She swallowed hard and clenched the skirt of her long white apron.

Taking a fresh grip on his patience, Sanford steadied his voice. “Getting too crowded here. Down there we could have 160 acres just for the taking.”

“Taking! Taking! We’d have to *move* there, Sanford.”

“My dear woman, it’s the only way we could ever have our own place.” He reached for Lucy’s hand.

Turning her back to him she whispered, “What’d we live in? A dugout? A soddy? A tent?”

He rose and took her frail shoulders gently in his big hands and said softly, “I can build you a fine house there.”

“Where’d little Frankie go to school? On the back of a wagon?” She dabbed her eyes with her apron.

“No, Lucy. Don’t fret yourself. We’ll build schools and make a place for our family.” He slipped his long arms around her waist and drew her to himself.

She began to cry softly. “Family! Am I supposed to have this new baby in a teepee like some squaw?” she sobbed into her apron.

“It won’t take long to build a nice sod house. If your folks go, we can work together.”

Whirling around Lucy looked at him through her tears. “After we move some Indian off his land. Think he’ll just hand it over to you?”

“Not at all. We don’t have to move anybody anywhere. These parcels are unclaimed. The government will *give* us the title to the land after we live on it for five years and make improvements.”

“Five years! And what if we don’t stay? Then where will you be? Besides, I don’t care *who* owns that land. Point is, we’re not *goin’*.” Wrenching away from his embrace she said, “Dad can go if he wants to. We’re stayin’. Has he talked to Mary about this loony idea? There’s no way in all of creation she’d leave Missouri and go to that God-forsaken place!”

Lucy snatched the freshly washed milk bucket and grabbed her woolen shawl off the nail beside the back door. It caught and ripped a hole. A fresh batch of tears coursed down her cheeks.

“Lucy. Wait.”

She flung the torn shawl around her shoulders and slammed the door, muttering to herself in the cold January dusk.

He knew he'd touched off a powder keg. It wasn't enough to carry the uncertainty of merely being a land renter, not a land owner. Now he had the unbridled ire of his lady-in-waiting to deal with.

***

Lucy stalked toward the barn. The very idea. He'd had some wild-hare schemes in the past, but this one beat them all. She thought he'd shed that love of wandering the summer he took off for the Washington Territory before they were married. At least that convinced him he didn't want to be a sheepherder for the rest of his life.

Brushing hot tears away she fumbled with the box of matches in the dark stall. Her hands shook as she lit the wick of the lantern, replaced the chimney, and hung the lamp on the peg overhead. The gentle glow filled the stall. Jers, their cow, ambled through the open barn door behind her, and sniffed the feeding trough while Lucy scooped out a generous portion of oats from the feed sack. She reached for the three-legged stool in the corner, sat and placed the wooden bucket under Jers. The cow's flank covered with a winter coat made a soft resting place for Lucy's head while she grabbed two teats and sobbed. Warm milk squirted against the bottom of the bucket.

"Jers, what's gonna become of us? If Dad wouldn't egg Sanford on, he'd forget this confound notion. Where'll all this end?"

Jers didn't answer. Just kept munching.

The cow's calmness seeped into her. By the time milk brimmed the bucket, Lucy's emotional cloudburst had ended. She picked up the milk, blew out the lantern, and led the cow out of the barn. "Good girl," she said, patting the cow's neck.

Lucy slipped back into the house and replaced her shawl on the nail. "I'll have to remember to mend that hole in the morning," she mumbled to herself. Was that Sanford whispering in the bedroom? Unable to make out what he said, she tiptoed closer.

From the light of the kerosene lantern in the kitchen, she saw Sanford leaning over Frankie's crib. He stroked the baby's blond ringlets as he murmured in his deep voice to his son. Oh, how she did love that man, in spite of his desire to wander. She leaned forward to catch his words.

"'Bout seven months and you'll have a little brother or sister. Somehow I'll find a way to feed us all. Promise. I'll find a way, in spite of everything."

In her heart, she was sure he would. She whispered, "Oh God! Just don't let that way lead to the wild land of the Oklahoma Territory."

***

The next Wednesday was the all-day quilting bee at Mary's, Lucy's stepmother. Lucy bundled Frankie in warm quilts while Sanford hitched the horses, Pete and Kate, to the wagon and brought it around for the short ride to the Estes farm. Her round sewing basket went into a crate along with the rising bread dough she promised to bring for the ladies potluck dinner.

"Let's go see Grandma Mary, Frankie."

He laughed and clapped his mittens together. "Bye, bye!"

"You're just full of words aren't you, little muffin?" His eyes sparkled as she plunked him on the wagon seat.

Sanford placed the box in the back. "Remember to keep these tight," he said as he handed her the reins.

"See you at the folks' tonight. Don't be late. You know how Father likes to eat his supper on time." Lucy clucked and slapped the reins on the horses' backsides. "Giddy up!"

"Don't fret, Lucy. I'll be there. Might even come early if I get my ax handle done," he said and smiled. "See you at supper." He watched his wife and child drive down the lane.

While the team plodded through the gray morning, Lucy rambled on to Frankie. "Maybe I'll share our news about our new baby with Mary today. Can't believe I'm in a family way again so soon. This time's so different from you. Then I wasn't sick even a day. Wonder if this one's a girl?"

A wave of nausea swept over her. She swallowed hard to try to will her breakfast to stay put. At the next turn, she pulled a quick jerk on the reins. "Whoa!" Before the horses stopped, Lucy wrapped the reins around the brake handle, swung down from the wagon, and threw up her breakfast in the ditch. Her hands shook as she wiped her mouth and climbed back into the wagon. Slapping the reins again on the horses, she clucked. "Get up, you two. Don't wanna' be late."

After the next mile section, she turned the team up the long lane leading to the wooden two-story home where Lucy grew up. Bare elms swayed in the wind along both sides of the rutted drive. In summer the trees were beautiful, but their shade made the dirt road slow to dry in spring rains. Mr. Estes had lived on this eighty-acre farm in Daviess County, Missouri since 1865, the year Lucy was born.

The memory of her mother rushed into her thoughts. Lucy's heart longed to see her mother stand in the door and wave a greeting again.

Wish Mom was still alive. My word. Been nine years now. If only she hadn't had Orris, she'd still be with us. Shame on me. Not Orris' fault. He looks so like her. She'd be so proud of him.

Lucy reined the horses toward the barn past the house and waved to Mary, her stepmother, standing at the kitchen window.

She thanked God for her. Her father wouldn't have made it if Mary hadn't come along. This new wife had her hands full with Orris and little Hanna, clear up to her elbows. Lucy's father spoiled half-sister Hanna so much. In Sanford's words, Hanna was liable to turn into a real ringed-tailed tooter.

Eleven months after Mary and H.W. were married little Hanna came along. At first Lucy had a hard time adjusting to a stepmother, especially one only a few years older than herself.

Lucy drove into the barn, grateful to be in out of the cold and looped the reins around the wagon brake. The smell of fresh straw warmed her chilled bones. She looked around the large barn as she unhitched the horses and tied them in a stall.

Father was better off than most. Why in the world he entertained the idea of moving to Oklahoma Territory to start all over again was beyond her. Lucy decided not to mention the subject to Mary. Maybe if no one talked about it, the idea would go away.

Lucy tucked Frankie under one arm, scooped the box off the wagon with the other, and hurried to the house.

***

Sanford watched Lucy and Frankie drive out of sight. *Gotta get busy on that ax handle. First, I'll ride Ginger to Winston to get the mail.*

Snow drifted as he drew his collar around his ears and shoved his Stetson more firmly on his head.

How am I going get my dear Lucy to move to Oklahoma Territory? Women sure are hard to get along with, especially when they're in a family way. I'll just have to figure a way–that's all there is to it.

Sanford hitched Ginger in front of the post office and slapped his hat against his thigh knocking the snow off as he slid in the door.

"Ooee!" Pulling off his leather gloves, he blew in his cupped hands, and rubbed them together.

"Getting kinda nasty out, ain't it?" the postmistress said as she poked letters into their appropriate slots.

"Reckon it'll get worse before it gets better."

She chuckled and nodded in agreement. In the small window of slot number 84 was a letter. With stiff fingers he tucked his gloves under one arm and turned the combination on the brass door. It was from his brother, Elwood in Walker, Missouri. It read,

Dear Sanford,

I've been asking around about some land. Mr. Fry's got some ground he's willing to rent for a year. Went out to take a look. There is a nice well on the place. Barn's in good shape, but it needs some repair on the south side. Just one drawback, the house is kind of small and run down.

I think you could get it if you act fast; told him we would let him know in a few days. Later I overheard somebody at the general store inquiring about it.

Write soon.

Elwood.

As Sanford unhitched Ginger, he shoved the letter into his shirt pocket. He'd not considered Walker as a possibility. Elwood seemed to like it there; probably because that's where Orilla, his intended was. With any luck, there might even be some land to buy.

Light snow laid a powdery blanket over the landscape as he urged his horse home at a gallop. Grateful for the cover of the barn, he tied Ginger in a stall, gave her a generous portion of oats, and went to work on his ax handle. His expert eye searched for just the right length of split white hickory in the barrel beside the workbench; one without knots and narrow growth lines would do best.

"This one'll make a good-un," he said as he pulled out a split log that came almost to his hip. Placing it in a vise he fashioned the ax handle with his drawknife. It wasn't long before he had a nice curve to the handle and chiseled the straight end just small enough to fit the hole in the ax head. He tried the ax head on. Perfect! Notching the top of the handle with the grain of the wood, he drove a small wedge in the notch to hold the ax head in place. Then he set the handle, head and all, to soak in a bucket of linseed oil to make the wood swell. Drawing his pocket watch out of his overalls, he popped the lid and checked the time. Four-thirty. Good. Just enough time do chores, wash up, and get over to the Estes' by six.

***

After a supper of roast beef, carrots, potatoes and Lucy's fresh bread, Mary cleared the plates while Lucy removed the remainder of the food.

"I'll fetch the dessert, Lucy. You go have a seat." Mary was always more at ease in the kitchen when no one looked over her shoulder.

"All right. If you're sure there's nothing more I can do."

"Oh, if you insist, take this cream in for the bread pudding."

Lucy placed the pitcher in front of her father and sat. Mary always served him first.

"Thank you kindly, Daughter," H.W. said as he placed his napkin beside his plate and leaned back in his chair. "Hanna and Orris, take Frankie upstairs to play. Mama'll give you dessert later." The children took off like a shot.

H. W. scooted his chair back, jammed his thumbs into his vest pockets, and stared at the table. After a moment, he looked up. A subtle grin played across his face. He cleared his throat. "What do ya'll think of this fine idea of us moving to the Oklahoma Territory?"

Lucy's dinner crept back up her throat. She swallowed hard. Can't get sick here. They'll know I'm in a family way again. She hadn't confided in Mary yet and she wanted to announce the news in her own time–certainly not like this.

She shot a quick glance across the table at Sanford that telegraphed her thought of "Tell him we're not going."

Avoiding her gaze he placed the bone china coffee cup in its saucer, wiped his handlebar moustache with his napkin and shifted in his chair.

"Don't think we'll be moving to the Oklahoma Territory with you all. My little woman's not of a mind to go."

That's the way, Sanford. Tell him we're staying right here in Daviess County. Another wave of nausea swept over her.

Sanford drew a letter from his shirt pocket, unfolded it and put it on the table in front of H.W. "Fact is, we might be moving to Walker. I got a letter from Elwood today. He said we might be able to rent some land from a Mr. Fry. I have to let him know right away."

Lucy couldn't believe her ears. What? What did he say? Walker! Where did this idea come from? Is the whole world against us staying put right here?

She felt her heart pounding in her ears. Sanford's voice sounded far away. His mouth was moving, but she couldn't comprehend his words. Then everything went black.

Sanford gently pressed a cool rag to Lucy's face while she came to on the couch in the parlor. Where was she? What happened? Then she remembered. Supper. Oklahoma Territory. Walker.

Her thoughts raced. This is not how she pictured this evening. Her plans to announce the new little one during dessert had gone by the wayside. Her Father and Elwood stole her thunder. Her news would just have to wait for a better time. God only knew where they would be by the time this little one was born.

Announcing Lucy needed to get home, they left without the bread pudding.

On the way home, he drove the wagon with Ginger tied to the back. Well-bundled, the baby slept on Lucy's lap. The snow had stopped and the sky was filled with bright stars. In the snowy silence the iron wagon wheels bumped on the frozen road. She wanted to say something, but no words made it past the lump in her throat.

Finally, Sanford coughed and spoke. "I should have talked to you about the letter from Elwood before I told your father. Sorry."

"I just don't know what's gonna happen to us," she croaked. Taking a fresh grip on Frankie she looked straight ahead. After a long silence, her pump was primed and she let loose. Words spilled out in a torrent. "Don't you understand? I don't want to move anywhere. Not even Walker. I know times are hard, but they'll get better. There's got to be some place near Winston. Maybe you could check around Kidder."

"No use. I've checked all the way to Trenton and back, my doe. Every place is spoken for. New people are settling here from back east every day. Land's as scarce as hen's teeth. I don't want to leave these parts, either. From the looks of things, we don't have a choice."

Trying to get a grip on her emotions, Lucy fought back the tears. His words stabbed at her heart like a flaming arrow. The silence hung like an icy blanket on the cold night air. Undisturbed snow radiated the brightness from the full moon.

Frankie coughed.

CHAPTER 2

February 4, 1887 - Going to Walker for a look-see.

Flopping on the feather-ticked mattress, Lucy watched Sanford pack his valise. "I wish you wouldn't go." The aroma of bacon and eggs filled the house in the half-light of early morning.

"Have to. Got to find some place to farm. I can't raise crops with no dirt to do it in."

"I know. It's just so lonely when you're gone." Lucy touched his hand. Her eyes rested on his steel blue eyes framed by his dark handlebar moustache and heavy eyebrows. She really hated being alone, even for a few days.

He took hold of her hand, and pulled her into his reassuring arms. "You'll not be lonely. Why, you'll be so busy with Frankie I'll bet you'll hardly even miss me."

"That's not like you being here, Sanford."

"I'll be back soon, my doe. Elwood says I've got to act fast on that parcel he's found to rent." He rested his cheek on the top of her head. "I don't want to go, but I've got to find someplace for us to be."

They headed for the kitchen, arm in arm.

She took his plate from off the warming shelf on the back of the wood stove, poured him a cup of coffee, and sat to watch him eat.

He paused before he took his first bite. "Aren't you having anything?"

Lucy shook her head. "Maybe later. The smell of bacon doesn't set too well." Mornings seemed to be the worst time for her nausea.

Fourteen-month-old Frankie awoke and climbed out of his small bed. He ran on unsteady legs across the rough kitchen floor in his bare feet and nightshirt.

"Daddy!" Frankie held up his arms.

Sanford scooped him up and let him sit on his lap while he finished breakfast.

Between bites he fed Frankie bits of bacon. "You be good for Mama, all right? Daddy has to go away. I'll be back soon."

Frankie coughed and rubbed his nose and eyes with his fat fist.

"Where'd you get that cough, little one? Mama better give you some elixir."

As Lucy finished the dishes she saw Henry, Sanford's dad, pull the team into the snowy yard. "Your dad's here."

Sanford pulled his watch out of his overalls and opened the clock's face. "He's running kind of late this morning."

Lucy grabbed Frankie before he could dart for the door. "Not so fast, you sneaky scamp."

Sanford wrapped his lanky arms around Lucy and Frankie.

"Hurry home. I hate it when you're gone."

"Don't fret. I'll be back before you know it." Sanford tousled his son's silky curls and said, "Take care of Mother while I'm gone, little man." Planting a kiss on both of them, he gave them one last squeeze, grabbed his bag, and hightailed it to Henry's wagon.

The February wind howled in protest against Lucy's effort to close the door. She kissed Frankie and frowned. "Liable to catch your death in that cold air, my sweet. I'll fix you some nice warm oatmeal in just a minute."

The swirling snow blurred her view as Sanford mounted the wagon, slung his valise behind the seat, and drew his collar up to his hat. Turning the team of mules toward the road, Henry waved a farewell. They disappeared into the blinding whiteness.

A powerful sense of foreboding fell over Lucy like a shroud. She shuddered. Running back to the door, she jerked it open, and called after them to come back. Only the wailing wind replied as she forced the door closed. Frankie coughed again.

"Father in heaven, bless little Frankie and keep Sanford safe on his journey," Lucy prayed as she sat Frankie on the floor and patted his head.

By noon, his cough sounded tighter, even though she dosed him with elixir. She rocked him in the walnut rocker, a hand made wedding gift from Grandfather Deering, but Frankie was not comforted. His cheeks burned in her futile attempt to break his fever with a wet rag to his forehead. He squirmed in her lap and pushed her hand away, crying.

"Little muffin, sounds like you're getting hoarse, or is it my imagination? Oh, that someone would stop by and fetch Doc Harris."

Through the afternoon, the baby refused to sleep or be comforted as she walked the floor with him. Finally, she laid him down. "Mama'll be right back, Frankie. I'll go to the well and pump some cold water. Maybe that'll cool you off."

Sharp wind seeped into her inmost being while she pumped water into her bucket. Back in the house, she heard Frankie's raspy cry. That sound tore at her heart. "God help us!" she whispered. If only Sanford were here.

Frankie refused to drink through the night. When she got a gulp or two down him, he threw it up. He was listless; slept for only short periods. His breathing came in shallow, rapid jerks.

"Maybe if I lay you down, you'll sleep."

His pitiful whimpers accompanied his waking moments.

What would Mother have done? If only she were here. She'd probably have some remedy. He's never been sick like this before.

What else can I do? Lucy could feel panic rising in her as the clock on the mantle struck two, three, and four.

***

Mid-afternoon on Saturday, Lucy's dad stopped on his way home from town.

When she came to the door he took one look at her and said "What's the matter, Daughter?"

She squared her shoulders and fought back tears. "Thank God you're here. I haven't slept since Sanford left. Baby's sick."

With hat in hand H.W. rushed into the bedroom and knelt beside the tiny walnut bed. Drawing off his glove he laid his hand on the sleeping child. Lucy followed close behind.

The look of alarm on her father's face caused Lucy's heart to skip a beat.

He stood. "I better go for Doc Harris. Saw him on the street in town."

"Send a telegram to Sanford, in Walker," Lucy called after him. From the kitchen window, she watched his buckboard light out for town under a thick overcast sky.

In the late afternoon the sky cleared. Long shadows cast across the snowy landscape. Would they ever come? Every bone in her body ached. At dusk, Doc Harris drove his buggy into the yard followed by H.W.

She met them at the door.

A shadow of concern crossed Doc's face when he heard Frankie's croupy, worn-out cry.

"Let's have a look. Lucy, you light the lantern." Tenderly, he lifted Frankie's blanket-wrapped body from his bed and put him on the kitchen table. Lucy held her breath as she watched Doc examine the boy from head to toe.

He asked, "How long since he ate or drank?"

"Yesterday morning."

H.W. and Lucy tried to read Doc's face. Lucy had to force herself to breathe. Frankie hardly resisted the many prods and pokes.

Doc took his temperature and announced, "103," as he wrapped Frankie again and handed him back to Lucy. "Got vinegar? I need to break the fever."

The vinegar sponge bath helped Frankie to keep down a few sips of water. He drifted into a fitful sleep.

"When's Sanford coming back, H.W.?" Doc said.

"If he caught the evening train, he'll be back in Winston tomorrow morning."

"Meet the train. Bring him home. I'll stay here."

From the tone of Doc's voice, Lucy knew the situation was grave. If only Sanford hadn't left, none of this would've happened. If he walked in the door this very minute, it wouldn't be too soon.

Her dad interrupted her thoughts. “I’ll swing by home and get Mary and bring her back here. Maybe she can help.”

“Don’t Dad. I wouldn’t want Hanna and Orris to get this fever. We’ll manage.”

***

Sanford received the telegram at brother Elwood’s just before supper Saturday evening. He barely made it on board the train just as the conductor announced, “Board! All aboard!”

Usually, the gentle sway and the clickity-clack of the steel wheels made Sanford sleepy. Not this time. Every time he closed his eyes his only child’s chubby face loomed before him. There seemed to be no end to the track from southwest Missouri northward. Each time the train stopped, his frustration grew. He wanted to pray, but wasn’t too sure God listened to people who only called on him in a pinch.

Early Sunday morning, the train chugged into Winston. Sanford squinted through the steam and spotted the Estes’ team and buckboard hitched beside the station. Before the train came to a final stop, he gathered his bag and jumped to the boot-worn platform.

H.W. was out the depot door like a jackrabbit, looking drawn and solemn, like the day his first wife died.

Sanford’s heart sank. “How is he?”

H.W. shook his head. “Ain’t good.” On the hour ride home, he filled Sanford in on the details in the pre-dawn darkness.

The heavy odor of vinegar made Sanford’s eyes water when he entered the house. Lucy slumped in the rocker beside Frankie’s bed, vinegar rag in hand.

“I thought you would never get here,” she whispered. “He’s so sick.”

Without a word Sanford sank onto one knee beside the bed of his first-born. Tears welled up in his eyes and spilled down his face as Sanford stroked Frankie’s hair. The baby burned with fever.

He whispered, “What a difference two days make. This can’t be happening. Must be a nightmare. My poor boy. My poor little man.” Sanford felt Doc’s hand on his shoulder. “Can’t you do something, Doc?” he asked as he stood to remove his coat.

"Gonna give him castor oil and a cool water enema. Gotta' get the fever down. Just keeps climbin'. Vinegar bath hasn't worked."

***

Sunday evening, Frankie's fever still refused to break in spite of Doc's best efforts. He even bathed him in a tepid bath in the galvanized wash tub. That didn't help either. Frankie was fading before their eyes. His once red cheeks were pale and sunken–his breathing shallow.

Although Lucy fought to stay awake in the rocker, her eyes drooped. She hadn't slept in a bed since Thursday night. Falling into a restless sleep, she dreamed. In the dream, friends and neighbors gathered in the front room in an eerie silence. What were they here for? Why were they so somber? In front of the fireplace was a small pine box on two sawhorses. The people parted, staring at her as she moved toward the box. Unable to make out their words, she peered inside. It was a child, a black opaque veil over its face. Lucy raised the veil to peek at the child. She awoke with a start. A stifled scream escaped from her lips. The child in the coffin was Frankie.

"Oh, God, no!"

"What's wrong? Sanford knelt on one knee beside the rocker and put his arm around her."

She buried her face in her hands and sobbed.

He drew her closer.

"What is it? Why did you scream?"

"Ohhhh... it was so real... it was Frankie's funeral."

She felt him stiffen. "Get hold of yourself, my doe. It was just a dream. I'll not have you talking crazy-like."

In her heart she knew it was more than a dream–that it wasn't crazy talk.

Tuesday morning Frankie's fever soared to 105 and remained there, despite Doc's remedies. The baby's body contorted in waves of convulsions, accompanied by diarrhea. His eyes rolled upward in his head; his pale face twitched; lips blue.

Neither parent could speak the unspeakable. They didn't dare even think it, but when they looked at their child, they knew.

Wednesday Frankie no longer cried at all. At one point he opened his eyes, stared at the ceiling and softly said "Mama."

"We're here, darling. Everything's gonna be all right," Lucy said. She stroked his forehead and gently kissed him. How much more could his little body take? She knew nothing short of a miracle would save him now.

Thursday evening Frankie's arms and legs grew cold. Lucy looked into the doctor's eyes as she stood. "Oh Doc! Maybe his fever's broke!"

Doc gently gripped her arm. "No Lucy. It's time to let him go," he said with a kind firmness.

"Lucy, Doc's right. We've done all we can do." He folded her into his arms.

Lucy pounded his chest with her fists. "Sanford! Do something. Our child can't die."

"Done all we can do, my doe." His voice cracked and his tears wet Lucy's hair. They clung to each other with a futile hope that maybe, if they just held one another tight enough...

A little past midnight Friday morning, Frankie's limbs suddenly straightened, then relaxed. With a shudder, he was gone, released from his suffering.

The kerosene lamp flickered on a nearby table as Lucy sat on the edge of Frankie's bed. Tears poured from her red, sleep-deprived eyes. She placed his tiny hand in hers and traced her finger across his dimpled knuckles.

Sanford knelt beside her in tears. He placed his left hand gently on his child's still chest and slipped his right arm securely around the shoulders of the woman who only two years ago was his lovely bride. She buried her head in Sanford's chest; her grief echoing in the darkened room. A part of her died inside.

"If only you hadn't gone, maybe none of this would have happened," she wailed.

CHAPTER 3

March 30, 1887-Tending to Lucy.

On Friday morning, word spread of Deering's tragedy throughout Winston and the surrounding countryside. Lucy's father and Sanford went to the sawmill to buy some pine lumber from Sam Youtsey for a tiny coffin.

"Sure sorry to hear of your boy," Sam said as he loaded the lumber into the wagon.

Sanford merely nodded his head and held out a silver dollar.

"Never mind, m'boy," Sam said as he waved his hand. "Just take the lumber, son."

"Thanks, Sam."

There was a knowing when their eyes met. Sam had lost his only child in a flood several years before. The boy and Sanford were best friends. Billy was only six when he was swept away by torrential spring rains in the river. They never found his body. After that, Sam always referred to Sanford as his "second son."

"Much obliged. Appreciate it." Sanford tipped his hat and put the boards into the back of the wagon.

"Least I can do."

Neither H.W. nor Sanford spoke until they passed the gravediggers in the cemetery.

"Ground's sure froze solid," H.W. said.

"Yup. Got their work cut out for 'em, fer sure."

"Get up there, darn ya! Ain't got all day." H.W. slapped the reins on the rumps of the horses. "Reminds me of the day we buried Martha."

Sanford nodded. "That it does."

"Sure be a glorious day when we don't have to do anymore burying."

"Yup." Sanford hoped he'd not see another burying day the rest of his life.

***

While the men built the coffin in the barn, Tom Haynes stopped by the house with a basket of fried chicken from his wife, Susan. Lucy opened the note pinned on the top of the basket. It read,

Lucy, so sorry to hear your sad news. I'll not be at the funeral. I've not told anyone yet, but I'm in a family way. Momma always said 'It's bad luck for a woman who's in waiting to go to a funeral.' I don't think I believe that tale, but I'm not taking any chances.

Accept this chicken with our deep-felt sorrow.

Love, Susan

P.S. I'll come by in a week or so to look in on you.

With shaking hands, Lucy sat at the kitchen table. She wished *she* could be excused from the funeral with such a note. After all, wasn't she in waiting too? Taking a deep breath, she picked up a needle and embroidery thread to finish sewing Frankie's name and death date on the corner of his black shroud.

The men finished the coffin before noon. The funeral was set for three o'clock.

Rev. Jameson arrived around two. Lucy sent Sanford out to greet him. She stayed in the bedroom pretending to get dressed, not wanting to see anyone. After all, nothing anyone could say could bring her precious child back. If she had her way, they could just dispense with the funeral all together. After all, she had already seen the funeral in her dream before Frankie died.

At three, Sanford knocked softly on the bedroom door. "Lucy, it's time."

The words made Lucy stiffen. No matter how hard she tried, her feet wouldn't move.

When she didn't answer, Sanford opened the door with a creek and extended his hand. The look of sadness on his face stung her heart. They walked together into the living room holding each other up till they got to the two empty chairs near the coffin.

Rev. Jameson led the gathered friends and neighbors in the hymn, "Shall We Gather at the River." Everything in Lucy wanted to be done with this life right now and gather at God's river with her son.

The reverend's remarks went unheard by Lucy. She kept a tight grip on Sanford's hand, her only anchor on reality. The nightmare of the Sunday before played out before her eyes. She felt limp, like a shirt boiled too long on the laundry fire.

After the funeral, Sanford nailed the lid on the coffin and carefully placed it on the back of the buckboard for the short ride to the cemetery.

A few close friends and neighbors followed. Winter dusk was about to swallow the last rays of daylight. In the gathering darkness, Reverend Jameson said a few words before the grave diggers lowered the coffin by ropes into the black hole. Lucy winced when the first shovel full of dirt hit the coffin. A slight scent of snow drifted on the crisp air that bit her ears. Lucy drew her wool shawl tighter around her shoulders.

On the way home, the thump of shoveled dirt on the coffin echoed in her ears. Her arms never felt so empty; her heart so wounded.

Finally she spoke. "I have no strength to go on. I'd curl up and die if I could."

"Don't talk like that. I can't lose you. Losing Frankie's enough for one lifetime."

With Sanford's help, Lucy struggled to get down from the buckboard and into the house. He hurried off to the barn to do chores.

Loneliness engulfed her as she sat in the dark kitchen. She folded her arms on the table and rested her head, too worn to cry. If only this was all just a bad dream. If only she could wake up. If only... if only...

Sanford came back from the barn, lifted the lid on the well, and lowered the bucket of milk into the cool water for safekeeping. Removing his boots at the back door, he felt his way into the dark kitchen. He set the half-full egg bucket on the table, took off his coat, and crouched beside Lucy. They held each other for a long time in the darkness. Words weren't needed.

***

Early the next week Susan stopped by. Lucy, still in her nightclothes and uncombed hair, opened the door a crack and squinted into the bright light reflecting off the new-fallen snow.

Susan held out a large pot. “Brought you some ham hocks and beans. Figure you don’t need to fool with cooking at a time like this.”

She was a nice enough neighbor, but Lucy was in no mood for a visit, not even with Susan.

Opening the door just wide enough to grab the bail on the pot, Lucy drew it inside. “Thanks. Appreciate it. Don’t want to keep you from your chores.”

She didn’t invite Susan in for tea, or even ask how she felt. Just closed the door in her face. Lucy sagged against the door and waited for her friend to leave. Shortly, she heard Susan’s footsteps on the steps.

Sanford came in from the barn and took off his coat, hung it on the peg by the back door, and removed his boots. “Thought I saw Susan’s buggy out front.”

“She brought our supper,” Lucy said as she stirred the simmering pot.

“Didn’t you ask her in?”

“Nope.”

“That’s a long drive on this cold day.”

“Yup.”

“We’ll have these ham and beans she brought for supper as soon as I make some cornbread. She set the pot on the back of the wood stove, opened the stove’s side door, and threw in another split log.

Lucy did feel bad about being so short with her friend. She just wasn’t up to listening to Susan go on about her new baby, or something she saw in the mail-order catalogue, or the news from town. Nothing mattered anymore. Not even the little life growing within her.

For two weeks Lucy refused to leave the house. She still had trouble keeping food down. Whether it was the pregnancy or the grief over losing Frankie, she wasn’t sure. When Sanford wasn’t there, the quiet of the four walls almost overwhelmed her. The house was becoming a tomb. Hers.

Before breakfast on Saturday, Sanford said, "Going to town today. Will you go with me?"

She opened the oven door, drew the cornbread out, and set it on the table. "Don't feel like seeing folks. Go ahead," she said while she stirred the ham and beans once more. She wasn't sure which was worse, going to town to face people or staying at home, imprisoned by the stillness.

Sanford waited for her answer. "Be pleased if you'd ride with me."

After a long pause, Lucy said in a quivering voice, "Might start crying. Don't forget to take the eggs. Trade them for flour." She dipped a ladle full of soup into a bowl and set it at Sanford's place and slid into her spot at the table.

Picking up his spoon he said, "Aren't you gonna eat? You're not taking in enough to keep a bird alive."

She gazed at the floor. "Not hungry."

A scowl shadowed his face. "Lucy, you need to think of that little one. If I see Doc Harris in town, I'm going to ask him to come by."

Lucy didn't answer. She stood and shuffled toward the bedroom.

"Rest up."

She called over her shoulder, "Haven't done much else. I'll try to have supper ready when you get home."

If she did have supper ready, it would be the first time since Frankie's death. Sanford had been the head cook and bottle-washer for two weeks now.

***

Trade was swift in Martin's general store on this late winter Saturday. Food stocks were waning for most folks and it was almost time to plant. Sanford didn't stay to visit with neighbors seated around the checkerboard near the potbelly stove. He traded the eggs for a sack of flour and a sack of corn meal and hurried to find Doc Harris. On the wooden sidewalk outside the general store he spied Doc entering his office.

"Doc! Wait a minute."

Doc turned and waved. "Sanford! Come sit a spell. How's Lucy? Haven't seen her in town since..."

Sanford's words spilled out in a rush. "I'm worried. Lucy's not bouncing back. She sleeps all the time; won't even see her friends and refuses to come to town with me. I need you to stop by and have a look at her, Doc. She looks awful peaked. On top of everything else, we're gonna have another little one come August."

Doc slapped him on the shoulder and shook his hand. "Well, well. Glad to hear about that little one, Sanford. Maybe that'll help her deal with her loss."

He nodded and took a deep breath. "She's sure been strange ever since Frankie's passing. Hope it's nothing permanent. I need my woman back. Don't know what I would do without her."

"Tell you what. I'm going out that way this afternoon. I'll look in on her."

"Thanks Doc. Appreciate it." Sanford made a hasty retreat homeward.

***

Lucy didn't get up later that afternoon when she heard voices in the kitchen.

"Have a seat, Doc. Mint tea all right?"

"Sounds good to me. Mint tea's a good remedy for any ailment."

Sanford poured hot water into the blue willow teapot from the kettle on the stove and called to Lucy, "Honey, come have some hot tea. It'll do you good."

Swinging her feet over the side of the bed she stood. The room seemed to whirl as she reached for her robe. Shuffling into the kitchen she sat across from Doc, rubbing her neck. It felt a little swollen. Sanford poured her a cup of hot tea, which made her feel better.

She could feel Doc's intense gaze.

"Sanford says you're feeling puny."

"No spunk, Doc." She peered into her teacup and avoided his eyes.

"You look a little pale."

Fiddling with the hem of the gingham tablecloth she felt tears rising from within. The stress of the past few weeks tumbled in on her. “Feel all washed out,” she peeped. Tears brimmed her eyes; her lower lip quivered. “Did Sanford tell you we’re having another one about August?”

Doc nodded. “He mentioned it.”

As Lucy reached over and poured Doc another cup. He touched her hand. It was hot.

Worry lines wrinkled his forehead. “How long you had that rash and fever?”

“Since yesterday, I guess.”

“Does the rash itch?”

Lucy nodded.

“Try not to scratch. It’ll leave scars.”

“What is it, Doc?”

He peered over his glasses at her. She felt like a bug under a microscope. “Looks to me like you got the German Measles, little lady.”

“That bad, Doc?” Sanford asked.

“Don’t think so. She may have that fever a few more days. It’s nothing to be concerned about. Rash’ll be gone soon. Just take it easy. Didn’t you have the measles as a kid?”

She shrugged. “Guess not.”

He turned to Sanford. “Keep her comfortable. She’ll be down for a few days. I’ll stop by when I’m out this way.” He drew out a bottle from his bag. “Give her one of these blood pills morning and night. It’ll help pink up those cheeks.”

Doc turned back to Lucy and winked. “We’ll have you up and about in no time, my dear.”

The rash and fever continued its course and was gone by the end of the week, just as Doc predicted.

***

The next Saturday Sanford brought news from town. “Saw Sam Youtsey today. He asked how things were.”

Lucy turned from the dishwater and dried her hands on a tea towel. “What did you tell him?”

“I admitted things were pretty tight. He said he could use some help at the sawmill. Told me to be over there tomorrow morning.”

Lucy's eyes met his and she nodded her head with a slight smile.

His heart skipped a beat. It was the first time his doe had showed any sign on life since Frankie's death.

"That's good. We could sure use the money to buy flour and seed... that is if we had any land to plant it in."

He continued, "We do! Got this letter from Mr. Dawson. His family isn't coming to Missouri for a while after all, so we can stay on this place a few more months."

Lucy's smile grew across her face. "That's wonderful! Two surprises in one day," she whispered.

"I'll have to plant after work but maybe the crops'll be decent this year. Then we could put some money by for a place of our own, if one came up for sale."

She put her arms around Sanford's neck and whispered, "I hope so."

***

The good news, the blood pills, and the spring air seemed to make Lucy feel better. She even began to eat again. The worst of the nausea had passed and she didn't stay in her nightgown all day.

The next week all the rash was gone. She made an angel food cake and took it to her friend, Susan. While there, Lucy learned Susan's baby was due in September, just one month after hers.

CHAPTER 4

October 15, 1887 - Butchered a hog.

Spring began to thaw winter's grief until Decoration Day in late May. Lucy and Sanford took some fragrant lilacs and blue bachelor buttons from the yard to adorn Frankie's grave for the occasion.

They knelt at the grave to pull the dandelions and other weeds. Lucy looked over the cemetery as she sat back on her heels. "Seems like yesterday when we were here."

Sanford continued digging dandelions with his pocketknife. "Or a hundred years. It feels like forever since I held my son."

Lucy stared at Frankie's headstone and rested her hands in her disappearing lap.

"What are you thinking about?"

She whispered, "Hope everything'll be okay with the new baby."

Sanford slipped his arm around Lucy's expanding waist and assured her, "It will, my doe. Don't you go fretting about it. Things are going to be better. Just wait and see."

In spite of Sanford's encouragement, doubt gnawed at Lucy like a tireless rat all through June and July. Fear sneaked up on her while she hoed the garden, cooked, or cleaned. The unsettling feeling lurked around every corner. There really was no basis for it. This baby was quite active. Still... doubt and fear reined in Lucy's heart.

One day over tea at Susan's, Lucy rested her hands on her swelling belly. Susan took another cookie from the plate and paused. "Awfully quiet today, my friend. Something bothering you?"

Lucy hesitated and then spoke as if she had a hard time finding the words. "Do you... do you sometimes worry about your little one, Susan?"

"Only if I let it." Susan offered her another cookie.

"I just can't shake this dread."

Looking at Lucy with a compassionate earnestness Susan said, "I'll pray for you, Lucy." She took a bite of cookie and asked, "Read your Bible much?"

"Mostly at church," Lucy shrugged.

"I find I have fewer fearful thoughts when I read my Bible and pray more."

Lucy took a sip of tea. "I'll have to try it."

***

One evening before supper, Lucy was aware of Sanford's intense gaze as she moved about the kitchen in her loose-fitting dress, tied at the waist. She looked at him and smiled. "Something on your mind, my dear?"

"Been thinking. I can't take time off from harvest to be home with you till the baby comes."

"And? ..." she turned and gave him a sideward glance while she rolled out the biscuits.

"Your time's coming soon. You might be eased a bit if you stayed with your folks till after the baby comes."

The prospect of boarding at someone else's house didn't excite Lucy, but she was not enthused about being alone when the baby came either. She finished cutting the biscuits, wiped her hands on her apron, and popped them into the oven. She straightened, rubbed her lower back, and put her hands on her hips. With a sigh she said, "Let's ask the folks on Sunday. This one seems to be resting lower than Frankie ever did. Maybe it'll be here soon."

***

The tiny choir sang with gusto in the small white wood frame church.

"What a friend we have in Jesus,
All our sins and griefs to bear,
All because we do not carry,
Everything to God in prayer."

After the choir sang, Lucy seemed to have new ears to hear Rev. Jameson's message. Certain phrases seemed to stick in her mind while he preached.

"If you've received Jesus into your heart and life, you are His sheep; He is your good Shepherd."

Lucy had heard that all her life, but today it took on new meaning.

"He's in charge of every minute of your life."

The bad ones and the good ones.

"Don't fret about anything."

Had he been listening in the window at Susan's house the other day when we had tea?

"Nothing happens to you without His permission. Learn to enter into the rest He provides in his everlasting arms."

I never thought about God having arms to rest in. Interesting.

Draw near to Him through reading your Bible."

Exactly what Susan said.

After church they gathered at the Estes' for a dinner of fried chicken, mashed potatoes and cream gravy, green beans with bacon, and a fresh blackberry pie.

Between bites Sanford asked, "Do you think Lucy could stay here till the baby comes? I don't want her to be alone when its time."

"Of course, Sanford. If you didn't bring it up, we were going to. From the looks of things, it might be any day now," H.W. chuckled with a twinkle in his eye.

By evening, Lucy was settled into the Estes' spare bedroom with her sparse belongings. It was the room she occupied before she was married. To be sleeping here again seemed strange in a way, but then again, comforting.

***

Early the following morning before daybreak Sanford joined other neighbors at the Owen's place to begin the harvest. He took time off from his sawmill job with Sam Youtsey, as did most everyone else because every available hand was needed in the field. They all worked as a team. When they cleared one field of hay, they moved on to another neighbor's field until all the hay was cut and stored in barns. Since Mr. Owen's fields were far away, Sanford and the other workers slept under the stars, instead of coming home at night.

While Sanford was gone, Lucy had time to let Rev. Jameson's message sink into her soul. Since childhood she trusted Jesus to save her from hell, but now she had a new peace–a deeper understanding–a new desire to read the Bible. Pastor's words bounced around in her head like a jackrabbit. *I'm His sheep; He's my shepherd. He's in charge.* A gentle joy began to well up within her.

***

On the first Friday in August, Lucy awoke before sunup. From the feel of it, today was going to be a scorcher. Try as she might, she couldn't find a comfortable position in the feather bed. From out of nowhere a sharp, cramping pain gripped her. She grabbed her belly, gasped, and whispered, "Today must be my baby's birthday."

Lucy raised to one elbow and attempted to sit up. Then between pains, she struggled to sit on the edge of the bed. "Mary... Mary... it's time," Lucy called softly, trying to keep a calm steady voice.

Mary was at the door in an instant. "Looks like we better get Doc out here in a hurry, girl." It seemed strange to Lucy that she called her "girl" because her stepmother was only ten years older than herself.

Bustling out of the room, Mary took charge. "H.W., get dressed. Go fetch Doc. I'll get some water boiling in the laundry kettle. Now Lucy, you relax. Everything's going to be all right."

From a bureau drawer, Mary drew out a box of clean rags she had tucked away for the birth. By now Lucy's little brother and stepsister were up. Mary poured each child a glass of milk.

"Hurry and eat your oatmeal and sourdough. Orris, soon as you're done, take Hanna and go down the road to Mrs. Babcock's. Don't come home till you're sent for. When you all come back you'll be an aunt and uncle again."

Lucy was relieved Mary sent them away. She felt children had no business hanging around the house when the birth of an infant was imminent, even if they were her own brother and half-sister. Laying back in the bed she tried to rest between pains–anxious to finally welcome her new little one.

Doc Harris arrived mid-morning. "Looks like we're gonna have a baby before noon, little lady."

"Sounds good to me, Doc. I'm ready."

Mary encouraged Lucy through each pain. "You can do it, girl. Just keep pushing... keep pushing."

"Glad you're here Mary. I appreciate a hand to hold," Lucy said. Deep inside she wished Sanford was here, but that wasn't possible. She'd just have to make the best of it. Before long, Lucy began to wonder just how much longer she could endure this constant, drawing pain.

She heard Doc say, "I'll have to keep you in mind, Mary, if I need an assistant. You're doing a great job. This'll be over soon."

Lucy held on those words while she gave yet another push. Gratefully, this labor was easier and quicker than with Frankie.

Little Nora Margaret was born according to Doc Harris' prediction, just before the walnut mantle clock struck noon. Little Nora was terribly blue, but pinked up with a few loud, lusty cries.

"Nothing to worry about. Just had the cord around her neck, that's all," Doc said confidently. He wiped the baby off with some terry toweling, wrapped her snugly in flannel sheeting and handed her over. "Here you are Mama. Meet your little girl," he said with a wide grin.

At last. Lucy's arms were full again. Gratefulness washed over her in waves. She marveled at each tiny finger, her button nose, and long graceful eyelashes. What a beauty.

Thank you, oh thank You, God.

Doc gathered his instruments in his bag while Mary picked up and straightened the room.

"Where's the father of this fine young lady?"

"He's harvesting out by the Owens' place."

"I have to look in on a young one out that way. I'll stop by and tell Sanford he has a 'Daddy's girl.'" In no time at all he was out the door.

Lucy put the crying babe to her breast. "She must have been born hungry, Mary."

"Sure looks like it from here, girl."

Soon Nora was asleep. Lucy's heart was so filled with love for this little girl she thought her heart would burst. "Thank you Jesus, for restoring my joy," she whispered.

On Sunday, Sanford arrived to meet his little girl.

"What a beauty," he whispered when he took the tiny bundle into his arms. "Looks just like her pretty mama." Sanford gazed into Lucy's eyes and touched her cheek. "Never saw you more beautiful, my dearest doe."

Lucy's joy spread all over her face. Sometimes Sanford knew just the perfect words to say. He was right; things had gotten better, in spite of the struggles of the last few months.

***

Lucy and Nora stayed at the Estes' for two more weeks while Mary fussed over her and Nora. It was hard to keep Hanna away from the baby. It wasn't that Lucy was afraid she would harm Nora, but a seven-year-old was not to be left alone with such a tiny one, either, especially not this seven-year-old.

Harvest would be over before too long. At breakfast the next morning Lucy announced, "I'd best be getting home, Mary. I'm missing my own place."

"I know how that is, Lucy. There's no place like your own." She added quickly, "But we hate to see you go. Sure enjoyed you being here."

"Thanks Mary, for all you've done for us. We'll come for a visit soon."

"Glad to oblige." Mary patted her on the shoulder. "Do come back soon now, you hear?"

H.W. drove Lucy and Nora home in the buggy. The late August morning smelled of fresh-cut hay. Lucy looked at her dad. Such a handsome man she thought. Although he was graying, he sat ramrod straight on the buckboard seat. She was proud to be his daughter. Her thoughts wandered through the past while they bumped over the dusty roads.

"Dad, Mary's such a blessing."

"Yep. Lucky I found her."

"I still feel sad I didn't get to tell Mom goodbye. She went so quick."

A deep sadness shadowed H.W.'s face. "That she did. You never know what tomorrow will bring. Gotta live each day to the fullest."

Lucy hugged her baby with a tight squeeze. "Un-huh."

Seems like just yesterday when you took over the house, Lucy. You had a lot thrown on you at thirteen. You did yourself proud, daughter."

Lucy laid her hand on her father's arm. "It was just good practice for having my own home I guess. Sure glad Mary came along when she did, or I might still be there," Lucy said with a wry grin. "Funny how things work out."

"Yep. If I hadn't needed someone to help you with the housework, I might never have looked twice at that new widow in church that Sunday. She's a good woman."

"Bet you never thought you'd have another daughter at your age."

"Nope. Sure surprised me," he said. A wide grin spread across his face. "Kind of like having you around all over again."

"Hanna's such a pretty child." Lucy didn't say what else she thought. Hanna was pretty all right... pretty spoiled. Dad would never have let the rest of us kids get by with what she does. Sanford and I will have to be careful not to spoil Nora Margaret.

***

The next week Lucy's friend Susan had a baby girl also. Lucy and Nora went for a visit and brought the blue and white baby quilt she made for the occasion.

When Susan opened the brown paper wrapping her face lit up. "Oh Lucy! It's beautiful! You are such a wonderful friend. We'll have to get together and sew little dresses for our girls."

Lucy nodded. "We can even dress them alike. Won't this be fun?"

***

After harvest was over there was little work to be found away from farming. Sam promised to hire Sanford back when he had a need.

Sanford and his dad, Henry, butchered a hog and hung the hams in the smoke house to cure. Winter set in with a vengeance.

One snowfall followed another. In order to get to the barn without getting lost in the driving snow, they had to run a rope from the back door of the house to the barn door.

During these long winter days, Sanford made a table of cut logs, chopped firewood and helped Lucy with the wash. When it was clear enough to hang the clothes on the line outside, the clothes froze before they dried. Lucy thought the long-handled underwear looked like ghosts flying in the winter wind.

In mid-January, Sanford came home with news. He found Lucy in the kitchen churning butter while she nursed Nora.

"I saw my brother in town today. He's moving his family down to Walker."

"What's James gonna do down there?" she said as she gave the churn a few final cranks.

Elwood thinks he can get him on at the Katy railroad. He says it sounds like Washington is close to opening the Oklahoma Territory. If they do they'll be lots of work on the railroads. Who knows, maybe we could even get us a place down there..."

Lucy paused in mid-crank, put the baby in her cradle, and looked at him with fire in her eyes. "Oklahoma! I thought you put that idea to rest a long time ago. You're not still thinking about that wild notion, are you?"

"Just because I haven't mentioned it, doesn't mean I've buried the idea. Things aren't any better here than they were a year ago. Maybe the winters would be milder there. Besides, when Mr. Dawson's family gets here we're out of a place to live, unless you want to move in with your folks."

"I love them Sanford, but don't want to live there. Don't want Nora learning Hanna's whiney habits."

"Well, Washington hasn't passed the bill yet. Some folks don't think it'll ever happen... but I can always hope."

"You can hope all you want, Sanford Deering, but you'd be hard pressed to get me and Nora down there."

Even though Sanford hadn't mentioned the dreaded word, Oklahoma, for several months, it was clear Lucy hadn't warmed any to the idea.

"Has James told them at Kidder he's quitting the sawmill?"

"No, but he said I could take his place. He's only been working three days a week, but that's better than nothing. I'll start over there come Monday."

"Maybe that'll get us through the winter. I was in the root cellar this morning. Not much left in there. Just a half a sack of potatoes and a keg of carrots and some turnips. Even the flour is getting low. I don't know if I can make it stretch."

"Well, we still got that small sack of beans and the little bit of pork in the smokehouse."

"If we're careful, maybe we can get by till spring." Pouring the extra milk off the butter she plopped the blob in a mixing bowl and began to squeeze the remaining milk out with a flat wooden paddle. "Next time you go to town, you can trade this butter for some corn meal. Thank goodness for Jers."

"We're not the only ones, Lucy. It's bad all over. Nobody's letting go of any money to hire help."

"We'll make it somehow, Sanford."

He nodded. "We'll have to."

CHAPTER 5

September 15, 1888 - Helped open a rock quarry.

Work was scarce at the sawmill in Kidder. The winter snow froze the landscape, not to mention commerce. During a late February thaw, Sanford was finally able to get out and go to the post office in Winston. Several letters awaited him. Among them was a scrawled note from Mr. Dawson. It read,

January 31, 1888
Dear Mr. Deering,

My family will arrive by the middle of March from back east. Please vacate the premises by March 15.

Sincerely,
Mr. Dawson

Stopping by the general store, Sanford traded the butter for a sack of corn meal, and asked Joe, the storekeeper, if he knew anyone who had any land for rent.

He scratched his head. "No, not that I've heard of."

Sanford headed for home with a heavy heart. Where to go next? With Lucy's stubborn attitude, he'd probably better check Oklahoma off his list. Maybe they could try Walker.

"That wind is sure sharp today." He dropped the logs in the wood box beside the stove, threw a couple of pieces in, and stirred the fire with a poker. The warmth felt good to his frozen body. "Got a letter from Mr. Dawson. You're not going to like it," he said as he unlaced his boots and placed them by the door.

Lucy finished kneading the large lump of bread dough and wiped her hands on her apron. "Mr. Dawson's family's coming, aren't they?"

"How'd you know?"

"Just figured. What'll we do next, Sanford?" Lucy covered the mound of dough on the kitchen table with a tea towel to let it rest and rise.

Sanford shrugged out of his coat and put it over the back of the chair. "I put the word out we're looking for a place to rent, but no one knew of anything, not even the storekeeper. Think I'll write James to see if there might be something in Walker."

Lucy mashed the potatoes and poured gravy on a large spoonful to feed Nora. "Wouldn't hurt to ask, I guess." Inside she thought, at least, it's not Oklahoma. With Sanford's two brothers and their families there, it might seem a little more like home.

Within a week James answered Sanford's letter.

Dear Sanford,

Things are better here in Walker than in Winston. I talked to the foreman on the Katy railroad. Sounds like he might have some work.

Come on down. You can stay with us till you find a place. Need some help with planting and general carpentry.

James

For a week Sanford and Lucy sorted through their household goods. She packed most of the things in wooden barrels with straw for storage in H.W.'s barn.

"Sanford, can't we can take our rocking chair?"

"Just put it in the barn. We'll send for it later. No need to pay shipping on a bunch of stuff we don't need."

Lucy stopped to wipe her face on her apron. "Sure is hard breaking up our house. Can't believe it's been three years since we moved in here. Where do you suppose all this plunder came from?"

Late one evening she finished packing a wooden box of linens and looked up at her husband as she sat back to take a rest. "Do you think we'll ever move back here to Winston?"

"Don't know, my doe."

She surveyed their small home. "Sure are a lot of memories here."

"Yep." Sanford nailed a lid on the last wooden barrel and put down the hammer. After a long silence he said, "Stopped by Frankie's grave on my way home this afternoon. I'll ask your dad to put fresh grass seed on it come spring."

"Leaving him behind is the most painful part."

"Yep." He drew her to him and wrapped her in his arms. " We'll be back for visits."

"Promise?"

"Promise," he said with a reassuring hug.

***

In the early morning of March 12, Sanford, Lucy, and Nora boarded the train at Kidder and headed for southwest Missouri. The train ride was filled with new sights and sounds. Lucy marveled at the number of small towns along the way. They made frequent stops to take on fresh water for the steam engine. The smell of the coal-burning locomotive was rather unpleasant. A thin, black dust covered everything in the coach cars. It burned Lucy's eyes.

"Looks like there's a town every whip-stitch. Where'd all these people come from?" she said as she brushed the coal dust from Nora's coat.

I told you it was getting crowded here."

Kansas City was their first long stop.

"This place sure is big. We must have been going through this town for a half hour," Lucy said as she stared out the window.

The train pulled into the station so they could catch another to take them to Nevada, Missouri.

"Yep. This state's getting more crowded all the time. Sure glad we don't live in a big city like this."

"No elbow room here, that's for sure," she said. They found a spot on a long bench in the waiting room. Mother and daughter took a catnap while they waited.

"Good day, Senator." Lucy opened one eye to see what a Senator actually looked like. A dapper man in a gray pin-striped suit and a starched collar with a black ascot tie sat near Sanford.

As the conversation progressed they learned he was a Senator representing Kansas in Washington, D.C. He was on his way home from the legislative session, which had just closed in Washington the week before.

Sanford wasted no time. He turned to him and asked, "Sir, What do you hear in Washington about the Oklahoma Territory?"

"No firm action yet. Congress is pretty well divided."

"Think it might be voted on next year?"

"Perhaps," he nodded. "Getting lots of pressure from all over to open it up, especially from a couple of groups in Kansas."

"We'd sure be interested in homesteading down there if it ever opens."

Lucy kept quiet and looked the other way. Nora awoke and squirmed on her lap. Sounded like Sanford was like that old snapping turtle Dad always talked about who, when he grabbed hold of something, wouldn't let go till it thundered. "Maybe Washington won't vote it in. Then we could forget this nonsense," she muttered under her breath.

At 6:00 P.M. the conductor called out, "All aboard!" They were on their way again. By the time the train reached Nevada, Missouri, Lucy was ready for some solid ground. The constant sway on the tracks made her feel a little sick. After an overnight stop with some childhood friends, they continued on to Walker.

***

In a letter home to her parents the next month, Lucy wrote:

April, 1888

Dear Dad and Mary,

James and Mattie have been very kind to open their home to us.

Sanford found a place for us to rent just a mile and a quarter east of James' place. We moved in last week. We're borrowing some furniture from them. It has a wonderful wood-burning cook stove in the good-sized kitchen on the back of the house. There is another big room with a fireplace and a bedroom besides. There's a loft upstairs for Nora over the fireplace room. It has a well just outside the back door and a nice sized root cellar beside the well. Be a good place to hide if a tornado comes.

The first few days we were here, Sanford hired on at the Katy, part-time. He's repairing rails with the road crew. It's hard work, but we're grateful for the job.

I helped him plant a garden the other day with cabbage, turnips, potatoes, green beans and carrots. Plan to plant some sweet corn, tomatoes, muskmelons and pumpkins later. Hope we get some good rains at the right time.

He and James built a chicken yard, hen house and pig pen at James' place. With the leftover scraps and some lumber he found behind our house he's gonna start on a chicken house and pig pen here at our place. We also found a roll of chicken wire behind a shed for a chicken yard.

James was right. There's more jobs here in Vernon County. Sanford hauled some coal for a fella last week and has a job plowing this week. Another fella asked him to build some fences when he had some spare time.

Nora's starting to crawl. Sanford thinks she'll be walking soon. Keeps me busy looking after her.

Been pretty wet here so far. Sure makes the garden grow weeds too. We wish we could come to Elwood and Orilla's wedding in Winston, but guess we'll just have to see them when they get back here.

Looks like Walker's getting pretty crowded with Deering's these days. Makes me feel more like this is our home with James and Mattie and now Elwood and Orilla living here.

I met a new friend at church. Her name is Rebekah Miller. She has a baby boy just about Nora's age and a newborn girl. Her husband, Uriah, works with Sanford on the Katy. We had a picnic after church Sunday. Met some other folks there too.

I'll write more later.

Love,

Lucy

There was little rain that summer. It was hot and dusty. When Nora learned to walk, Lucy had to keep her eye on her every minute. She found more to get into than three children. Still the garden had to be hoed, laundry done, and harvested food stored for winter.

July 6th Lucy wrote a post card to her parents.

Dear all,

Nora started walking. Falls a lot. Keeps me busy. No rain here. Sanford working long days.

Spent the 4th of July in Walker. S. helped build a lemonade stand and dance platform for the celebration. There was a band, politicians spoke, and our church furnished ice cream. Our nation's come a long way in 112 years.

Love,

Lucy

***

The next week Sanford went to town to trade eggs for chicken feed at the general store.

"What's the word from town Sanford? Any mail?"

"Lucy, I hope you're not feeling too settled here."

She put Nora down and frowned. "Don't like the sound of those words, Sanford."

"Your dad sent word. He needs help with the oat harvest. He's not been feeling too good. He wants to know if we'd be willing to come for a spell."

"Who's gonna take care of the chickens and the garden?"

"I'm sure James would be glad to lend a hand. Besides, Mary says she wants to see you and the baby. I bet your dad put her up to saying that."

"I guess we don't have a choice. I'm not too anxious to move in again with Dad and Mary; especially Hanna."

Within a week, they were back on the train; Walker to Nevada, Nevada to Kansas City, Kansas City to Gallatin. H.W. picked them up in the buckboard.

"How's my little sweetheart?" H.W. said as he held out his arms to Nora. She toddled unsteadily to him. "We've sure missed you all." Nora rode in his lap all the way home to Winston.

***

Summer seemed to vanish like a chunk of ice in searing sunshine. Sanford and H.W. were out threshing every day. At night they came home to be with the family instead of staying in the fields. Most of the time H.W. came home with a cough.

"That dust is getting to me, the older I get." H.W. blew his nose, shoved his handkerchief back in his hip pocket and sat at the kitchen table.

Lucy looked up from kneading her bread dough. She hadn't noticed before how bald he was, not to mention the graying of his hair. In the last few months he seemed to have aged at least five years. She hated to see her oh-so-handsome father going the way of all the earth.

"What you looking at girl?"

"Oh, nothing; just resting for a minute."

***

After they had been there a few weeks, Lucy took Nora to visit her friend Susan.

"Nora sure is a busy little person, isn't she?" Susan watched Nora chase a chicken around the yard.

"Yes. Into everything," the chicken disappeared around the corner of the house, clucking out her desperation and flapping her wings.

"Little Martha isn't quite that busy. Most of the time she's content to sit and hold the blue quilt you made her while she sucks her thumb. How do you get anything done?"

"It's not easy. The other day when I was baking, Nora got into the sack of flour. She had it all over herself and the floor, in the wink of an eye. Hanna thought it was funny. She ran out to tell Mary who was in the garden."

"Bet that didn't make Mary too happy. She's such a housekeeper." Susan drew Martha onto her lap.

"Almost to a fault. Nora, stop chasing that chicken. You'll wear her out! I tried to clean the flour up before Mary came in but I wasn't fast enough."

"What did Mary do?"

Nora sighed. "She just emptied the mess of turnips from her apron onto the table, looked around on the floor, frowned, and went back to the garden without a word. I think Hanna's kind of jealous of Nora. Nora! Let go of the cat's tail. He's going to bite or scratch you."

"Tough living with other folks sometimes."

"I think we've about worn out our welcome after only a month. I'm feeling like it's time to go back to Walker. I know father likes having us here, but I think the stress outweighs the help Sanford is to him."

"Lucy Deering. I never thought I'd hear you say you'd want to leave here!" Susan laughed.

Lucy continued, "It's more than that. Nora's not sleeping too good. Her bed is a dresser drawer. Sanford set it in the corner of our room. In the night she gets out and wanders around in the dark sometimes. I lay awake at night, worried what she might get into."

"I hate to think of you going Lucy, but I know I'd hate to be in that fix."

"I can't say much so long as Sanford's working. We'll need the money, come winter; we really had to tighten our belts last year."

***

Sanford's cousin, Molly, had a baby just after Nora's first birthday. The birth was difficult. Little Rosa was born six weeks early. On the Sunday after she was born Lucy and Sanford went for a visit.

On the way home Lucy said, "Don't remember Nora ever being that small."

"Or that quiet."

"I wonder if something is wrong."

"Maybe. She looked kind of blue to me."

Both fell silent. The memory of Frankie's illness and death rushed into Lucy's mind. She was afraid to say anything, but she was sure Sanford's thoughts matched hers. How quickly those emotions surface and the pain of those dark days returned at the sight of a struggling infant.

Two weeks to the day from her birth, little Rosa died.

"I can't go to the funeral Sanford." Tears welled up in her eyes. Even though it had been a year and a half, all the memories of that awful day at the cemetery flooded over her.

"I'd just as soon stay home with you, but I've got to go."

When he came home he took off his Sunday jacket, changed into his overalls and work boots, and went out to chop wood without a word. He didn't come back till supper. Through dinner, Lucy kept quiet. She knew the day's events were heavy on his shoulders.

Silently she prayed, *Help him, Jesus. Please surround him with your comfort.*

***

Harvest wound down. Few jobs were available at Sam's sawmill.

Although Mary didn't say anything, their relationship in the too-close quarters was strained. Hanna grew more jealous of Nora every day. One day Lucy saw Hanna pinch Nora, although Hanna denied it.

Soon winter would set in. Travel would be more difficult.

In mid-September Sanford was gone all day to help open a rock quarry near Winston. He came home late, dirty and dog-tired.

Lucy warmed his dinner in the skillet while Sanford washed up. After filling his plate she sat near him so she could quietly share her thoughts with him.

"I've been thinking, Sanford. I'd like to move the last of our goods to Walker. I miss being in our own home."

Sanford nearly choked on his bite of stew. He looked at her wondering if he heard her right. Resting his fork on the edge of his plate he said, "I never thought I'd hear you say those words. I'm ready to go any time you are."

During the first two weeks of October they sifted through their things stored in the barn, and chose the most necessary items to ship to Walker. It was a difficult choice to make.

"Sanford, can we take the table you built?"

"No. I can make another when we get back to Walker. It'd be more trouble to ship it."

"But it's such a nice table. I hate to sell it."

"We can use a couple of wood crates till I can make another, Lucy. We just can't take all this stuff."

She moved a box from the rocker and sat in it. "How about this rocker Grandfather Deering made us?"

"We can get another. We only have so much space in the boxcar."

"Sanford Deering. Your own grandfather made that for us. I'll not sell that in the auction."

"Suit yourself," he shrugged.

They contacted an auctioneer and set a date for the following week. On the day of the sale Lucy went to Susan's for the day. She couldn't bear to see her things sold.

After the sale, Sanford busied himself around the house. He repaired the caning on a chair and put a new handle on Lucy's butcher knife while she packed their few remaining items. He even helped her with the washing.

"Looks like we're about ready to go, my doe," Sanford said. As Lucy hung the last pair of long-handles on the line, he slipped his arm around her waist. They watched H.W. play with Nora in the swing he made for Hanna in the side yard in the big oak tree. Hanna stood by and whined; she didn't like sharing her swing with her niece.

"Dad's gonna miss Nora, Sanford. Maybe we can have them come for a visit at Christmas."

"Think you want to put up with Hanna?"

Lucy laughed. "After these past three months, I think I could put up with about anything."

***

By the 16th of October, Sanford took the farm implements and their packed barrels and boxes into Winston for shipment to Walker. By the 20th, the rail car was loaded with a few household goods, including their bed *and* the rocker. Lucy felt a strange excitement to be on their way, but she had one last thing to do before they left Winston. She had Sanford stop by Frankie's grave.

With a cool nip in the air, they walked through the brilliant red and yellow maple leaves. Sanford carried Nora while she chattered, unconcerned that no one was listening to her.

"You know Sanford, I feel a new peace here."

He scowled. "What do you mean?"

"Don't know. A new assurance. Frankie's not here, but we'll see him again."

"Unhuh."

"Wherever we go, he'll still be waiting for us in heaven."

Sanford nodded his head in agreement but wasn't as sure as Lucy seemed to be. He hugged Nora and Lucy to himself. A sudden gust of wind blew the colorful fall leaves into a swirl around them.

By evening the train was underway, headed for Kansas City. The next day they were back home in Walker. It took all day to unload the plow and farm implements, the boxes of household goods... and the rocker.

***

Through the following week Lucy seemed to be extremely tired.

"Sanford, I can't seem to get these boxes unpacked. Every time Nora lays down for her nap, I can't resist laying down beside her."

"Well, it was a long trip. Just take it easy for a while. No need to fix breakfast. I'm going to James' place early. We're gonna butcher a beef. I'll be back before dark."

By late afternoon, Sanford was home again. "Here Lucy." He placed a bucket of fresh beef liver on the kitchen table. "We better eat this for supper. James sent along some fine onions from the garden, too."

With one look at the liver, Lucy bolted for the outhouse. When she came in, she was a sickly white.

Sanford looked at her with alarm. "What's the matter with you? You look like you've seen a ghost."

"Nothing's wrong. I'll be better in about seven and a half months, I reckon'." Lucy went straight to bed to get away from the stench of liver and onions.

A slight smile played across his face. He didn't say a word while he cooked dinner, fed Nora, and got her in bed. "Maybe this one will be another boy," he said to nobody in particular.

CHAPTER 6

December 25, 1888 - Everyone met at our house today.

In early November, Sanford's parents, Henry and Malinda came for a visit. The root cellar was full of harvest bounty.

At dinner their first evening, Sanford asked, "What brings you down here to Walker, Father?"

Henry took a fork full of mashed potatoes and said, "Thought I might look at some land I heard about over near Eldorado Springs." He popped the bite in his mouth and continued. "I had hoped to homestead in Oklahoma, but I'm afraid I'll be too old by the time those fancy fellas in Washington ever get around to opening it."

Sanford buttered a slice of sourdough. "How does Maggie feel about all this moving talk?"

"I'm afraid your little sister's digging her heels in." She has her heart set on staying near that George Smith over near Tipton."

"Do you think she'll marry him?" Lucy asked.

"Oh, eventually. He's a good solid farmer. Said he'd like to get in on the Oklahoma deal too."

Lucy lowered her eyes but kept her mouth shut. From the sound of it, Oklahoma Territory was going to have to be as big as heaven itself to fit in all the people who planned to stake a claim.

Sanford cut off another piece of ham and flopped it in his plate. "The way that Senator from Kansas talked at the train station, this next session might be the one to crack it open. You better hold off for a while. Then we could all go to the Territory together."

"My waiter's worn out, Son. Want to go with me to look at that place at Eldorado Springs?"

"Nothing better to do. When?"

"My bones tell me it's going to be a good day tomorrow. We could catch the train in town and be back by nightfall."

"Sounds good to me."

***

After the men left the next morning, Malinda and Lucy picked out enough pecans from the shells for a pie. They put a beef roast in the oven, complete with carrots and potatoes, and spent the rest of the day making little dolls from dried cornhusks.

"These little beauties need something else," Malinda said as she held one at arms' length.

"What about making them some aprons? I think I have some scraps in a bottom drawer of the dresser."

Lucy laid the snippets out in front of Malinda.

After she felt each one she held up a bright red and white scrap. "This is just what the doctor ordered. Gingham aprons will put the finishing touch on these little ladies."

"These'll make perfect Christmas gifts," Lucy said.

"It'll be here before you know it, Lucy. Don't you just love this time of year?"

"Sure do. It's such fun making surprises for everyone."

Mid-afternoon, Lucy finished stitching a little apron and set the coffee pot on to boil.

Malinda paused her sewing and studied Lucy for a long moment. The delicious aroma escaped the grinder as she turned the handle. "You look kind of peeked. Are you all right?"

Malinda's question took Lucy by surprise. I'll have to be careful what I say or she'll guess I'm in a family way again. It's too soon to tell that news. Maybe I can change the subject.

Lucy turned from the cabinet and said, "What makes you ask?"

"Oh, you seem to be awfully quiet today for some reason."

"Just have a lot on my mind."

"Like..."

"Well, for one thing, I'm worried about Sanford's itch to move to Oklahoma. He refuses to let go of that notion. What if they open that place? He'll be the first in line."

Malinda smiled and nodded.

I'm just not of a mind to move down there. Not now, nor next year, or even the next. We're just getting settled here. I'm finally beginning to feel like this is home." She turned away to steady her voice.

"I understand, but as long as you've known Sanford he's always had a hankering to be on the go somewhere. Why I'm surprised you all stayed up in Winston as long as you did."

Lucy's vision blurred as she poured the ground coffee into the boiling water. "I figured when he went out to Washington Territory to herd those sheep for Uncle Tom, he got traveling out of his system."

"I don't know, my dear. It may have just given him a worse case of wandering fever."

"Lord, I hope not." Lucy poured coffee and picked up the scissors.

"Who knows, it might be a real adventure for you and Sanford. You all are young. Wish we were. Life flies by so fast," Malinda resumed her sewing.

Lucy took a sip and stared in the cup. "I don't call living in some dugout with little kids an adventure."

With her needle in mid-air Malinda cocked her head as if to hear better. "Kids? You meaning more than one?" She leaned forward. "Something you want to tell me?"

Oh no! I let the cat out of the bag. Me and my big mouth. Lucy swallowed and said, "Hadn't planned on telling anyone yet, but... ah... next June we'll be having another."

Malinda bounded around the table and gave Lucy a big fat Malinda bear hug. Patting her hand she said, "Oh, honey. That's wonderful. I'd hate to think of little Nora being brought up alone. Are you feeling okay?"

"Just tired. Some stuff makes me sick, although it's getting better." Lucy looked up with a weary smile.

Malinda sighed and straightened. "Goes with the territory, I guess."

"That's for sure."

Lucy was grateful for the encouraging sympathy, but disgusted with herself about the slip of her tongue. There probably was no keeping the secret, now that her mother-in-law knew.

Malinda went to tend to Nora. Cleaning up the table from their project, Lucy got the dishes out of the pie cupboard for dinner. The disgust over her little slip gave way to the nagging words from last night about leaving Missouri. They chased her like a hound after a coon. She made the biscuits and finished the gravy.

In the dusk, she spied the men-folk in the yard. "Here they come."

"That's how I get Henry home from town," Malinda said with a chuckle.

"How's that?"

"Just finish supper and here he comes." Malinda took the pecan pie out of the oven. "I swear, that man can smell his supper from ten miles away."

"I'll have to remember that. Maybe I can get my man home earlier that way," Lucy said with a hint of a grin.

Lucy mused as she dished up the gravy and set it on the table. I love Malinda's sense of humor. And nothing ruffles her feathers, no matter the circumstances; even if it's moving to Timbuktu or new babies. Besides, I don't usually like hiding things from people.

While the men washed up at the pump outside, Lucy poured the stiff, black coffee. "We're ready when you are," she called.

Henry rubbed his hands together and looked over the table like a half-starved vulture. "A Deering's always ready, Daughter. Especially when it comes to eating," he said.

The men sat down and tore into the roast beef, carrots, potatoes, biscuits and gravy.

While Lucy broke apart pieces of meat for Nora, she asked, "What's the story on Eldorado Springs, Henry?"

"It looks to be pretty fair land. This piece is flatter than in Winston. Appears to be rich soil with a good well on the place. Pass the strawberry preserves."

Malinda passed the jelly and said, "Did you buy it?"

He took the bowl and dumped a generous spoonful on a slice of roast. "Of course. You never knew me to pass up a square deal did you, woman? Old man Lawson was pretty anxious to get rid of it. Set me a good price. His daughter wants him to move to Arkansas with her. Now we can be closer to the boys and their families down here."

Lucy took a bite and thought, great! Maybe if Sanford's folks are here he won't be so anxious to move. "And Maggie?" she asked.

"Oh, she'll come around. If George is the one for her, a little distance won't make much difference."

Sanford took another slice of bread to sop up the beef juice in his plate. "So are you gonna sell your place in Winston?"

"I'll get it up for sale by spring. I need to get someone to repair the house before I can sell it. We'll move down here right away before winter sets in, I reckon. That way we'll be ready for planting in the spring."

"Well, that's wonderful. We'll be able to see you all more often," Malinda reached across the table to give Lucy's hand a squeeze and a knowing wink.

Lucy could feel her face flush.

"What's the hand squeezing for, Malinda?" Henry looked from one face to the other.

"Can I tell him, Lucy?"

Lucy shrugged. "Might as well. He'll know soon enough. You're going to be a grandpa again, Henry."

He pushed his chair back and laughed. "Well, I'll be switched! Congratulations, you two. That's the finest news I've heard all day."

Sanford chimed in, "Even better than Mr. Lawson's price?"

"Even better than that, my boy!"

The next day Sanford took H.W. to the pecan grove down by the river. The two of them picked all day. They each came in that evening with a 50-pound feed sack on their back loaded to the very top.

"Looks like you fellas are going to have your work cut out for you for the next several days," Lucy said as she surveyed the haul.

"Not me. I have to high tail it back up to Winston if I'm going to get packed up to move. I'll just save all that work for you and Sanford," he said with a broad grin.

"Squirrel them away in the root cellar. We'll get to them when we can. Don't want to keep them in here. Nora will have them all over the floor in a jiffy." Lucy said.

True to Henry's words, they left the next morning to prepare for their move.

During the next weeks, Lucy made sure she had a bowl filled with uncracked nuts sitting on the kitchen table with the nutcracker and picks conveniently placed near an empty mixing bowl.

"Think we'll ever get through these pecans, Sanford?"

"Oh these are nothing, my doe. When I was a kid we had a grove of pecan trees. We never had less than half a dozen sacks to go through come fall. We'll have these done in no time."

Christmas promised to be quite a celebration. Lucy invited H.W., Mary and Hanna to come. Their acceptance came by return mail.

Sanford's folks and Maggie moved into their place in Eldorado Springs according to Henry's plans in early December, despite Maggie's objections. Everyone, including Sanford's brothers, James and Elwood and their wives, agreed they should have Christmas at Sanford's place.

In spite of Lucy's overwhelming tiredness, and her child's constant care, she somehow managed to get some window coverings made from flour sacks, as well as a dress for Nora for Christmas from the leftover curtain material. Without Sanford's knowledge, she had salvaged the material and her mother's fine china from their auction in Winston, by packing the dishes in the flour sacks and placing them in the bottom of the barrels marked "kitchen."

It was a week before Sanford noticed the curtains. When he did, he said, "Have we used that much feed? Where'd you get all this material?"

"I just found it in our stuff." After all, Lucy knew men don't always know what the *really* important stuff is.

She folded her arms and surveyed the warm surroundings. "This place really *is* beginning to feel like home," she mused.

Christmas Eve day, Lucy prepared pumpkin for pies, fresh from the garden, and mixed the filling for the pecan pies from the nuts they had picked out.

With the aroma of fresh bread and roasting ham, the house seemed to burst with the bounty. When Sanford came in from feeding the stock and milking Jers, he had a load of wood in one arm and small pine tree in the other. Leaning the tree against the wall, it was no taller than Nora. He dropped the wood in the box beside the stove and added more fuel to the fire.

"I decided we needed a tree for our celebration; cut it along the railroad tracks."

"Oh Sanford! It's beautiful." She gave him a big kiss and hug.

He set the tree in a bucket of sand beside the fireplace. "What do you think, Nora? It's your very own Christmas tree."

Nora squealed with glee. "Tree! Tree!"

Lucy headed for the kitchen and called over her shoulder, "We'll have to decorate it after dinner. Sanford, come pull the ham out of the oven, but no picking on it. Gotta keep the lid on to keep it warm. I'll just pop these pies in the oven, quick."

The rolls baked to a golden brown, lima beans simmered on the stovetop, while she lopped another heap of butter on the potatoes. "Suppose the train was late getting in to Walker?"

"I heard it come through. They'll be here soon. Don't fret, my doe."

"Maybe they missed the train. Your father said he'd pick them up at the station on his way out. Maybe they had trouble on the road."

"Lucy, quit it, you worry-wart. You're making a mountain out of a molehill."

"It'll be dark before you know it, and it's starting to snow." Lucy peered out the window toward town. She placed the lid on the mashed potatoes and moved it to the back of the stove to keep warm.

Suddenly, Lucy remembered her mother-in-laws' recipe for getting folks home in time for supper and smiled. "Set the those glasses around the table. They'll be here soon. Here's the butcher knife and the platter so you can cut the ham. I'll fill the jelly dish with strawberry preserves and then we'll be ready."

"But we don't have folks here yet."

"We will." She drew the strawberry jam out of the cupboard.

"What changed your mind? A minute ago you were worried sick."

"I remembered what your mother said last time she was here. 'Put the dinner on and they'll come.'"

Sanford shook his head. "Must be true if Mom says it." He gave her a playful swat on the bottom.

"Sanford Deering! Behave yourself! Get busy with that knife."

After he dutifully set the glasses on the table and cut the meat he looked out the window. "Well, I'll be crackie! Here they come." He grabbed Nora and said, "Come on, baby. Let's go open the door for the folks."

They piled in, shaking the fresh smelling snow off their coats and hung them on the pegs by the back door.

H.W. leaned over the pies on the warming shelf on the stove. "Those pies smell good enough to eat, Daughter."

Lucy shook the meat fork at him. "All in good time. I'm watching you. No tasting till after dinner, Dad."

Henry rubbed his hands together and held them out over the stove. "It's starting to flurry, Sanford. The way my bones ache, there's a storm brewing."

"A Christmas snow. Won't that be wonderful?" Mary exclaimed.

After dinner, pie and coffee, they all lingered at the table to sing Christmas carols while Sanford played the old harmonica that had been his Grandfather Deering's before he passed.

Some of the guests strung popped corn with a needle and thread while others fashioned a paper chain for an additional tree decoration. Henry read the story of Jesus' birth from the Bible while the women dressed the tree.

Lucy passed Sanford and whispered, "Can you believe how well Hanna is playing with Nora. Hope it lasts." Hanna actually seemed glad to see Nora and didn't tease her even once. Before long, Nora began to rub her eyes.

"Looks like you're ready for sleep, little one," Malinda said. "You want Grandma to put you to bed?" She was too tired to resist.

When Lucy came to kiss her daughter good night, she found the two girls curled up together in Nora's feather bed, both sound asleep. This visit was turning out to be a joy. Covering them she tiptoed out of the room.

After the dishes were done, they bid good night to Sanford's brothers and their families while the remainder of the guests got several quilts and found a place on the floor near the wood stove for a Christmas Eve rest. The wind howled outside, but there was a warm glow indoors, not only from the burning wood, but also from the gratefulness of being together.

At dawn the next morning Lucy arose to discover a thick blanket of snow. She tiptoed carefully around sleeping relatives, and refueled the stove and fireplace. In the quiet, she nestled into the rocker Grandfather Deering made for them. On a square of butcher paper, Lucy placed Nora's finished dress and tied it with string. There was a warm muff of otter skin for Hanna. She quietly hummed Christmas carols as she carefully placed both packages under the small tree beside the fireplace.

She surveyed the room. *Now. I'm finally ready for Christmas morning* she thought. *Oh, one more thing–the three oranges all the way from California that I hid in the dresser. They'll be so surprised.*

Drawing out three of Sanford's white socks from the drawer, Lucy popped an orange in each stocking and laid them on the mantle; one for Nora, Hanna, and Orris.

Finished! No, not quite. From under the bed Lucy pulled out the cornhusk dolls she and Malinda had made the month before. She set each one on a branch of the tiny tree for Mattie, Malinda, Orilla, Maggie, and Mary. One was left over. "I'll put it on the top for Sanford and me," she whispered.

Lucy dressed, secured the last loose wisps of hair with her tiny hair combs on each side of her tightly drawn bun, and tied her apron. *A blessed Christmas indeed*, she thought.

Sanford's brothers and their families arrived soon after breakfast, laden with roast beef from the cow James and Sanford had butchered in the fall. They also brought a wild turkey Elwood shot as well as baked sweet potatoes from Mattie's garden and more pies, cakes and bread pudding. There was enough to feed a threshing crew.

After dinner, the men folk sat back to let their dinner settle. Lucy caught little snippets of conversation here and there while she cleared the table. The dreaded word "Oklahoma" came up several times. Everyone had another theory about when "the opening " would be.

"What are those men talking about in there, Lucy?" Malinda asked while she washed the dishes in the white porcelain pan in the dry sink.

"More Oklahoma talk," Lucy said as she dried another dish.

"Doesn't surprise me. From what I've heard, most everybody knows someone who's planning on staking a claim."

"I think half the church is talking about going," Orilla sighed as she put another plate on the dried stack.

"We have several neighbors gathering goods in order to go," Mattie, chimed in as she took out the broom and swept the wood floor. "This country might look pretty bare, by the time all the folks run off to Oklahoma."

Lucy added, "Well, if there's that many going down there from all over, I doubt they'll be enough land to go around. Some folks may just come up empty-handed."

Maggie murmured as she dried a cup, "Sure hope George gets a claim."

"What's that you say?" Lucy said. "You better think twice, girl. I hear that place is pretty wild country. If George does get a claim, you better think about picking another man."

Maggie didn't say anything to her sister-in-law. She just kept wiping.

"Elwood better not decide to go. I'm not of a mind to leave my folks," Orilla whispered.

"You sound like this Oklahoma move is just crossing your mind, for serious, right now Orilla."

"Lucy, you don't suppose Elwood would really consider it, do you?"

"Don't know. I never gave it much mind 'til Sanford got the fever. Now the thought haunts me day and night. Seems like that Oklahoma word is on everyone's lips."

"Mary, you've been awful quiet. What's H.W.'s plans?" Malinda asked.

Mary sighed as she placed the stack of dishes in the pie cupboard. "Think he's got the fever, too. He's talking pretty serious. I'll have to go wherever he does. I don't have much say about it."

An eerie silence settled on the women. They looked from one face to another. A new reality set in. This might be their last Christmas together... in Missouri, anyway.

CHAPTER 7

April 22, 1889 - Oklahoma Territory opened today.

The night before Lucy's folks were to head back to Winston, Lucy overheard her dad and Sanford talking quietly by the fireplace while she did the supper dishes. Mary busied herself getting the girls ready for bed.

"Still making plans to homestead in Oklahoma, Sanford?"

The words sent a chill through her, knotting her stomach. Waiting for his reply, she dried her hands on her apron and held her breath. She and Sanford hadn't spoken the dread word "Oklahoma" to each other directly for weeks–keeping an uneasy truce.

Lucy crept closer to the darkened doorway in order to catch even the slightest whisper. The men's reflections danced in the firelight in flickering shadows across the floor.

Sanford took a sip of his coffee before he answered. "Don't know. It'd help if we knew exactly when it was gonna open. With that new little one coming in June it kind of puts a kink in my plans. 'Course, Lucy's been against it from the git-go. If I mention it, she gets her bowels all in an uproar."

"Women are funny that way. I think they got deeper roots than us men."

"Yeah. Guess you're right. Hadn't thought of it that way. Then again, if women had their way, we'd all still be sitting across an ocean somewhere."

H.W. rubbed his chin as he gazed in the fire. "That's true. Guess we better never give them a chance to vote. We'd all be in trouble, for sure."

"Now there's a scary thought!"

Women? Voting? That was a novel idea. Lucy wondered how different things would be if women could vote. She continued to eavesdrop.

"Hope your new one's a boy."

"Me too. Love my daughter, but I miss my boy."

"Shoot. We might be dead and buried, and that son of yours growed up, by the time they ever make up their mind in Washington."

"Hope not. That's the only way we'll *ever* own some land. Ever been down that way H.W.?"

"Nope. Hear it's mighty purdy. Rich soil, too. I heard in town that some fellers went to Washington the other day to work on getting it opened up for settlers."

"You still making plans to go H.W.?"

"Sure thinking about it. Have to sell our place before we could go. Got a feller interested. Not sure he can come up with the cash for the down payment though."

Lucy crept back into the kitchen, her mind racing. These men of hers were as determined as a freight train headed to a fire. Was there no stopping them? It seemed their path was set in granite. Only God Almighty could change things now.

***

In early February, Sanford went to town, but was back early.

Lucy met him at the door with Nora on her hip. "What's your rush, Sanford? You rode in here like the devil's chasing you."

He sported a wide grin and pulled out the Walker Herald from inside his coat and spread it out on the kitchen table. "Something to show you, Lucy."

The headlines read, "OKLAHOMA BILL PASSES HOUSE 147-102."

She sank into the nearest chair and let Nora slide to the floor, staring at the newspaper in disbelief. The words seemed to swim before her on the page while she snatched it up and tried to read it. As near as she could understand, the legislators in Washington had passed the resolution and now President Grover Cleveland had to sign the bill and it would become law.

"Maybe the President won't sign it, Sanford. He's in office only a few more weeks."

"Have a lot of people down his back if he didn't. Everyone wants this. No holding folks back on this one."

"Not *all* people want this. I know of 103 that don't."

He pointed his finger at the headline. "Paper says 102."

"They didn't count me. I make 103 against it," Lucy said with a frown.

Sanford hung his coat at the back door. "Woman, are you touched in the head? This was bound to come. The Indians aren't doing a dang thing with this land. It's just sitting there going to waste when we could put it to good use. Now, it's just a wide space for cattle drives and a hiding place for outlaws."

She knew there was no use for words. His ears were deaf to anything his woman might say.

"So when is all this going to take place?"

"Don't know. Soon, I hope. This year, maybe."

How in tarnation did he think they could possibly move with a baby coming in June? Men sort of overlook the minor details of life, for sure. If I didn't love him so much, I'd just let him run off and rot there.

***

The next month at the general store, Lucy was surprised at the number of folks buying enormous amounts of feed, flour, beans, and bacon. Addie, the general store owner was as busy as a hound dog with new pups trying to fill everyone's order.

"What's going on, Addie?"

"Looks like Oklahoma Territory's going to open up like a pumpkin, Lucy. Haven't you heard? President Cleveland signed an order that added some of the Creek and Seminole land to the Unclaimed Territory."

"So there will be more land available?"

"Yep. When President Harrison takes office in March, he'll set the date to enter.

Lucy set a bolt of material on the wooden counter. "I hadn't heard about this before. You sure?"

"Everybody's talking about it. It's even in the *Kansas City Star*." Addie shoved the paper toward Lucy's protruding belly.

Lucy's hands began to shake as she read.

Addie continued. "Why, people who hadn't even given homesteading a second thought are coming in here loading up provisions for the trip. Business has never been better. They're getting ready. Says here they think he'll set it for the 22nd of April."

Lucy looked up from the paper with a frown. "That's the day after Easter, Addie."

"Yup."

Lucy left her dry goods on the bolt, unpurchased and hurried for the door.

On the way home she calculated the date of the land grab; six weeks before the new baby was due. Oh Lord, don't let Sanford drag us down there!

***

After church, the last Sunday in March, Lucy's friend Rebeka Miller called to her. "Lucy, you and Sanford going to the opening?" She shifted her baby, Lula, to her other shoulder and grabbed two-year-old Charles by the hand.

Sanford handed Nora to Lucy on the seat of the buckboard. He could feel the ire of his woman rising, even from this distance.

Lucy gave him a quick glance, stood, and put her hands on her hips. "Nope. Can't see us going down there in the shape I'm in. By the time this little one comes, all that land'll be taken up, anyhow."

"Don't seem like you're too upset about missing out, Lucy."

"I'm not. Missouri's a *fine* place to live out my days. So you're going, Rebekah?"

"Uriah says we'll make Oklahoma or bust. It'll be hard, but 160 acres is more than we could ever own up here. Five years and its ours."

I wonder how Uriah got his wife to think like that? I'll have to ask him when I see him... that is *if* I ever see him again.

Lucy fired back. "Five years is a long time."

"What'll we have here after five years? A broken back and nothing to show for it. I hear it's beautiful country. Better pack up and go with us."

Lucy sat and said, "I wish you well, Rebekah. Missouri's beautiful country too. We'll be staying right here. Write and tell me about it."

"Let me know if you change your mind. We all could go together, you know."

The ride home was quiet except for Nora's chatter. Sanford struggled, trying to find words that would somehow make Lucy see things his way. You'd think with her folks planning on going, she would want to go. Finally, he gave up.

Maybe with all those folks going to Oklahoma, there would some land for sale here. If he had good crops for the next three years, and picked up some extra work on the railroad, he might be able to save enough for a down payment on something here. Lucy was the most stubborn woman he knew. Why, she was even more stubborn than a Missouri mule.

No matter how hard Sanford tried to reason his dream dead, it kept coming back. In resignation, he made plans to plant his crops as soon as the weather let up.

Every day Lucy watched more and more families pass her home in wagons down the deeply rutted, rain-soaked roads of southern Missouri headed for the Oklahoma border. The wagons carried everything from farming implements to bed steads; books to chairs; babies to old folks. Some had saddle horses and milk cows tied on behind.

Lucy looked out the kitchen window while yet another wagon went by. "Sanford, it seems the whole world is headed for Oklahoma."

"Lucy, we're missing the chance of a lifetime. How about if I go stake a claim and come back and get you and Nora?"

She turned and faced him, stood on her tip-toes in order to get as close to his six-foot eye level as she could and looked him straight in the eye. Grabbing the front of his shirt, she whispered, "Sanford Deering, I've lost little Frankie. I'm not losing you in some crazy land grab. Besides, what if this new baby came while you were gone? Who'd fetch the doctor? Little Nora?"

Clasping her hands in his he said, "There's no talking to you, woman. If you have your way, we'll just be poor dirt farmers all our lives–living in one rented place after another. Don't you see? I want better for us."

"No. *You* see. We *have* a place to be. It's here in Missouri. I don't give a hang if the whole world goes off to the moon. I'm not going. I'm not leaving."

Hot tears coursed down her face. She turned her back on Sanford and stepped away. With trembling hands she wiped her eyes on her apron.

Sanford slipped his arms under hers and gently placed his big hands on her swelling belly. "I'm sorry, my doe. I didn't mean to upset you. I just want what's best for us all."

"Then leave it lay, Sanford. Just leave it lay."

As much as he wanted his dream, he knew at this point in his life, at least, it was not to be. To go to Oklahoma for a claim would cost him his family, and he was not willing to pay that price. With a deep sigh, he dropped his hands to his side, turned, and walked away.

On Palm Sunday, Pastor Smith had special prayer for those who planned to enter the Oklahoma Territory the next week to stake a claim the day after Easter. Lucy prayed especially for Rebekah and Uriah who had left two weeks before. The whole week before Easter, Sanford was very quiet. Lucy didn't press him for conversation. She knew where his mind was and she didn't want to start another "discussion."

A couple of weeks after the opening, Sanford brought a fat letter home from the post office addressed to Lucy. It was from Rebekah. Lucy put the beans on the stove to boil, dried her hands on her apron, and sat at the kitchen table. Sanford leaned against the wall and listened as Lucy read.

May 6, 1889

Dear Lucy,

We finally got down to Arkansas City, Kansas and camped near Walnut Creek. I think everybody and their brother must have been there waiting to stake a claim. At the end of the first week, we had a terrible rainstorm. Lightening crashed all around us. Thunder sounds louder here. Maybe because we're in a wagon and not a house. We slept in the wagon because it rained so hard it flooded our tent.

The morning after the rainstorm, Lt. Foster of the Cavalry announced we had one day to get ready to move across the 60 miles of the Cherokee Strip to the north border of the territory. We were to enter from there on the 22nd. Lucy, you never saw so many wagons and tents in one place. We looked like a great fleet of ships. Some folks even traveled in buggies. Others were on high-powered racehorses. Guess those folks got a claim before anyone else.

We had some trouble crossing some of the rivers because of the rain. Lt. Foster saw to it that we got over safely. At one place we had to cross a railroad trestle bridge. One man tried to lead his racehorse over. The horses' foot slipped and broke its leg. The man had to shoot him.

In order to get across, Lt. Foster ordered the men to tear down a railroad building and put the boards over the open tracks. They had to lead each team across and pull the wagons by hand. Men stood solid on both sides of the bridge so the horses couldn't see the open spaces on the sides and spook. It took a long time. We got to the border the evening before the run.

I've never seen so many people in one place in all my born days. At noon on the 22nd Lt. Foster signaled his bugler to start the race. Before he even got the bugle to his lips, the men on horseback took off in a great rush. We came along behind. It was a frightful time. Everyone drove their horses as fast as they would go. I hung on to the kids real tight. I was afraid they might bounce out of the wagon.

We entered just about ten miles west of the Santa Fe tracks on what they call the Black Bear Trail. We passed a fancy racehorse with his leg broke. Uriah said the horse most likely stepped in a hole.

One of our neighbors told us he was with some folks that came in by rail. He said they jumped off the car while the train ran down the track in order to get a claim.

Our claim is up by Ephriam Creek west of a town called Alfred. We began work on a dugout right off. The next day Uriah went to the land office in Guthrie to register his claim. He didn't come home that night. I was afraid something happened to him. Turns out he had to stand in line all day, and night and part of the next day at the land office to declare his claim.

While he was gone, some fellas came up and tried to tell me I was digging on their claim. They said if I paid them $25.00 they would let me have it. I put the baby down in the wagon and drew ole' Betsy out real quick and told them I knew how to use it. When I cocked it and drew a bead on them, they took off like scared rabbits. Guess they didn't expect a woman to know how to use a gun. Hope that's the last we see of those claim jumpers.

The neighbors are real friendly. On the quarter section just to the east of us are some folks that came all the way from Ohio. To the west, some Kansas folks. They have two young ones, like us. South of us is a large family from Illinois. Haven't met any other neighbors yet.

The children are fine. Our dugout faces south. Uriah has gone to the stream nearby to cut some branches to use for a roof. We'll cover the branches over with sod. He's going to Alfred tomorrow to buy some lumber to make a door and a window frame. I'll have him take this letter to the new post office.

Miss you. Write soon.

Love,

Rebekah

Glancing up at Sanford, Lucy put the letter on the table. "She doesn't say anything about how beautiful it is."

He avoided her eyes. "Well, maybe she just left out that part."

Lucy stood and stirred the beans. "Maybe living in a wagon in hopes of moving to a hole in the ground with sod for a roof isn't as much fun as she thought."

"A sod roof is still a roof, Lucy."

"I prefer a real roof, thank you very much." She put the lid back on the bean pot.

"Sounds as if they're getting things together, though."

Putting down her spoon, she said, "How together is getting water from a stream? Think I'd rather draw my water from a clean well instead of a creek somewhere."

Sanford didn't say anymore. He knew he had already said too much. No use stirring up a hornet's nest. His feet were in Missouri. That's just the way things were. The sooner he resigned himself to that fact, the better off he'd be. It was too late now anyway. He made one last resolution to kiss his dream good-bye.

"Guess I'll go slop the hogs," he said as he grabbed the bucket of potato peels from breakfast and headed for the door.

CHAPTER 8

June 14, 1889 - Birthing day for Lucy.

Lucy didn't take time to write back to Rebekah right away. The garden had to be planted, the wash done and spring cleaning. And then there was keeping up with Nora who was into something all the time. Lucy wondered how she would ever manage another one in just a month.

Sanford didn't speak of Oklahoma anymore. Hopefully, that idea of his was dead and gone. Maybe now they could get on with the business at hand; adding a new member to their family.

A couple of Sundays later, Addie met Lucy at the church door. "You just about ready to hatch that young 'un?"

"Another week or two."

"Seems like babies are everywhere this year. I heard Doc Morgan telling someone in the general store he's delivered three babies this month already. Must be something in the water here abouts."

Lucy laughed. "Might be. Never can tell."

She didn't tarry long after church. "We need to get home, Sanford."

"I thought we were gonna stay for the picnic today. You even brought that fried chicken."

She shot a "Let's go" look at Sanford and said, "I'm light-headed. Think I need to lie down." She leaned heavily on her husband's arm.

Sanford grabbed Nora with his free hand. "Come on Nora. We're going home."

Nora squalled. "Stay, Papa."

"Another time, little one."

Sanford put her into the buckboard despite her strong protests. Lucy pulled out a drumstick from the picnic basket and handed it to her.

"Here short stuff. Maybe this I'll keep you busy for a while."

Sanford helped Lucy climb into the wagon and hopped in himself.

"Get up there, you two." He slapped the reins on the team's backsides. "Think it might be time?"

"Don't know. I'm feeling kind of funny."

"Think we should send for Doc Morgan?"

"No. Let's wait a while. I might be better when I can lie down."

Even though Lucy rested, she wasn't better that evening or the next day.

"Could you stay close and help me with the laundry today, Sanford?"

"Sure. I'll fill the laundry boiler and get it going."

Reaching out she touched his hand. "Could you kill a chicken too?"

He nodded. "You look a little peaked. Any pains yet?"

"No, just a bad backache."

Sanford put water on to boil for the laundry while Lucy put on a pot of water to loosen the chicken feathers. "Looks to me like you're carrying that little one awful low this time."

"Feels like it too." Lucy arched her back, stretched, and headed for the bed.

Sanford grabbed two buckets and headed outside to pump more water.

Trying to find a comfortable position was next to impossible. Every way she turned was wrong. A warm breeze blew the flour sack curtains away from the windowsill. The songs of barn swallows and meadowlarks lulled her into a light sleep.

The sound of squawking chickens in the yard aroused her. Sanford grabbed a Rhode Island Red hen by one leg and wrung its neck. After he hung it on the clothesline for a while, he brought it inside and plunged it in the boiling water on the wood stove. The hot chicken feathers smelled like burning hair. It made Lucy sick to her stomach. She rolled over, planted her feet on the floor, and made a quick trip to the outhouse.

When she came back in, Sanford took one look and reached out to steady her.

"You all right?"

"My water broke. Get Doc Morgan. Hurry! Take Nora with you."

Sanford saddled Ginger while Lucy fetched Nora out of the yard. In no time at all, Sanford was headed down the road with his little girl perched in front of him in the saddle.

Lucy set the pot of boiling chicken off the fire. The pains started in something fierce when she bent down to put more wood in the stove.

"Lordy! Think I better get to the bed."

She tried to rest a while, to no avail. "Guess I better get some things gathered for this birthing."

Over the next hour between pains, Lucy gathered her sewing basket, some sheeting, newspapers and towels, and placed them on a chair near the bed. She checked the clock on the mantle. How long had Sanford been gone? Shouldn't he be back by now?

After another hour and a half the pains were solid with no letup. Lucy knew the time was near. Panic set in.

"Oh Lord, please help me! I'm gonna end up birthing this baby alone!" she cried. She wished Mary were there. She had been such a comfort before. Suddenly, a calm came over her. Instructions as clear as if spoken, came in doable order. "Prop some pillows behind your head. Lie down. Don't panic. Relax."

She could feel the baby coming. Everything seemed to be in slow motion. She strained her ears to hear the arrival of help. Nothing.

"Here we go, Lord. I can't hold this little one back any longer." Grabbing her knees, she took a deep breath, bowed her head to her chest and pushed. After two long hard pushes, the baby's head was born. She rested a moment before another strong pain bore down upon her.

Lucy looked at her precious babe lying between her legs. It was a boy! The lusty cry of this fine child filled the house. At the end of his spindly arms his minute fingers reached out to grab the warm summer breeze with each squall.

With shaking hands she reached for her sewing basket and drew out a small wad of darning thread and tied off the cord. One more short pain and she expelled the afterbirth. With a few quick snips of her sewing scissors, she cut the cord.

Tears streamed down her face and she cried, “Oh, thank you Lord. A boy! Another boy for Sanford!” From the nearby chair, she grabbed a towel and wiped him off.

“You sure have powerful lungs, little one.” She wrapped him in flannel sheeting and lay back exhausted, cradling him on her chest.

While Lucy rested the baby fell asleep. The house was quiet until she heard the faint “clippity-clop” of horses hooves and the iron wheels of a buggy on the dirt road.

“Lucy! You alright?” Sanford burst into the bedroom followed by Doc Morgan.

“Well, lookie here! What we got?” Doc Morgan said with a wide grin. “Guess we were a little late, weren’t we? Here. Let me take a look-see.”

“It’s a boy, Sanford,” Lucy said when she saw her husband.

Sanford was without words. Joy welled up from deep within him. He stroked her hair and gave her a big hug.

Doc unwrapped the baby at the foot of the bed. “This sure is a little-un.”

Finally Sanford found his words. They tumbled out in a torrent. “A boy. Another boy. Wait till your dad hears. He said he was hoping for a boy. Sorry I’m so late. Had to go all the way to the Ham’s place to find Doc. She delivered late this morning.”

Doc examined the baby with a fine-toothed comb. “I’m guessing their baby must have weighed about ten pounds. I was called out there last evening. Took her all night, but she finally came around.”

“Not like this one, huh, Doc?”

“No. You got to call this one, ‘Greased Lightnin’”

Lucy laughed. “We haven’t decided on a name, but I don’t think that will be it. I didn’t dare hope for a boy. Guess we’ll have to think of one.”

“How about William?” Sanford said.

“Or Albert?” she said.

“William Albert. How does that sound?”

She looked at her new son and said, "William Albert. He kinda looks like a William Albert, don't you think?"

Sanford nodded and beamed. "William Albert it is."

"Can I call him Albert? "

"Fine with me, my doe." Sanford's moustache seemed to stretch from ear to ear.

Doc rewrapped Albert and said, "He's a fine healthy one, though the Ham's baby would make two of him. Don't worry. He'll grow." He handed him to Sanford. "Congratulations, Daddy."

With the baby cradled in the crook of his arm, Sanford knelt beside the bed, parked his hat on the bedpost and beamed at his tiny son. Tears welled up in his eyes. "Another son," he whispered. He kissed Lucy and held them both.

Suddenly, Lucy raised on one elbow. "Where's Nora?"

"Oh. I dropped her off at James and Mattie's place on the way to town. I'll have to go around and pick her up. She needs to meet her new little brother.

***

A few days later, Lucy took time to write to Rebekah.

June 20, 1889

Dear Rebekah,

Sorry I didn't write sooner. Had a boy on the 14th. William Albert. He is a little one. He's growing already. Nora likes him. She thinks he's her doll. Likes to poke at him, especially his eyes. Sanford sure is proud of him. He's a good baby. Sleeps a lot. Gives me time to weed the garden. I got a good stand of green beans this year.

How are you coming on the dugout? Got a door on yet? Do you ever see any Indians? Think of you often. How far are you from town? Do you have to haul water?

Sounds like you all are having a real adventure, though I don't envy you much.

Sanford has stopped talking about Oklahoma–for good, I hope.

Got any crops in? Ever bothered by those claim jumpers anymore? I would have been scared out of my skin if those fellas had come up on me. You're so brave, Rebekah.

Write and tell me how you're fairing.

Love,

Lucy

CHAPTER 9

July 6, 1889 - Got a letter from Uriah.

Lucy didn't have long to wait for another letter from Oklahoma, but this one was from Uriah instead of Rebekah. Sanford unfolded the letter. It was written on the back of a bill of sale for a door and a window.

July 6, 1889
Dear Sanford and Lucy,

Glad you had another son. We celebrated the 4th with a shindig in town. I found out some of the land around here isn't taken yet. How about you all coming down here to look things over? You're welcome to stay with us while you search. Albert is the nearest train station–only five miles. You could be here by train in just one day from Walker.

We have turnips and beans coming up; a pretty good stand. Dirt's a little redder here than in Vernon county. I got the dugout done. Rebekah is fancying it up with one of those checkered curtains at the window. Hope to start digging a well next week.

Uriah

Lucy's heart sank. Sanford's grin was as wide as the Missouri River.

"Did you hear that? There's still land! We still have a chance to get some for ourselves. Let's give it a whirl."

She snipped the threads on the baby dress she was sewing. "And take off with a six-week old baby and a 22-month-old holy terror on a wild goose chase to look at some dirt?"

"But..."

She cut him off quicker than an ax to a lamb's tail. "You have a place here. What about your crops? I thought this idea was dead."

"I didn't think there was any chance now that the rush was over."

"Our people are here. We've begun to make our home here. I don't want our children growing up so far from family."

"Well, maybe we could *all* go down. If there's land still available, maybe we could find claims real close together. I'm gonna write your dad. Maybe that fella is still interested in his place at Winston."

She couldn't say anything. Her chest hurt so bad she couldn't get her breath. What good were words anyway when you've married a deaf man? The baby began to cry. He was hungry... again. Nora came inside covered with dirt. Oklahoma? Lordy, there was too much to deal with right here.

Within the week, Sanford had a reply from Lucy's dad. It read,

Dear Sanford and Lucy,

Got your letter today. Mr. Gibbs was over last night wondering if I might still be interested in selling my place. Said he came into some money and had enough to make a down payment. Mary, Orris, Hanna and I are ready to pull up stakes here and move closer to you all. If you're of a mind to go to Oklahoma, we'll give it a try.

Take the train down there, Sanford and give it a look-see. We'll come down to Walker next Monday and stay with Lucy and the babies while you're gone. We need to see that little son of yours. Bet he's a fine one.

H.W.

Sanford read over the letter again. "Now doesn't that just beat all? I think this is a golden opportunity, for sure. It's set then. I'll go down for a look-see on Tuesday."

Forcing herself to stand, she grabbed the wooden bucket beside the back door and headed out to pump water from the well on wobbly legs. She could feel anger boil up within her with each downward stroke of the handle.

***

Over the next few days, Sanford's head swam with all the suppressed thoughts and plans tumbling over one another. *Would there really still be land when he got there? What if it wasn't suitable for farming? What would he do if there wasn't enough for he and H.W? Would they want to share a homestead? If it was all true, when would they leave? Would there be enough time to get a shelter built by winter?*

Lucy's parents came the following Monday as promised. They all loaded into the buckboard to see Sanford leave on the morning train bound for Oklahoma on Tuesday. While they stood on the wooden platform, the engineer yanked twice on the train whistle. "Toot, tooooot." The conductor called out "Board! All aboard," as he picked up the step stool and boarded the train. Hot steam rolled from beneath the engine's wheels.

"Take care, my doe." He reached down to kiss her. "Go with God," Lucy said with a sad resignation. She watched him bound into the coach as the train rolled forward. She strained on tiptoe for one last glimpse.

If a thief had stuck a gun in her ribs, she couldn't have felt any more robbed. She turned. Empty. Trapped. Alone. Forsaken, because of this lust for land she couldn't halt, any more than she could stop the wheels on the steam engine.

"Best be going, Daughter," H.W. said with a pat on her shoulder. "Be time for dinner before you know it."

All the way home, she fought back the tears. Where would this madness end?

When they got home H.W. took Nora to the barn to tend to the animals while Lucy put the baby down to sleep. Mary removed the blue willow cups from the pie safe. When the teakettle whistled, she poured hot water on to mint leaves in the teapot.

"Albert's sleeping sound," Lucy said as she took a seat at the table.

Mary replaced the teapot, sat, and ran her hand over the wrinkles in the blue checkered table cloth. Mary looked a long time at Lucy and then softly said, "Girl, why are you having such a hard time with this?"

Lucy took a sip of tea and thought for a moment. "I just can't abide the thought of moving into Indian Territory. Our lives are good here. I can't even imagine what Rebekah and Uriah are going through." Lucy slammed her fist on the table and made the teacups jump. "Darn it, Mary. I want Nora and Albert to grow up in civilized country. Aren't you having a tussle in your mind with this move?"

Mary fiddled with the spoon in her saucer. "I did at first. Then I began to remember my covenant with H.W. I promised to be his helpmate. I'm yoked to him. Can't help him if I dig my heels in. Have to go where he goes; do what he feels is right."

Lucy was quiet for a long time. She stared at her hands in her lap. Mary's words struck deep in her heart. These were not the words she wanted to hear. Hadn't she been a good wife to Sanford? Lucy had never been one to keep silent if she had a differing opinion. Did she have to agree with Sanford all the time?

She opened her mouth to protest Mary's statement, but no words came out. Instead, only a silent prayer. *Oh Lord, help me be the wife you want me to be. I turn this whole thing over to you and your will. Have I been so busy telling Sanford I wouldn't go that I've been working against Your will for us?*

The thought had never occurred to her that maybe, just maybe, Oklahoma was exactly where God wanted them. This idea was going to need thinking time. Maybe by the time her man got back, she would have some clear answers on this new thought.

CHAPTER 10

August 7, 1889 - Arrived in Alfred; now called Mulhall.

Sanford settled into a spot on the train with his valise under his seat. He could hardly believe he was finally headed for Oklahoma Territory on the Atchison, Topeka and Santa Fe.

The train swayed in a certain rhythm on the southwest-bound tracks as he watched the landscape whiz by. This is the adventure of a lifetime. *A month ago, I never dreamed I'd be sitting here headed for Oklahoma Territory. If I'm lucky, they'll still be some land left.*

The conductor held out his hand for Sanford's ticket.

"Heading for Mulhall, are ye?

"Alfred."

"Changed the name last week. Now it's Mulhall," the conductor said as he punched his ticket.

"Well, sir, I don't really care what they call it, long as I get some free land."

The conductor chuckled and handed the ticket back to him. "Good luck to you."

As morning turned to afternoon, Sanford reached into his valise for a ham sandwich Lucy had wrapped in butcher paper and tied with a string. The image of his doe holding their new son was ever before him. He missed her and the children already. If successful, his family would soon be on this train together, headed for their own place.

The hard wooden seat afforded little comfort for Sanford's bony frame during the long train ride. He awoke through the night each time the train stopped at small towns, which weren't much more than a water tank and coal bin.

At one stop, a husband and wife boarded with a crying baby who refused to sleep or be comforted. Finally, Sanford gave up hope of sleep and watched dawn break. As the sun rose, he squinted to get a view of the countryside. The large oak, sycamore and cottonwoods of Missouri and Kansas had disappeared. They were replaced with only scrawny miniatures over gently rolling hills of tall prairie grass. A warm breeze blew in the window.

"Mulhall! Mulhall next stop!" the conductor called as he strolled through the car.

Sanford gathered his things. Even though he slept little, he wasn't tired. The excitement of walking on Oklahoma soil gave him boundless energy.

The train pulled into the depot as Sanford stood and brushed the cinders off his clothes. Would you look at that! They've got buildings up already! There was a hotel, a bank and a general store with a lumberyard down the street. It all looked like a regular town, except all the lumber was new.

He stepped onto the depot platform and took a deep whiff of new-cut hay. Such beautiful country. Uriah was right when he talked about red dirt. "Oooeeeee." Sanford shook his head and muttered to himself, "Hell's dirt couldn't be much redder than this, if hell has dirt."

He first stopped at the general store.

"How can I help you, mister?" The clerk peered at Sanford over his wire-rimmed glasses.

"I'm looking for a Mr. Miller. Uriah Miller. Any idea where I might find him? He said he lived about five miles west of here."

"You got business with him?" the clerk said as he eyed him suspiciously.

"He said I might still find a claim. We're friends. From Missouri."

"Mebbe. Miller... Miller." The clerk scratched his beard. "Let's see. I think there's a family by that name out there somewhere. You might take the trail down from the station a bit. Don't rightly know the exact location."

"Thanks. Is there a livery stable around here?"

"Yep. One block over," the clerk said as he pointed east."

Sanford found his way to the stable. “Got any horses to let?”

The blacksmith put down his hammer and shoved the horseshoe back into the glowing fire with his tongs. Taking out a handkerchief from the back pocket of his overalls, he wiped his bald head as he pointed toward the back. “Sure. Got a nice filly back here. How long you need her for?”

“Few days maybe. I’m looking for some unclaimed land. Hear there’s some out west of here.”

The blacksmith nodded. “Here and there.”

“I’m looking for a Uriah Miller from Missouri. Ever heard of him?”

“Nope. But then I’ve not heard of most folks around here. Everybody here is from somewhere else.”

The blacksmith went to the back and saddled the black mare. “Here you go.”

“What do I owe ya?”

“Jest leave me $2.00. We can settle up when you get back. “Few days you say?”

“Depends on how long it’ll take me to find a claim.”

The blacksmith extended his hand. “Well, Good luck to ya... what did you say your name was?”

He shook his hand. “Sanford. Sanford Deering. Walker, MO. And you are...?”

“Ike Munsey. Tennessee. Good luck, Sanford. Hope you find all you’re looking for.”

Sanford swung his valise onto the saddle horn, mounted, and started out of town on the rutted trail to the west.

By mid-afternoon, Sanford passed at least a dozen dugouts, huts, and several campsites dotted along the rolling landscape. He stopped by a stream for a cool drink. While the horse drank, he broke the shells on two hard-boiled eggs Lucy had packed for him. As he ate, he heard someone sawing nearby. Finishing his lunch, he walked to the next ridge and spotted a dugout just beyond, near a gulch.

“Howdy,” Sanford said.

The man stopped sawing and wiped his forehead, face and neck with a red bandana. He extended his hand. “Howdy, stranger. A real scorcher today, ain’t it?”

“Yes. Guess you could say that.” Sanford shook his hand.

"Looking for someone in particular?"

"Looking for a fella by the name of Uriah Miller. Might he live hereabouts?"

"From Missouri?" The man wiped his forehead again.

"Walker."

"They're just over the next hill. Friend of yours?"

"Yes. He told me there's still some land available."

"A little. Some parcels were claimed by city slickers who gave up and went home already. Then there's pockets no one's claimed yet. Check with a real estate office or the land office in Guthrie. Those fellas keep up on what land's available."

Sanford mounted his horse and tipped his hat. "Thank you kindly, sir. 'Preciate it."

Over the next ridge, Sanford recognized Uriah's horse tied under some cottonwoods near the edge of a stream.

"Uriah! You here abouts?" he called.

"Who goes there? That you, Sanford?"

He walked toward the voice coming out of a hole in the red earth, squatted down and peered in. "Looks like you're in up to your neck old buddy. Need some help?"

Uriah scrambled up the ladder and gave Sanford a bear hug. "You're a sight for sore eyes. I never turn down good help. You came just in time. I could use another pair of hands. You were to let me know when you were coming."

"Thought I'd surprise you."

"That you did," Uriah said as he wiped his hands on his pants. I've been digging several days. I figure I ought to hit some water soon."

Sanford glanced around. "Where's Rebekah and the kids?"

"They're spending the day at a neighbor's. Quilting bee. Have any trouble finding me?"

"Nope. Just headed west out of town. Where's all this land you're hollering about?"

Uriah bobbed his head toward the hole in the ground. "Help me with this well and I'll tell ya."

"I knew this information would come at a price, you old fox."

"Just a small one," Uriah chuckled.

They worked for a couple of hours with no sign of water and sat down to rest under the shade of a scrawny tree.

"You sure there's water down there, Uriah?"

He wiped his forehead with his sleeve, raised one eyebrow and looked at Sanford for a long moment. "You may not believe this, but an old water-witcher fella helped me out."

"A water-witcher? You believe that stuff? I've heard tales about those fellas, but never thought it was a for sure thing."

"Figgered I needed some extra help before I started digging. He sure made a believer outta me."

"Yeah? How?"

"He cut off this forked willow stick down by the creek and held it in each hand with the point sticking up. Then he walked back and forth across this patch here. All of a sudden, the point on that willow stick twisted down to the ground like somebody was pulling on it. Peeled the bark clean off that switch."

"And you dug there?"

"Right where we're a diggin'. Folks swear by him around here. Ever place he tells them to dig, they find water. He's busier than a maw-cat with a new litter of kittens."

"What's he charge? I might better get my name on his list."

"Better get a claim first, my friend."

"Can't do that till you tell me where to look, Uriah. From what I saw on the way out here, there's not much to be had."

"I've got a couple pieces spied out within five miles of here. We can check 'em out tomorrow. If it fills the bill, you can go on down to Guthrie and claim it."

"I'd like to find some for my father-in-law and brother-in-law too."

"Don't want much, do ya, ole buzzard?"

"About the only way I'm going to get Lucy down here is to bring her whole family."

"That letter she sent Rebekah didn't sound like she had any intentions of coming."

"You didn't have to read between the lines much to figure that one out. I finally gave up any hope of claiming any land till I got your letter."

"Well, I'm glad I wrote it then. I hope we can find you something."

"Me too." Sanford got up and looked in the well. "Hey. Lookie here. Some water's collecting in here. That old water-witcher might be right after all!"

They dug with renewed fervor. After an hour of steady digging Uriah said, "Hallelujah, Sanford! Looks like we got water!"

"Guess that witcher fella knows what he's talking about, Uriah! This ought to put a smile on that wife of yours."

"She'll be one happy woman, for sure."

By late afternoon, Rebekah and the children came home. "Well I'll be. Look what the wind blew in!" she said as she rode into the yard. "My Lord in heaven! Is it really you, Sanford? You were gonna let us know..."

"I know, I know. Just call me an Oklahoma surprise."

"This place is full of those, but never expected you to be one of 'em. I better get you fellas some dinner. You best get cleaned up now, hear? I don't let no mud pies come to my table." Rebekah handed them a big bar of lye soap and pointed toward the stream.

Sanford looked at his hands and said, "This is gonna take some doing."

"You don't know the half of it. This stuff sticks like stink on manure."

After scrubbing his hands and face in the stream for a few minutes, Sanford understood exactly what Uriah meant.

"Suppose this is why the Indians are so red, Uriah? I think this mud must sink in permanent-like."

"Could be. Rebekah sure has an awful time getting it out of the clothes. I hear about it plenty. Don't say anything about it at dinner or you'll be hearing about it all evening."

Rebekah warmed a pot of vegetable soup and made some corn bread in the iron skillet nestled between hot coals outside the dugout.

"How's Lucy? Changed her mind?" Rebekah said over supper.

"Nope. But if I found some land for us and her family, it might help me to change it for her. Uriah said he was gonna show me some that's kind of out of the way he thinks might work. We'll go out there in the morning." He took another piece of cornbread. "Right nice dinner, Rebekah."

"Thank you. You got a good guide there. Uriah seems to know about those things."

Uriah shot Sanford a grin and then said, "Rebekah, guess what we found down that hole today."

"Buried treasure, no doubt."

"Well, you could say that. By the time rains come in fall and the water table rises we could have water just for the dipping."

"You hit water? Why didn't you tell me? This is wonderful!"

"Don't get too excited, woman. We got to line it with rocks. That's our next project."

"While I'm in Guthrie, you all gather rocks and when I come back, I'll help you line the well."

"All help is greatly appreciated. I know the little woman will be most obliged. Who knows, by fall, I might be able to return the favor on your place."

"Hope that's a true prediction, for sure."

"So do I, neighbor."

CHAPTER 11

August 12, 1889 - Staked my claim in Guthrie today.

Early the next morning, Sanford and Uriah saddled their horses and headed southeast just after first light.

"Got a good little stream running through this quarter, Sanford."

They came up over a rise. A slight breeze and the early morning sun greeted them. It shed a gentle glow over the prairie grass, dotted with small trees along the stream. A meadowlark greeted the peaceful morning.

"What do you think, Sanford? Think Lucy'd like this place?"

"Don't know why she wouldn't. Pretty as a picture. Good soil. We could put our dugout over there. Looks like a fine place to me, Uriah."

"Let me show you the other place I had in mind. It's the next quarter section just south and east of here."

"I can't believe these places aren't taken."

"Well, you'll have to check at the land office. Maybe they were saved just for you. Who knows."

The second quarter section was lower in elevation but as beautiful as the first.

"This'd be a great place for Frank and his family. Do you know of any more open claims?"

"Well, I'm not sure. There may be one on the southeast corner of this section. Folks were camped out on it for a few days but I don't know if they ever claimed it. We can check the corner markers to see if there is a name on it. You can check on it in Guthrie."

"These would fill the bill for sure. Guess I better high-tail it down there before someone else claims it."

"You're welcome to stay with us while you build a dugout."

"Thank you kindly, Uriah. After I get back from the land office I may stay here a couple of nights, but I'll be back up your way. I'll help you however I can before I go."

Uriah bid him good-bye and good luck and headed for home and Sanford set out for Guthrie.

Sanford rode over the rolling landscape, through small creeks, and past numerous homesteads on the way to Guthrie. A train whistle blew in the distance. He sang a little song to himself.

Going to find my way,
This very day,
Going to find my way,
That's what I say,
Going to find my way,
This very day,
Oh happy day.

"Yes sirree. This land feels like home," he whispered. By the time the sun passed overhead, he reached Guthrie and tied his horse outside a local eatery. He enjoyed a slab of smoked ham, a glass of milk and a piece of blackberry pie for two bits.

After dinner, he asked the waiter, "Where's the land office?"

"Down the street a block. Staking a claim?"

"Yep."

"Good luck to ya."

The square wooden clapboard building was perched on a rise just before the train station.

"Can I help you, young fella?" the clerk said.

"Hope so. Looking to stake a claim. I want to sign for me, my brother-in-law and father-in-law."

"Whole clan on the move, are ye?"

"You bet. I spied out some claims up in Rose Hill township."

"Well, let me see here." He unrolled a large land plat on the table. Each little square was divided into four equal quarters. Names were penciled in on the already claimed quarter sections.

"Got some open spaces up there. Let's see now. Here's one up in Rose Hill. Southeast corner of quarter 11, in section 18, range 3."

"Put Sanford Deering on that one. Is the one southeast of there open? I told my brother-in-law I'd sign him up too."

"Yep. It's open."

"Make that one for Franklin Estes."

"The clerk penciled Frank's name on 13-18-3.""How about the southeast corner of that quarter?"

"No name on it. Want that one too?"

"Yep. H.W. Estes. That'll fill the bill. Thank you kindly. We'll be moving in as soon as we can load out stock and possessions."

"I need to warn ya, if nobody shows up to prove up these places within six months this transaction is no good. With winter coming you need to get a move on."

"We'll be here. You can count on it."

"That'll be $14.00 each for the filing fee. Good luck."

Sanford paid the filing fee and tipped his hat. As he walked out of the land office he glanced at the papers in his hand and noted the date. August 12, 1889. A day to remember... forever.

Stopping by the general store he bought some jerky to eat on the trail and a shovel to start on a dugout. The sun cast long shadows by the time Sanford headed back to his claim.

He slept on the open prairie that night and at first light, pointed his mount toward Rose Hill township, homestead of Sanford Deering and company.

By noon, Sanford made it to his claim. His first task was to find the corners of his claim and mark them with the proper names. Near the place he chose for the dugout, he found a patch of turnips gone to seed. After he harvested the turnips, he re-planted the seeds.

"This oughta make the little doe happy. She loves turnips."

Next, he chose a shaded area by an outcropping of rocks to start a dugout. "This'll do for shelter till we can get a soddy built."

He dug a ten foot square down about four feet. On the fourth day he finished digging and hunted large dead branches to help hold up the roof of the dugout. He planned to bust some sod or buy a tarp to lay over the branches when he returned.

In the afternoon he took some time off to go hunting for a wild turkey. It wasn't long before he bagged one. For supper that night he roasted the bird and some turnips over the open fire, while he whistled "Turkey in the Straw" softly to himself.

"Now this is living," he said as he leaned back on a rock and enjoyed his feast.

The fire lighted the gathering night. He rolled out his bedroll on the red earth, rested his hands behind his head, and looked up at a sky filled with what seemed to be a million stars. Cicadas rose in a cacophony. Sparks flew up into the cool night air.

His thoughts turned toward home. *Lucy, I hope I can get you down to this place. It's the next best place to heaven you'll ever see.*

The following morning Sanford was at Uriah's early.

"Find something, my friend?"

"One for each of us."

Uriah slapped his knee and gave a hoot. "Oooee! You ole' turkey! You must be Irish, seeing the luck you got. Rebekah, we got us a new neighbor."

She paused her scrubbing, looked up from the washtub and grinned. "It will be nice to have some home folks around here."

"Just blind luck." Inside, Sanford hoped that luck didn't run out before he could get Lucy down here. That would be a miracle for sure.

"Blind luck or whatever it is, it sure is powerful! When you coming down?"

"Soon as we can reserve a car from the railroad and get our plunder organized. Got some milo and cane to cut. I imagine Lucy'll have a list as long as my arm of things to do before we can leave."

"What's the earliest you all can be down here?"

"We'll have to come in a month if we're going to get a soddy built before winter, don't you imagine?

"Yep. You'll have to step lively to get it done."

Sanford picked up a rock. "You ready to line that well yet?"

"Well, to be honest, I need help haying more than lining the well right now."

"I'd be pleased to help you."

"That's real neighborly of you, neighbor!"

After two weeks, Sanford announced at supper, “Best be a getting home. Lucy’s gonna wonder if some Indian got me. Sure doesn’t feel like I’ve been here this long.”

“Come back anytime. I appreciate the help.”

“Glad to do it, neighbor,” Sanford said with a grin and a hardy handshake.

The next morning, he dropped the rented mare off at the blacksmith’s shop. Then he sent a telegram to Walker asking H.W. to meet him the next morning at 4:30 A.M. He was homeward bound, on the 6:30 train that evening.

He could hardly wait to tell Lucy and the others about his find. Hopefully, she would resign herself to her new location without too much fuss.

CHAPTER 12

October 3, 1889 - Loading the boxcar.

The train pulled into the Walker station in the moonlit night as a dog barked at the hissing steam engine in the pre-dawn darkness. H. W. waited on the platform for Sanford to appear.

"Welcome home, my boy!" he said as he shook Sanford's hand and pounded him heartily on the arm. "So, did you find us a claim in the Territory?"

"You bet I did. One for you, Frank, and me. All in a diagonal. Nice rolling hills."

They walked to the wagon together. "When you figure you'll get down there?" H. W. said as he shoved Sanford's bag in the back of the wagon.

"Soon as possible. We'll each have to reserve a boxcar. When do you figure you can get your land sold in Winston?"

"The fella wants it as soon as we can move. I'd like to go in a couple weeks, maybe. Winter will be on us before you know it. Frank and Anna won't come till they can sell their land. Said he had someone asking about it earlier in the year. Maybe those folks are still interested."

They climbed into the wagon and turned the horses toward home. "Frank has six months before he has to be there. He might want to wait till late winter. Be easier for all of us if we only had to build two houses instead of three before bad weather sets in."

"You may have a point there, my boy."

"Two weeks might be rushing it, H. W. It'll probably take more like a month for us. Gotta sell my corn and haul some cane."

"I guess the missus and I better head for home today on the afternoon train so we can get started," H. W. said.

"I'll let you know when we're about to go."

On the way home, Sanford watched light begin to dawn and wondered just how he was going to get Lucy to finally agree to go. He might have a real fight on his hands.

H.W. pulled the team up to the house just as the sun peeked over the horizon. Lucy had bacon and eggs and gravy on the stove and biscuits in the oven.

"Wooee! Sure missed those biscuits and gravy, Lucy."

"Just the biscuits and gravy?"

"No. Missed you too, my doe." Sanford grabbed her waist and hugged her tightly whirling her around the kitchen. He buried his head in her neck and took a deep breath. "Seems like forever since I smelled your sweet lilac cologne," he whispered in her ear.

"Missed you too, Sanford," Lucy whispered as she hugged him extra tight. "I was beginning to wonder if you forgot where you lived."

"Couldn't forget that." He tiptoed into the bedroom to touch his sleeping children. "What have you been feeding Albert? He's so much bigger," he whispered.

"Well, if you hadn't stayed away so long, you could have watched him fill out. He eats all the time."

H. W. leaned back in a kitchen chair and called into the bedroom. "Better pack your bags, Mary. I think it's about time to leave these two alone." He chuckled and winked at Sanford.

With all the commotion, Nora and Hanna awoke. Nora ran for Sanford, arms open wide. "Daddy! Daddy!"

He scooped her up and folded her in his arms. "My princess! Did you miss me?"

She nodded her head while she snuggled down into his embrace.

Nora ate breakfast sitting on Sanford's lap while he recounted each step of the journey and described the land in a selective way. He emphasized the fact that all three plots were together in an attempt to reassure Lucy, but carefully left out certain facts like Rebekah's dislike for the red dirt. No use stirring Lucy up over minor details. His wife was surprisingly quiet and cheerful as she heard about their new home.

Sanford and H. W. sat at the kitchen table most of the morning making a list of things they needed to take and another list of things they needed to buy when they got there.

It was late morning when Sanford loaded Lucy's folks' things into the wagon. Sanford took H. W., Mary, Orris and Hanna to the station just in time for the early afternoon train headed for Kansas City and points beyond.

Sanford wondered if a real set-to was about to happen when he and Lucy got home alone together.

He entered the kitchen and grabbed the list of supplies jotting down a few more things that came to mind. Lucy boiled some thick black coffee and looked over his shoulder. She put a steaming hot black cup down in front of him.

"Looks like your list is growing awfully long, Sanford."

"Just the important stuff we need to take. Not gonna have a lot of room in that boxcar by the time we get the stock loaded."

I want to talk to you a little," she said as she poured herself a cup and sat down across from him. At first, Lucy didn't say anything–just looked into her coffee.

Sanford could hear it coming. All the arguments why they shouldn't go. In his mind he was formulating a list of counter-arguments to the protests he had already heard a hundred times before.

Finally she spoke. "Sanford, I... I think the Territory's exactly where we're supposed to be."

He was dumbstruck. What in the world happened? Had he heard her right? Did she say she was in favor of moving? He was sure he was going to face another Civil War when he got back, and now she was agreeing to go? Just like that? He was curious, but at the same time he didn't want to upset the apple cart by asking too many questions.

He cleared his throat and whispered, "You're willing to go? What... brought this on?"

Her eyes met his. "Mary and I had a talk. She reminded me that you and I are yoked together as a team and that I am your helper. If you feel we should go to the Territory, that's where God must be leading us."

Was this a dream? He sat there in stunned silence and then willed his feet to come around the table and kneel beside Lucy's chair. Tears welled up in his eyes.

Words tumbled out his mouth. "Lucy, you're gonna love it. It's so beautiful. I already started on a dugout. I gathered branches for the roof and cut a pile of firewood. And I planted some turnips, too, just for you. This place even has a stream nearby and a nice stand of trees."

Even in his haste he noticed the word "dugout" disturbed her a little and made a mental note not use that word again. After all, he wouldn't want her to change her mind at this point. No siree. No turning back now. Oklahoma, here we come!

***

Over the next month, Sanford made arrangements for the boxcar with the railway and got their belongings together. He sold his corn and hauled it to town and cut and hauled his cane.

Lucy helped dig potatoes and dry peaches. She was busy deciding which items to pack and which to sell at the auction. When she wasn't tending the children, she packed barrels. When Lucy's back was turned, Nora had great fun unpacking small wooden crates already packed for the trip.

She set the packed items to go to Oklahoma on one side of the fireplace along with a few pieces of furniture. All the rest went on the other side of the room.

Sanford came from cutting the last of the cane just in time for supper. He dried his hands and stood in front of the fireplace.

"Is this the pile to sell?" he said.

"No. That's the 'take' pile."

"Lucy, we can't take all this stuff. It'd take two boxcars to move all this plunder. I'll make you some new furniture when we get there."

He grabbed the walnut dresser and pulled it to the other side of the room to the "sell" pile. Grandfather Deering's rocker was the next to go. When he picked up a wooden crate marked "Mama's dishes" Lucy shrieked, "Stop!"

Sanford almost dropped the crate. He turned to look at her in dismay. "What in the world is wrong with you, woman? You look like you've seen a ghost."

"Sanford Deering. Put that crate down." Lucy's eyes looked like they might pop out of her head. She wrung her hands in her apron. The veins in her skinny neck bulged in blue lines. "I'll not have some stranger eating off of Mama's dishes. Those'll belong to Nora some day. We're not leaving Mama's dishes *or* the rocker."

"We got to have room for the plow and the farm stuff in the boxcar, woman. This house stuff is not essential. It can all be replaced."

"You can't replace Mama's dishes or that rocking chair. It may not be important to you, but it is to me. We're not just going to build a farm. We're going to make a home."

Sanford knew he better back down in a hurry or he would be in the same place where all this started with an unwilling wife and broken dreams. He set the crate down in the rocker and drug them back to the "take" pile.

"Guess I'll be taking a little less equipment to the Territory than I figured," he muttered under his breath.

***

By October second, all their goods were packed. At daybreak the morning of the third, Sanford's brothers James and Henry helped make several wagon trips to town to load the boxcar. In the afternoon, Sanford came home for the final wagonload.

"Is that all?" Sanford called to Lucy while he lashed the last barrel down.

"Nothing left in here Sanford, except one wife and two children," she said from the front door.

"Don't know if there's any room for them on this wagon," Sanford said through a grin.

"Well, you're just going to have to make room. We're going," Lucy said with a laugh.

Sanford tied Ginger's reins to the back of the wagon while Lucy plopped into the seat and placed Nora between them, holding Albert on her lap. Lucy sighed as she took a long look at the last civilized home they would have for a long while. Everything in her fought back the urge to jump down off the wagon and announce she changed her mind. After all, she never envisioned herself as a pioneer woman.

On the way to town she said, "This must be the way sardines feel all squished in a can."

Sanford laughed. "Never thought about the feelings of a sardine."

James and Henry worked a good portion of the day to load their belongings into the boxcar. In mid-afternoon, Sanford rode Ginger back to the farm to drive Jers, the milk cow, and two hogs to the railroad station. Sanford milked Jers, and took the milk to the hotel dining room for part payment on their room. The kitchen help gave him some potato peels to feed the hogs. There was barely room for Ginger, Jers, the hogs and the wagon in the space left in rail car.

Meanwhile, Lucy settled the children in the hotel room. She sat on the edge of the feather bed and watched the children sleep. She wished she could take this soft mattress with her to her new home. From here on, it would be a bed of straw on a dirt floor in a dugout.

She wondered, "Have I made the right decision?" Panic began to rise in her until she remembered Mary's words, "I'm his helpmate. I must go where he goes." The words calmed her fearful heart.

Sanford made one last trip to take the team of horses to the person who bought them at the sale. He lived just east of Walker.

"Hope you're pleased with them, Homer. They'll make you a good team," Sanford said.

"I'm sure they will, Sanford. They're a fine match. Wish you all the best in the Territory. Come see us if you ever get back up this way."

"Much obliged." Sanford tipped his hat and turned his face toward their new home.

CHAPTER 13

October 7, 1889 - Met Mr. Jeremiah Jump.

Just after four the next morning, Sanford had Lucy and the children up, ready to meet the 4:30 train at the depot. The children slept on Lucy's lap in the waiting room. They awoke with a start when the train pulled into the station. The engineer gave a long blast on the train's shrill whistle. Albert started to cry.

After Sanford made sure their boxcar was coupled to the train, he hopped aboard as they pulled out of the depot and headed for Nevada, Missouri. They reached Fort Scott, Kansas just after sun-up. The day passed in a blur of corn and wheat fields, punctuated at regular intervals with frequent stops to take on fuel and water for the steam engine.

The last faint rays of sunlight found them near the Kansas border, about to enter Indian Territory, somewhere south of Wichita. The cool fall evening breeze carried the hint of an early winter.

Lucy slept, or at least tried to, knowing they were scheduled to arrive at 2:30 A.M. in Mulhall. She awoke somewhat disoriented when Sanford shook her shoulder. He took Nora off her lap and said, "Lucy, we're here. Grab your bag. We've got five minutes. I've gotta make sure they leave our boxcar on the siding."

Stumbling to her feet she juggled the baby and their bag. On the depot platform, she tried to see her surroundings. It was pitch black.

The conductor pointed across the street. "The hotel's that way ma'am."

Soon Sanford came alongside with Nora asleep on his shoulder. They walked quietly to the hotel together.

"I'll have to get a teamster in the morning to help us move the goods. Just wait till you see this place. You'll be so surprised."

Morning came all too soon. Sanford was dressed and gone before Lucy awoke. She decided to let the children sleep as long as they would.

Quietly creeping to the window Lucy peered out to get a glimpse of her new homeland.

"My heavens! What red dirt! I thought south Missouri dirt was red but this is unbelievable. Even the rocks are red!" she mumbled to herself.

***

Sanford was back before 8:00 A.M.

Lucy's first words to him when he walked in were "This dirt's so red. Looks like someone took barn paint to it!"

"Redder than Missouri. That's fer sure." He decided to not say anymore than he had to about it. She would find out soon enough how hard it was to get out of the children's clothes. He quickly changed the subject.

"Found a fella who's gonna help us carry our goods tomorrow. He's new in town. Drove down here with his mule team and wagon from Nebraska. He thinks it might take three or four days to get all our stuff hauled out there."

"How far is this place?" Lucy asked.

"Oh, about five miles west and a quarter south of here. Uriah and Rebekah are only about five miles north of us. Maybe we'll go to see them soon. I bought big tarpaulins at the general store this morning to put over the branches on the dugout. We'll tie another one to some trees to make a shelter to store our stuff till we can get the house built."

After a long silence he continued, "I have the dugout almost ready. Just needs some sod on the roof and a trap door."

"You mean a hole in the ground."

"Yeah. It'll make a good root cellar once we get the soddy built."

Lucy didn't say anything but her head was a mass of swirling thoughts. *Lordy! We might as well be a bunch of ground hogs living in a hole in the ground. Somehow, that's not my definition of a house. Oh, Lucy Deering. Hush. Be glad we've got some shelter over our heads. You're here now. Make the best of it.*

***

The next day Sanford and the teamster unloaded the pigs, Jers, Ginger, and the wagon from the boxcar. He boarded the animals for two bits a day plus the milk Jers gave. The animal's temporary home would be at the livery stable next to Ike Munsey's blacksmith shop until Sanford could drive them to their homestead.

Lucy was torn. She didn't want to stay in town with the children, but she didn't want to be alone in unfamiliar territory while Sanford went into town for another load, either. Sanford was anxious to show her the place he had chosen. Finally, she decided to go on the first trip out. There was no use putting it off. She made sure the rocking chair and Mama's dishes were on the wagon with them. The nonessentials could come later.

At dawn the next morning, Sanford filled the water barrels from the pump on the main street. He left enough room in the wagon for two sacks, one of flour and one of cornmeal. Next to them he put a side of bacon and some canned beans he bought at the general store. He wedged his rifle on the side of the wagon behind the seat.

"Never know when I might need this," he mumbled when he felt Lucy's eyes on him.

Sanford pointed their wagon pulled with a rented team of horses out of town on the western trail. The teamster, Thomas, followed behind in his wagon.

On their way over the rolling hills through tall prairie grass, they passed a few colorful fall trees where a stream wound its way through the hills. All the foliage was smaller than in Missouri. Every so often they passed a dugout or a soddy with smoke curling out the chimney. Many had corrals and a lean-to for a barn.

Lucy thought to herself. *If we had come in the rush in April, we'd already have a shelter up now.* Even though the sun was bright, a cool gust of wind blew red dust into her eyes.

After an hour and a half, they turned south. "Just another quarter mile," Sanford said. He slapped the reins, "Get up there."

Lucy's bottom hurt from bouncing on the buckboard and her arms ached from holding the baby. Just as she opened her mouth to ask Sanford to stop, he pulled the team up on a ridge.

"There it is," he said as he stood and swept his hand across the landscape. "Our very own homestead. Isn't it just a sight to behold?"

She surveyed the rolling hills of brown prairie grass dotted with scrubby trees poked into the red dirt. It did indeed have a stream, but the water in it was as red as the earth. Not a house in sight. Just a hole in the ground by a pile of branches near an outcropping of red limestone rocks. Maybe it would look better by spring with a sod house on it, if she was lucky.

Lucy struggled to say, "Yes, Sanford. Pretty as a picture." On the inside she thought. *Lord! How will this place ever become our home?*

The men tied a tarpaulin to four trees to form a shelter for their goods close to the dugout. They unloaded the wagons and built a fire just beyond the tarpaulin.

Lucy opened a can of beans with a jackknife, and heated them while she made cornbread in her iron skillet in the hot coals. She went to lie down under the shelter beside the sleeping children for a few minutes until the men were ready to eat. It had been a long day for them all. She drifted into an exhausted sleep.

While Sanford and Thomas unloaded the last of the wagons, he saw something move out of the corner of his eye. It was an old man. He appeared out of nowhere. Drat! My rifle is on the other side of the camp.

"What you boys think you're doin'? This here's *my* place." The scrappy old fellow had dirty long white hair tied with a piece of rawhide at the back of his wrinkled neck. His felt hat was ragged around the edges; looked like he might have used it for a pillow it was so misshapen. Buckskin leggings covered his skinny frame complete with a red flannel shirt and moccasins, a rusty old lever-action Winchester in his hand.

Sanford said, "Afraid you're mistaken, mister. This is *my* place."

The old man raised his rifle to his shoulder and cocked it with his thumb as he took a bead on Sanford. "I beg to differ with ya."

"Now hold on there, old fella. I got papers to prove it."

"I don't care what you got. This here's *my* place. See these turnips? I planted 'em."

Sanford eased closer to him with his hands raised in the air. "Got proof of that?"

"I don't need no proof. I been living here since '65. Stand back or I'll put a plug right square in your middle. Now get off my place 'fore I shoot ya dead."

Sanford knew he was lying, but lie or no, he'd be just as dead if this old buzzard let loose on that trigger. From the looks of that gun, it might even blow up in the old man's face if he shot it.

Unnoticed by the old man, Thomas circled around behind him. He signaled to Sanford and they made a dive for him together. In the scuffle, the Winchester discharged. Ricocheting off the rocks just above the dugout, pieces of red limestone pelted the tarpaulin. The shot woke Lucy and the children. Lucy sat up with a start and stifled a scream, while the children erupted in loud squalls.

He was a tough old bird–put up a heck of a fight. But Sanford and Thomas overpowered him and tied him to a tree until they could take him into town the next morning.

They tried to offer him some beans and cornbread, but he'd have none of it. He seemed a bit confused. Needless to say, no one got much sleep all night while they listened to his ranting.

Lucy even tried to sleep in the dugout, but she couldn't see him from that vantage point. About midnight she snuggled in next to Sanford under the tarpaulin. She tried to keep one eye open in his direction, but it didn't work. Her open eyes closed along toward morning, in spite of her best efforts.

At first light, Sanford and Thomas plopped the old boy in the back of Sanford's wagon and tied him securely, in spite of his colorful protests.

"Gimmie my gun, you dad-blamed thieves! This ain't no way to treat a bonafide landowner! Where do ya think you're taking me, anyway?"

"Taking you in to get this land ownership thing cleared up," Sanford said.

"Here, Thomas, you be in charge of his gun."

Before they left, Sanford quickly tucked his own rifle beside Lucy.

"Wake up, my doe," he whispered. "I'll be back as soon as I can. Don't expect you'll have to use this, but just in case..."

Lucy lay there in stunned silence turning over Sanford's words in her head. Surely this must be a dream. Her hand fumbled through her blanket to the cold hard steel barrel nestled in beside her. A big tear rolled down her cheek.

Sanford's recent words of "You're going to love this place," echoed in her mind. Somehow, this wasn't quite the image she had envisioned. Was this what she had come all this way for?

Just a few days ago, her greatest problem was how to get all her precious belongings into a boxcar. A week ago, she slept in a bed with a feather mattress under a secure roof in a real home in a civilized land. Now, here she was, alone with her children with a hole in the ground to sleep in, an open fire for a kitchen and a gun to defend them from who knows what.

"Oh Lord! Have you forgotten us? Please protect us in this wild place," she quietly cried.

CHAPTER 14

October 8, 1889 - Nora got lost today.

Sanford and Thomas stopped under the sign "Mulhall Jail ~ Sheriff Jim Hensley." Thomas stayed with their "cargo" while Sanford went inside.

"Sheriff Hensley?"

"The same."

"Sanford Deering. Just moved out to our claim from Walker, Missouri. My helper, Thomas and I, got an old buzzard out in my wagon. Swears my homestead is his property. Know anything about him?"

Sheriff Hensley stepped to the window. "Oh, I see you've met our local loco, Jeremiah Jump."

"Know him?"

The sheriff laughed. "He adds a little spice around here. Getting to be a regular nuisance, though."

"Is that what you all call 'spice?' He darn near shot us with that old rifle of his."

"Well, that's a new twist. Usually he just scares the wits out of new settlers."

The sheriff went outside. "Jeremiah, going to have to lock you up again. Last time I let you out, you swore you'd head back to Indian Territory. This fella here says you about plugged him. I'll have to run you in. Have to keep your weapon, too."

Thomas handed the rusty relic over to the sheriff.

"These fellas camped out on my place. I'm plugging anyone who takes my land, including you, Sheriff," Jeremiah said.

"With that kind of talk you'll end up in the pokey for a *long* time. Better watch your lip."

"Better watch yours, Sheriff. That's *my* land."

The sheriff wrangled the old coot into the jail cell and sat down to talk to Sanford and Thomas.

"He's pretty feisty for such an old buzzard," Sanford said.

"Yeah. I'll keep him locked up for a few days. Maybe his head'll clear by then."

"Never seen him, Thomas?"

"Nope. I just come down here from Nebraska. Don't care if I never see him again, neither."

The sheriff motioned his guests to sit and continued, "The story goes, he's an old Civil War soldier who was captured after he took one to the head at Wilson's Creek up by Springfield. After the war he came out here and lived off the land. With all these settlers moving in, he's kind of misplaced. Can't figure out where all these 'Yankees' are coming from."

"He always this cantankerous?" Sanford asked.

"Nope. Some days he's as sane as you or me. Other days he's as confused as a chicken with his head cut off."

"Yesterday must have been one of his 'chicken' days. I'm sure my Lucy would rest easier if you just 'forgot' to let him out. Had enough trouble getting that woman to come down here. People like him sure won't help her stay."

The sheriff placed Jeremiah's old gun in the cabinet on the wall and shoved the lock shut. "I'll make sure I keep hold of his rusty ole' rifle when I let him out. That ought to keep him from hurting anybody."

Sanford shook the sheriff's hand. "Much obliged. Hope you keep him in here for a *long* while."

Sanford turned to Thomas. "Soon as we get our next load ready to roll, I think I'll tie Jers to the wagon. Lucy's gonna need some milk to drink in order to feed Albert."

Before he left town, Sanford stopped by the railroad station and telegraphed H.W. and Mary.

WE'RE HERE STOP
ADVISE OF YOUR ARRIVAL DATE STOP
SANFORD

***

While the menfolk were gone, Lucy fed the children and arranged wooden crates to construct a makeshift kitchen. Nora played at Lucy's feet while her mother kept a constant eye out for strangers. Yesterday's episode set her in a nervous twitter. Her mind rehashed her friend, Rebekah's, encounter with the claim jumper when Uriah was gone. Each time Lucy moved to another area of the tent, she kept the rifle close at hand.

Nora picked up various rocks and brought them to Lucy for her to admire. Lucy stopped her work to take a dipper-full of water from the barrel, wiped her forehead on her sleeve and squinted at the sun.

"Must be noon already. Albert will be awake soon. Have to nurse him and get some dinner for Nora. Nora. Where is she? She was just here a minute ago."

"Nora! Nora!" Lucy called.

No answer.

"Nora! Where are you?" Panic made Lucy's throat feel tight and her breath came in short jerks. A knot formed in her stomach.

"Where in the world has that child gone? She was just here a minute ago!"

Lucy grabbed the baby and ran toward the stream. "Nora! Nora! Where are you?"

All she could hear was the moaning of the prairie wind and the gurgling creek. She ran to the stream and half slid down the short, but steep embankment as she looked to the south. Nothing. She headed north, stumbling over red rocks and gnarled tree roots next to the murky water on the muddy bank.

Could Nora have fallen in the stream? "Oh, Lord! Please help me find her. I couldn't bear to lose another of my precious children. Show me where to look, Lord. Maybe some Indian stole her. Oh, my God! I've left the gun back at the tent. What will I do if I run into some savage or another loony? Oh God! Help me!"

Lucy tripped on a half-buried root as she clamored over the slippery red soil. Splat! She barely avoided falling on the baby, landing on her shoulder instead. Somehow she managed to hold on to Albert without dropping him. He wailed. She lay there, stunned for a moment. They were both a mass of sticky red mud.

"Why did I ever agree to come to this God-forsaken place?" Lucy wanted to lie there and cry, but she had to find Nora. She scrambled to her feet and stumbled up the creek-bed.

"Nora! Honey, where are you? Answer Mama!"

Albert refused to be comforted so Lucy stopped a moment to feed him. Maybe that would calm him. She tried to find a clean place on her skirt to wipe her hands. He wailed louder. Lucy fumbled with the buttons on her dress and finally got Albert nestled into his dinner. Tears streamed down her face while she walked slowly calling, "Nora! Nora!" Oh where could that little girl be?

Between furtive calls, Lucy thought she heard something. Was that someone singing? There. She heard it again. Was it just wishful thinking? No. She heard it again. She urged her stiff and sore body on around the curve in the stream. There Nora sat with her feet, shoes and all, in the water singing "Jesus Loves Me" while she rubbed her hands over the slimy red, mud beside her. Nora's face and flour-sack smock were smeared with the slimy goo.

"Nora!" Lucy sobbed.

"Hi Mama!" She grinned from ear to ear.

Lucy laughed and cried at the same time.

"Nora... Margaret... Deering," Lucy said between sobs, "Don't know... if I should... skin you alive... or wring your neck! Don't you *ever*... go away from Mama... like that again."

The sharpness of her mother's voice frightened Nora and caused her to wail. Scooping Nora up, Lucy marched back to the tent with the filthy children in tow.

Everybody got a quick sponge bath in the dishpan. They were a mass of drying red mud. "How am I ever gonna get you clean, girl!"

After dinner they all curled up for a nap in the shade of the tent. Lucy kept a tight grip on Sanford's rifle with her right hand while her left arm encircled the bodies of her dear children.

The men arrived at the campsite late in the afternoon. Lucy had their supper of roasted turnips, hot beans and a little beef jerky ready and waiting. "Glad to see you *and* the cow," she said.

Sanford milked Jers while Thomas watered the horses.

Over supper, they had a lively conversation sharing the day's events around the campfire. When Sanford and Thomas finished their account about Jeremiah, Lucy was very quiet.

She pulled her shawl tightly around her shoulders, gazed into the fire and quietly said, "That poor old man. What a lonely life he must lead. Can't help but feel kind of sorry for him."

Conversation lulled. Lucy bowed her head and began to pray aloud. "Heavenly Father, thank you for helping me find Nora today. Thanks for sparing us from any ill at the hands of Jeremiah. Bless him, Father. Grant him a clear mind. Bless Dad, Mary, Orris, and Hanna. Give them safe passage to Oklahoma. We pray all this in Jesus' name. Amen."

Without a doubt, this place was filled with more surprises than any of them ever dreamed.

CHAPTER 15

October 13, 1889 - Busting sod.

The next afternoon, Sanford and Thomas came back from town with the last of the goods, including the two hogs and a coop full of chickens. As the wagon creaked to a stop, they climbed down and surveyed the wagonload of work awaiting them.

"Let's get the hogs outta there first," Sanford said.

Thomas nodded in agreement. "Gonna be dark before you know it."

"What in the world is that thing?" came a voice.

"What you talking about?" asked Sanford, his arms full of goods.

"That thing up there." She pointed to the back of Sanford's wagon. "Some kind of newfangled plow?"

Sanford laughed and looked over at Thomas. "Told you she'd say something. " He put his arm around her and looked into her questioning eyes. "That, my dear, is a sodbuster."

"A what?" She craned her neck to get a better look.

"A sodbuster. Got it at the general store."

"Do we *need* it?"

"You bet we do. It's going to cut five inch deep strips of this lovely red sod to finish the roof on the dugout and provide bricks to build our house. Thomas has agreed to help us."

"Built one in Nebraska, Miz Lucy, before I came here," Thomas said as he unloaded a sack of feed off the wagon onto Sanford's back.

"We're gonna get started tomorrow morning, at first light." He kissed her cheek. "Oh, by the way, got a telegram from your dad." He rolled the sack off his back and onto the ground and pulled the message from his shirt pocket. "They're coming late next week."

She read it. "Doesn't say if Frank and Anna sold their place. Was kind of hoping we'd all be down here this winter."

"They may be waiting till spring. Thomas, let's get these porkers outta this wagon before one of them jumps out and breaks his neck."

The pigs wriggled and squealed while the men wrestled them back to solid ground. One of the pigs ran a few steps and then stopped to root at something underground.

"Quick. Take this rawhide and tether one of their back legs to a stake, Thomas. That ought to hold them till we can build a pen.

Sanford set the coop full of chickens on the ground. "Now we'll have some eggs to go with our bacon."

"It's a joy to have our goods all in one place again," Lucy said as she pulled the washtub off the side of the wagon. Now I won't have to wash Albert's diapers in the stream."

Nora ran to the chicken coop. Picking up a small stick she poked it through the chicken wire. "Chickies! Chickies!"

The chickens squawked and scrambled over one another trying to get away from Nora's prodding assault. Chicken feathers flew everywhere.

Lucy took the stick out of her hand and led her away from the fractious hens. "Leave the chickies alone, Nora. We don't want to get them upset."

"Why, Mama?"

"Upset chickies won't give us eggs. Now go find something else to do, and don't go far. Papa and I have to unload this wagon."

Lucy pulled the wooden box off the wagon marked "kitchen items" and the tripod for the big iron pot and asked, "How big are you going to build our house, Sanford?"

"Oh, I figure about 16x20 feet. That'll be big enough for all eight of us to stay in till we can get your dad's house built." He hoisted another gunnysack onto his shoulder from the wagon and set it on the ground. "Got some wheat seed to sow before frost. All this work will pay off one day."

"It won't pay off if you work yourself to death," she said as she watched him reach for the sodbuster.

He didn't respond while he propped this strange looking tool against the wagon wheel, put the chickens back on the wagon, and covered them with a tarpaulin. "Hopefully, that'll keep the coyotes away from you tonight, you little cluckers."

He turned to Lucy. "Woman, hard work's good for an honest man. He winked at her as he folded her into his arms. "Besides, I just want the best for my family. You just wait. It'll be the best place around."

"Unhuh," Lucy nodded and shut her eyes tight as she gave him a squeeze. Even in her wildest dreams she had never envisioned a *red* house before.

The next morning, the menfolk were up before dawn. After a quick breakfast of bacon, eggs, biscuits and gravy, they hitched the horses to one of the wagons, set the chickens on the ground, and loaded the buster.

"Let those chickens out this morning; their feed's in the sack under the wagon seat," Sanford called over his shoulder as he headed for the field.

All morning she arranged the sacks of flour, dried beans, sugar and coffee into their proper place in her makeshift kitchen while she kept one eye on the simmering pot of ham and beans.

The dew-filled prairie grass looked like it had tiny crystals all over it in the early morning sunshine. "Thomas, you hitch your mule to the buster. I'm going to see where's the best place to start."

As the sun gave full light to the new day, Sanford shoved his new implement into the virgin soil. "Let's give her a whirl, Thomas." He whistled at the mule. "Haw! Git up there!"

The animal jerked to a start. As the mule moved forward, the buster peeled a width of grassy soil about as wide as a man's forearm, finger-tips to elbow. The air was filled with the aroma of freshly-turned earth.

"Nothing smells any better, hey Thomas?"

"You betcha, Mr. Sanford."

If Sanford could have put this moment in a jar to save it forever, he would have. This longing that had rested in his heart for so long was finally becoming a reality. If he didn't know better, he would have sworn he was dreaming.

After about half an hour he stopped to wipe his brow. "This stuff isn't like cutting hot butter, that's for certain."

Thomas nodded. "Wearing out? I'll take over for a while."

"Go right ahead. Won't stand in your way," Sanford chuckled. "I'll just rest here a spell in the shade of the wagon."

The sun was high overhead when Lucy looked up from her pot of ham and beans. They bubbled in the big iron pot suspended over the open fire. Cornbread baked in the iron skillet in hot coals below. She heard the wagon creak under the heavy weight of the first load of sod from the crimson fields. Soon these bricks would become a roof for the dugout and walls for her new home.

"Smells good, woman. I'm starving."

"Step right up folks. Soup's waiting." She dipped up their ham and beans and poured them each a tin cup of black coffee while they washed up.

"That stuff's like carving clay, Miz Lucy. Makes a man hungry as a bear." Thomas took his plate and a slab of cornbread and sat on a nearby log before he shoveled in the first bite. "Thank ya kindly, ma'am. Gonna take us a spell to bust that sod."

While Sanford ate, he was busy figuring with a pencil and a scrap of paper.

"What are you writing?" Lucy asked.

"Well, I figure we're going to have to bust right at an acre of sod before we'll have enough for our house. Those dense prairie roots bind that soil together like iron.

"That's why they make houses with the stuff," Thomas said, smiling.

"As near as I can figure, we'll be at this busting business a week or more."

Thomas reached for another piece of cornbread. "I didn't say it was gonna be easy, Mr. Sanford."

"We'll need to get a couple of windows and a door next time we're in town. I've got to keep at this. Once that ground freezes, they'll be no more harvesting sod."

Before dinner was over, Sanford had consumed three plates of ham and beans and corn bread. Both men lay back against a short tree, hats over their faces for a few minutes of rest before they began to place the sod on the dugout roof.

Their siesta was interrupted by the sound of squawking chickens and flapping wings. Both sat up with a start.

"What in tarnation . . .?" Sanford said as he jerked his hat off his face.

Thomas scrambled to his feet and yelled, "One of the hogs is loose and he's having a chicken dinner!"

"Well, if that don't beat all. Guess we'll have to dig us a hog pit before we can get to anything else." Sanford grabbed his shovel.

"Yep. Once he's got the taste of chicken, he'll not quit till they're all gone."

The men re-tethered the hog and dug a large, rather deep hole near the stream to make a secure place to keep the rascals. Trees were too precious to use as fencing for hog pens. By late afternoon they had the swine in their new home and spent the rest of the afternoon roofing the dugout.

"Let's see if we can set those corner poles for the house before dark."

"We'll sure be ready for some of Miz Lucy's fine supper by then," Thomas said.

"Fer sure."

"That way, we can start cutting sod for the house at first light tomorrow."

Through the week the men worked steadily cutting each strip of sod and then dividing the strips into one-yard lengths with a shovel. They loaded each yard-long piece onto the wagon. When the wagon was full, they hauled it into the campsite. With the strips grass-side down, they placed them in a staggered pattern like bricks to form the walls of the house. Every day was harder, as the walls grew higher.

After three days the walls were so high they off-loaded sod straight off the wagon directly on to the walls.

"What do you figure these little bricks weigh?" Sanford said as he pulled his hat off and wiped his forehead with his shirtsleeve.

"About fifty pounds or better, I'd say."

"They're beginning to feel more like a hundred."

Friday afternoon, Sanford and Thomas had the walls almost as high as the top of the window holes, just below Sanford's eye-level.

"Soon we'll be ready for a roof, Lucy. We'll go to town and get you a couple of windows and a door. Then you'll have a *real* house."

"That'll be a day I'll never forget. Think I'll sleep better when there's a solid door between me and those howling coyotes. Don't forget to fill our second water barrel. We're running low. You'll have to get several yards of cheesecloth for the ceiling."

"Thomas, help me to remember to leave word at the general store for that water-witcher fella. Need to know when he plans to be out this way."

Thomas nodded as he counted off the fingers of his left hand. "Windas, door, water barrel, cheesecloth and water-witcher fella."

The next morning, Sanford handed Lucy his rifle without a word before he turned to mount the wagon.

"Hurry back." Lucy forced the words through her tightening throat. Bidding Sanford good-by in this place wasn't getting any easier. She wondered if Oklahoma would ever really feel like home.

In late afternoon, she saw a wagon pull over the rise. Then a second wagon appeared over the ridge.

Sanford called, "Look what I found in town!"

"Dad! Mary!" She ran to hug them. "I didn't look for you for a few more days."

"We just wound up earlier than expected, Daughter. Didn't want to miss all the fun," H. W. said with a broad grin. He took off his hat and surveyed the work. "Right fine looking house you got here."

Eleven-year-old Orris leapt off the wagon with nine-year-old Hanna not far behind. Little Nora squealed and ran to grab their hands. "Come on, Nora. Show us our new home."

"Nora, you stay away from the stream, you hear?"

"Yes, Mama."

After supper around the campfire, they silently watched the sparks fly upward as the flames warmed the chilly night air.

Lucy finally spoke, "Mary did you have a good trip from Winston?"

"Oh girl, I was wondering if we were going to get here in one piece," Mary said.

Lucy sat forward and threw another log on the fire. "Was it a rough train ride?"

"Now, wife. Don't make it more than it was," H.W. said as he raised his hand in the air. "We just had to pull off the main line for a little while just after we crossed from Kansas at Arkansas City into Indian Territory's all. Nothing happened."

Mary looked at him with wide eyes. "I don't call that nothing."

He slapped his knee. "Aw, woman, now don't get your bowels in an uproar. We just had to hold up a piece. The engineer got word there might be some train robbers about. They were just being extra cautious. Turns out our train was carrying the government's yearly payment of $70,000 to the Indians."

"I *never* would have got on that train if I'd a known we were carrying that kind of cargo," Mary said as she wagged her head and stared into the fire. I sure did wonder what all those armed federal Marshall's were doing on that train, for sure."

"Got through alright, didn't you?" Sanford said.

H.W. answered quickly. "That we did, with no sign of robbers."

Mary rubbed her backside and said, "Those wooden train seats sure gave us a sore backside."

H.W. poked a stick into the fire. A partially burned log fell apart into the flames. "The stop did made us kind of late, though. We didn't pull into Mulhall till about noon."

"I was beginning to wonder if we would *ever* get here," Mary said.

"Well, it was better than coming down by wagon."

Mary chuckled. "That's your father, girl. Always looking on the bright side."

Lucy nodded with a grin. This place didn't seem so foreign, now that her family was here. Maybe this could be a real home after all.

Through the night, Lucy awoke frequently, dreaming of train robbers. Then she'd snuggle in closer to Sanford on the hard ground and assure herself, that all's well.

CHAPTER 16

November 3, 1889 - Uriah brought the water-witcher.

Within the week, the three men and Orris framed in the door and windows and cut supports for the roof from cottonwood trees down by the stream. Over the poles, they laid a layer of grass and brush with a final layer of sod carefully butted together, right side up.

Nora chased a chicken in front of the house. Lucy grabbed her to distract her.

"Look here Nora. See the house your Papa built for us? Isn't it wonderful?" Nora gazed at it for a long time. Then Nora looked at her mother and pointed to the roof.

"Look, Mama. It's got hair."

Lucy threw her head back and laughed. "Yes short stuff, our house even has hair."

While the men put the finishing touches on the house outside, the women rolled out cheesecloth across the floor inside. Lucy stood on the humpback trunk and nailed the cheesecloth to the rafters while Mary stood on the floor, feeding her the material.

As Lucy hammered she said, "I hear this works pretty good to keep the loose dirt from falling onto everything. I hope it works."

Handing her another strip of cheesecloth Mary said. "Wonder what happens when it rains?"

"Don't know. Guess we'll find out, come spring." She hammered the last corner to the cottonwood pole ceiling.

Sanford and H.W. constructed beds of cottonwood logs while Mary and Lucy sewed mattresses of striped pillow ticking and stuffed them with clean straw. H.W. suspended the mattresses on ropes lashed tightly across the bed frame.

"There." Lucy slowly turned near the center of the soddy for a final inspection. Grandfather Deering's rocker was in a front corner near one of the windows on the dirt floor. Mama's dishes occupied the humpbacked trunk beside the rocker. Sanford and H.W. had even made a small table complete with five big chairs and three smaller ones, which occupied the center of the room. The cheesecloth was firmly in place overhead.

"Lucy, this is beginning to look like a real home," Mary said. She surveyed the interior with her hands on her hips. "Soon as we make some curtains this will look like a regular home. Don't you agree?"

"Not bad for a red house with hair." They both laughed. Lucy hugged her step-mother. "Thanks Mary, for all your help."

"My pleasure." Mary grinned.

Lucy's folks bought a cast iron laundry stove with two burners on top to cook on. The men set it near the back corner of the soddy opposite the rocker and installed a metal stovepipe.

"Now you ladies can cook in style," H.W. said.

Mary flicked her husband with a tea towel. "And you men can eat fancy, my love."

"Don't know if I'll remember how to cook indoors anymore." Lucy said.

The thought of his wife's cooking made Sanford's mouth water. "Fire it up and give it a try on some of your stew, woman."

"Need some wood first."

"Now that might take some doing." Mary leaned out the door and called to Orris and Hanna. "You all go get us some prairie coal."

"Prairie coal. What's that?" Orris cocked his head sideways.

"Cow pies. You can bring buffalo chips too, if you can find any. We'll use them for fuel in the stove."

"Mama, can't we just cut some wood?" Orris asked. "Who wants to pick up cow poop? "

"That's gonna be your job from now on, Son. Wood's too precious here to be burning it, even if it is for cooking."

"Ick! Can't Orris do it, Mama? I don't want to collect cow poop."

Mary handed them each a bucket and said, "Hush with you now. Be careful. Only pick up the dry ones, mind you."

***

The cold weather brought unwelcome guests. Mice... and more. They burrowed through the sod looking for a warm place to winter.

One afternoon, Mary and the older children went to town with the men. Lucy took advantage of the quiet and laid down with the little ones at naptime.

"I'll just lay here a minute and then get on with my chores," Lucy mumbled to herself.

She awoke to the sound of Nora's periodic giggles. Nora peeked over the edge and then drew back, over and over.

"What's so funny, short stuff?" Lucy rose on one elbow to encounter a cottonmouth coiled on the floor playing hide and seek each time a face appeared over the edge of the bed.

Lucy let out a blood-curdling scream, jumped off the end of the bed and grabbed a hoe from behind the stove. The snake headed for a hasty retreat out one of the mouse holes. Each blow missed the serpent despite Lucy's best efforts. After a thorough search of the entire room, ceiling to floor, for any of his friends, she spent the rest of the afternoon stuffing rags in every mouse hole she could find– as if that would keep the varmints out.

***

In early November, Uriah and Rebekah came for a visit. They brought the water-witcher to divine for water.

"Oh, Lucy, it's so homey. You've really been busy here, girl," said Rebekah.

"Thanks. We've got a long way to go before we're done."

She wanted to ask Rebekah if she had any trouble with snakes, but didn't want to frighten her, if she hadn't. With any luck, none would find their way into the house while her guests visited.

After a cup of tea, Rebekah suggested, "Let's go watch the witcher-fella. Beats all you've ever seen."

Lucy jumped at the chance to get her company away from the house on the outside chance a snake might appear. On the way out the door she grabbed a shovel, if she encountered a snake outside.

"You gonna start digging right away when he finds a spot?" Rebekah asked, and laughed.

"I just might," Lucy said. She didn't want to tell her friend it was really her snake weapon.

They spent most of the morning watching the witcher walk back and forth over the ground on H.W.'s place with a forked willow stick. He grasped the branches of the fork firmly in each hand with the fork pointed straight up in the air. The stick formed an up-side-down v.

"I'm sure we'll find water on at least one of these three homesteads," he said with confidence. "Feel it in my bones."

He walked back and forth across the ground until the point of the stick took a dive downward, as if some unseen thing were pulling it toward the ground. The witcher-fella held tightly to the branches. The bark peeled off the stick in his hands.

"This is a good one. Dig here," he said with authority as shoved the willow branch into the hard red earth to mark the spot.

Before the day was over, he marked three spots–one on each homestead.

"Start on H.W.'s well first. It'll be the best one. Then you can all use out of his 'till you get the others dug."

Sanford paid him his fee and bid him good day.

"Thank you kindly." He mounted his horse, tipped his hat, and was gone in a flash–off to another hopeful homesteader.

November passed quickly. Sanford, H.W. and Thomas dug a well on and off through the month when they weren't working on H.W.'s wood frame house. The water-witcher was right. It was a good one. Within a month after they completed it, they had drinking water–enough for them all.

H.W.'s house was built of "store-bought" lumber. The weather in Oklahoma was somewhat milder than in Missouri so the three men and Orris were able to work on his place most every day. It even had a wooden floor.

The day H.W. moved and Mary moved into their house, Thomas made an announcement at supper.

"Guess I'll be moving on."

Questions fired at him from all directions as fast as a Gatling gun. Thomas had almost become a part of the family. No one wanted to see him leave.

"What in the world are you going to do that for?"

"Where you going?"

"What's wrong with here? Someone make you mad?"

Thomas held up his hands. "Hold on, there! It's nothing personal. I just think I'll drift on to Texas. Kind of got a hankering to see what's down there."

"We'll miss you, Thomas. You've been a real help. Couldn't have done it without you. Especially in those first few weeks," Sanford said.

"Much obliged for your help, Thomas. Hate to see you go." H.W. reached out and shook his hand.

"When I came to the Territory, didn't really intend to stay here. Just got this Texas itch I gotta scratch. I'll miss y'all too. Would you be interested in my wagon and team, Mr. Sanford? Think I might travel faster if I just had a saddle horse. Besides, I figure those mules feel like this is home by now."

"I'll give you a fair price for them, Thomas."

"Let's consider them sold then. You have more use for 'em than I do."

"It's a deal. Much obliged. And if you don't like it down there in Texas, you just come on back. You're welcome here, anytime."

"I'll keep that in mind, Mr. Sanford."

The next morning, Sanford took Thomas to town to buy a horse he had his eye on at the livery stable. Everyone was unusually quiet at the homestead that morning.

"Seems like one of the family's gone," Lucy said.

H.W. sighed. "We'll miss him, for sure. He was a fine helper. Kind of thought he might stay on as a permanent hand."

***

A week before Christmas, H.W. picked up a telegram from the railroad office. It was from Frank and Anna. It read,

SOLD PLACE STOP
OKLAHOMA BOUND STOP
FRANK

They arrived just in time for Christmas, and set up a tent not far from the edge of H.W.'s place. It only took two wagonloads to bring them from town, but they brought some very needed commodities, another team of mules, and an additional plow.

"This'll be a great help when it comes to spring planting, Frank," H.W. said.

"Can't wait to get some crops into my very own place."

The family's Christmas celebration was a very simple one. Sanford shot a wild turkey for the occasion. They all gathered at H.W. and Mary's place on that snowy Christmas day. Their little house was filled with the aroma of baked sweet potatoes, roast turkey, sage dressing, and a ham.

Lucy placed a small doll for Nora and a booden top for Albert under the scrawny cedar tree. She made the doll from leftover rags. It had an embroidered face, with hair made out of string and a loose-fitting jumper made from Lucy's leftover window curtain scraps. Nora was delighted.

Frank and Anna spent most of the rest of winter with H.W. and Mary in their house. Occasionally, Frank and Anna came for short visits with Sanford and Lucy. Sanford and Frank were full of plans for spring planting and improvements to the land.

On milder days, the three men worked together on each other's places to build stock pens, chicken coops, out houses, and a lean-to for the horses and mules. On the few extremely cold days Sanford was forced to stay inside, he made a bed for Nora and a cradle for Albert from small saplings. He also fashioned extra ax and hammer handles and sharpened his tools in preparation for spring planting.

Through the winter, Lucy worked diligently to keep the mouse holes stuffed with rags in her new home. Anytime she went outside the soddy, she carried a trusty hoe with her... just in case.

"You never know when those critters might come out of hibernation, you know," she told Mary.

CHAPTER 17

March 3, 1890 - No rain.

Oklahoma Territory had little snow during the winter of 1889-1890. March arrived with a blast of dry wind, and no prospects of rain in sight.

"Don't look good, Sanford. I remember back in '73. Spring started this way in Winston. Like to never got a crop that year."

Sanford searched the sky in every direction. He took off his felt hat and beat the dust off against his trouser leg. "No cloud in the sky. Hope you're wrong, H.W. That wheat'll never make if it doesn't get moisture."

"Not going to be able to bust that sod open to plant anything else but those turnips we got in, either."

"Well, maybe tomorrow."

Every tomorrow brought no rain. The stream was down to a trickle, the well, almost dry.

"H.W., if we don't get some rain soon, we're going to have to take the barrel to town to fetch water," Mary said as she kneaded bread dough.

"I plan to go to town in the morning."

"Turnips the only thing planted so far?"

"That's it."

"I'm not that fond of turnips."

"If this keeps up, that may be all we'll have."

"It'll rain soon."

The next morning H.W. and Sanford and Frank went to town for the water. H.W. surveyed the landscape.

"At this rate, even the grass won't green up. May end up having to sell off our stock. Have no hay for them come winter."

The dry wind blew dust in their eyes. “You can barely see the road, Sanford. Suppose we ought to turn back?”

“Can’t turn back. Need the water.”

Later in the month it still had not rained and the menfolk went to town again for water. Lucy saved just enough to boil Albert’s diapers.

“Sure will be glad when you don’t wear these anymore, little one. Mary says you’ll be grown before I know it.” Out of the corner of her eye, she watched Albert play on the dirt floor. Meanwhile, she carved shavings from a cake of lye soap and stirred the dirty diapers with a stick, in the oversized iron kettle. Now that he had learned to crawl, he was into everything.

“You poor baby. There’s not a spot on you that’s not red dirt... except behind your ears, maybe,” Lucy said. She picked him up off the floor, spit in her hand and smoothed the blond hair out of his eyes. “Oh, you’re getting to be quite a load, my little man. I bet you’ll slim down just like Nora did, now that you’ve started to eat some big people food.”

Nora busied herself in the corner, poking something with a stick.

“Short stuff, what are you up to over there?”

“Fuzzy bug, Mama.”

She glanced over and thought, *at least it’s not a mouse*. “Let me see, honey.” With Albert wriggling on one hip, Lucy pulled Nora back so she could get a better look. “Eeeeek! Get away, Nora! It’s a tarantula!” Lucy grabbed Nora with her free arm and tossed both children on the bed. “Stay there. Both of you. Don’t move.”

Lucy grabbed her ever-present hoe behind the stove and hacked at the dirt floor with a vengeance. “Get out of my house, you devil! I’m going to get you. Where did you go?”

The tarantula managed to scurry into a crack in the sod wall. Lucy cried and shook uncontrollably. Her reaction frightened the children; both wailed, eyes wide with fear.

“Mama, what’s wrong?” Nora asked between sobs.

Lucy got on the bed with them. “It’s alright, hon. You just don’t want to play with those fuzzy bugs. They might be poison.”

“What’s poison mean, Mama?”

"That means they're not good. They might hurt you."

Lucy rocked Nora and Albert back and forth on her lap as she sang softly and stroked them. Calm began to reign again. Would they would ever have a civilized home in this territory? "Oh God," she whispered, "this is such a wild place. Are you sure this is where you want us?"

Long after both children fell asleep, she was still unwilling to step a foot on the floor. She wondered if the spider she saw was the kind that rots the flesh where it bites. "I'll have to ask Sanford. Think his mother was spider-bit once," she whispered.

Finally, she took a deep breath and said, "Enough of this. I must get on with the laundry." Lucy gently laid the children down and forced herself to take the basket of diapers outside. She spread them on bushes to dry.

A voice from behind startled her. "Ma'am?"

"She jumped and turned to behold a man as skinny as a skeleton. His filthy buckskin trousers and jacket hung on his frame like a scarecrow. His sleeves hung beyond his wrists. Lucy stifled a scream, hand over her mouth.

"Didn't mean to scare you. Could ya spare some grub?" he asked in a raspy whisper.

His voice sounded somewhat familiar. He held a beat-up felt hat loosely in his hands.

Her mind raced. Who is this poor soul? I can't quite place his face. Is he a neighbor?

He murmured, "Need some vittles. Ain't et in days."

Then it hit her. Jeremiah Jump! "What are you doing out of jail?" Her voice came out in a squeaky, high-pitched tremor.

"Jail? Ma'am, I ain't been in jail. I'm jest a hungry traveler, asking fer a handout."

He looks for all the world like Jeremiah, without his gun. There's something different about him though. His voice is so soft. He doesn't have that wild look in his eyes. Whoever he is, he looks like a half-starved dog. "Sit under that tree over there. I'll make you a fried egg sandwich."

"Much obliged, ma'am." He slowly turned and made his way to the budding cottonwood tree.

Lucy dipped bacon grease from a tin can on the back of the stove. The grease popped while she cracked two eggs in the cast iron fry pan. While they sizzled, she wondered if this was the same old fella who nearly scared them half to death last fall.

She peered at him through the window. The wind blew his long white hair into his eyes. “He looks so frail; I’ll bet a big wind could blow him away like a tumbleweed.”

After slicing four pieces of her sourdough bread, she placed the fried eggs between the slices, and wrapped the sandwiches in a piece of butcher paper. She grabbed her hoe from the end of the bed and took the sandwiches to him under the tree. “Sorry. We’re out of water.”

“No matter. Jes’ grateful for the grub, ma’am. Bless ya.” He attacked the sandwiches like a starved dog.

If this *is* Jeremiah, maybe this is how he is when he’s in his right mind. It must be terrible to have no one. Poor soul.

Lucy watched him for a moment, picked up the laundry basket and headed for the house. She looked over her shoulder every few steps and quickly shut and bolted the door with the two by four; replaced the hoe behind the stove and put the basket in the corner. When she looked out the window again he was gone. “Strange, really strange.”

CHAPTER 18

March 14, 1890 - Fought a prairie fire today.

Lucy waited until Sanford pulled the wagon up to the yard before she unbolted the door. She was so relieved to see them finally home again.

The men unloaded the first water barrel and set it near the corner of the house.

"I'll bring your wagon to you, Sanford as soon as we can unload the other two at my place."

"Never mind. I'll come down and get it in the morning. No use making another trip, H.W."

Lucy and Nora came out to greet them. "Thanks, Dad. We were plumb out of water. Used the last of it to wash Albert's diapers today." Lucy surveyed the landscape with a quick glance and hurriedly gathered the diapers while Sanford picked up Nora.

"Daddy! Found a fuzzy bug! Mama says it's poison."

Sanford shot a quick glance at Lucy. "What was it, a tarantula?"

Lucy nodded her head. "Was that the kind that bit your mother?"

"No her's was a slick brown one. short stuff, Mama's right. Don't play with those. They bite." Sanford hugged Nora close as he went in the house and put her down. Nora immediately began to look for more bugs. "What's for supper, my doe?"

"Beans and cornbread." She said as she re-bolted the door.

"What are you bolting the door for?"

Lucy took a deep breath and leaned against it. "We had a strange visitor today while you were gone." Lucy took the bowls from the cupboard and dished up the beans.

He scowled. "Oh? Who?"

Handing him a spoon she said, "I'm not for certain, but I kind of think it was that Jeremiah Jump."

"You mean to tell me that old goat is on the loose again?" Sanford stood and stepped to the window. "Wouldn't you recognize him for sure?"

"Well, he... he had the same buckskin trousers, but he seemed so different."

"How?"

"He didn't have that wild look like before, skinnier too. He had on a buckskin jacket. Looked half-starved. I gave him a couple of sandwiches."

"Guess I better start leaving the gun loaded above the door when I have to be away. He might show up some day when he's having one of his 'chicken days.'"

Lucy put the bowl of beans at Sanford's place and cut the cornbread in the iron skillet. "Chicken days?"

Sanford put his arm around his wife. "Never mind, Lucy. Nothing to worry about."

For the next few days, Sanford kept very close to home. Lucy wondered if he was concerned about Jeremiah's re-appearance. She wanted to say something, but was afraid of his answer. The water barrel was almost empty again.

"Going to have to go to town tomorrow to get water. I want you and the children to go to your dad's while I'm gone."

"Why? Does Mary need help with something?" Lucy braced herself for his answer.

"Oh, I just thought you and Mary might like to spend the day together."

"And the *real* reason, Sanford?"

"You know the real reason. I don't want anything to happen to you while I'm gone. There's safety in numbers. Don't forget to take the gun."

Lucy felt a big knot in her stomach. Maybe it was the lack of rain or the stress of the encounter with Jeremiah Jump, but fear began to creep in. She prayed, *Lord, protect and help us.*

Sanford deposited Lucy and the children at Mary's early the next morning. The men left immediately for Mulhall.

"I thought we might work on that quilt today, Lucy. Got the pieces all cut. Frank said Anna would be over soon."

When Anna arrived, the women sat outside together in the spring sunshine. Their nimble fingers stitched each piece of the wedding ring quilt with the expertise only seasoned quilter's possess.

Mary called to the children. "Hanna, you make sure you and Nora stay close to the house now, you hear?"

"Do you think it was Jeremiah that asked you for food the other day?" Mary finally asked as she stitched two tiny squares together.

Lucy rested her sewing in her lap and thought a while. "You know, the more I think about it, I'm sure it was. He was so different though. I can't explain it."

"He must have been a real fire ball the first time you met," Anna said.

Lucy laughed as she remembered. "I was ready to pack up and go back to Missouri right there on the spot. There was just one problem. I'd have to leave Sanford behind."

"You couldn't do that, now could you?" Anna chuckled.

"Not in a million years. Still, that Jeremiah makes me uneasy. Just because he was calm the other day, doesn't mean he'll stay that way."

"I'd feel better if he wasn't out and about somewhere," Mary whispered as she glanced around the yard. "Lawsey! Who knows when he might appear again?"

The thought of him coming back made Lucy shudder. It was as if she could see and hear him standing before her all over again. "I can't imagine what a confused, lonely life he must lead. No family. No friends. Not even a right mind to call his own, sometimes."

"Must be an awful way to live," Anna sighed.

"Makes you grateful for what you have, doesn't it, Mary?"

"That it does, girl. That it does."

An unusual wind blew out of the northwest.

***

In mid-afternoon, Sanford, H.W., Orris and Frank headed the team westward for home with the filled water barrels.

H.W. urged the horses on. "Get up there you two. Maybe that northwest wind will blow up a rainstorm."

"Sure would be welcome, but there's not much chance it would do my wheat any good if it did. I'd plow it under and plant corn if I had money for corn seed, and if there were any prospects for rain."

"Is it that bad?"

"Afraid so."

When they came up over a steep ridge thick black smoke arose from the prairie.

"What the..."

"Prairie fire! Looks like it's down our way. Let's high-tail it."

The fire had already consumed Sanford's wheat field. The hungry flames licked the dry prairie grass like a swift devouring behemoth from hell. By the time they caught up with it, it had already spread to H.W.'s place.

The men raced to get feed sacks to dip in the water barrels on the back of the wagon. Beating the flames they saw it was futile. Acrid, black smoke stung their eyes and made it impossible to see anyone or anything.

"Lucy! Mary! Anna!" they called. No one answered.

Sanford cried out in short gasps, "Oh my God!..." Where were they? Had they been consumed in the fire? If the wind would only shift the southeast!" In their own strength, he knew their attempts against this hell-fire devil was futile.

As he tried to beat the flames he discovered his arms wouldn't work; he couldn't get his breath. What was happening to him? He tried to run but fell.

***

When Sanford came to, he was flat on his back. The stench of scorched earth filled His nostrils.

He opened his eyes and struggled to focus on the soot-stained face of his sweet doe. Had they died in the fire? Was this Heaven? She cradled his head in her lap and wiped his face with a wet rag.

A little wail escaped Lucy's throat. "Oh, thank the good Lord! I thought the smoke got you for sure."

Sanford tried to speak but only a long series of coughs came out. H.W. stood by peering at him, hands on his knees.

"You alright, boy? That fire nearly got ya."

Sanford looked around wildly for the fire.

Lucy laid a reassuring hand on his chest. "It's alright, Sanford. A big wind whooshed from the southeast and blew the fire back on itself. Sure saved out necks, for sure. Burned clear up to the house."

"The children?" Sanford choked.

"They're fine, thank God," Lucy said.

H.W. took off his felt hat and wiped his sweating forehead with his sleeve. He looked out over the smoldering, scarred earth. "Sure burned the dickens out of the prairie grass. Your wheat field, too."

Mary came out of the house with a child in each arm. The fading daylight and the blackened landscape cast eerie shadows on the consumed prairie.

Sanford struggled to sleep. When he laid down, his cough was worse. Anxiety gnawed at him in the long night hours. How are we going to make it here if we have no rain? Maybe I should have listened to Lucy's reluctance to come here. Maybe I was wrong all along.

In spite of his apprehension, a quiet assurance began to grow in him. The wind *had* turned and choked off the fire. Their lives *were* spared. Maybe God *does* hear and answer prayer sometimes. Maybe he'll make a way for us here in this tough place.

***

Mid-afternoon the next Monday he and H.W. went out to survey the damage to their homesteads in the wagon. The charred earth stretched as far as they could see.

"Sure burned a far piece."

"I thought you were a goner for sure. Never saw someone so taken by smoke before."

"That was the strangest feeling. I wanted to move but I couldn't. It was like the flames and black smoke were out to eat me. Hope to never go through that again."

They rode in silence for another half mile to the northwest edge of the charred earth without a word; each man deep in thought.

Sanford pointed to a lump on the horizon. "What do you suppose that is over there, H.W.?"

"Looks like a burned animal, maybe. Suppose it got caught in the fire?"

"That looks kind of like a campfire."

H.W. got down off the wagon to get a better look. He kicked an iron pot with his foot. "There's a *man* here, Sanford. Suppose he was trying to cook something?"

Sanford jumped off the wagon. The stench of burned flesh made the men gag. Sanford turned the small burned body over with his foot. Both men looked at each other in disbelief. It was Jeremiah.

"My God, Sanford. He must have been the one that started the fire. The sparks must have gotten loose in the wind."

"Why didn't he run away, you suppose?

"Maybe he died before the fire took off."

"Could be."

"Shall we bury him here?"

Sanford removed his hat and smoothed his mustache with his hand. "Don't know how Doc McPeek would feel about us burying someone on his place."

"You're right. We better load him up and take him to town tomorrow." H.W. glanced at the sinking sun. "It's getting too late to start out this evening. We'll ask Sheriff Hensley what to do with him."

CHAPTER 19

April 4, 1890 - Plastering the soddy.

When the men came home, Lucy was in the yard with the children.

She waved a welcome and headed for the wagon. "My land, Sanford! What have you got in the wagon? You been hunting skunks? You smell like the dickens."

Sanford jumped off the wagon and grabbed her arm. "Don't go back there, Lucy. It's Jeremiah.

"What is he, sick? That old geezer never smelt that bad."

"We found him dead. Burned on the prairie west of here on Doc Mc Peek's place. We're gonna take him in to the sheriff in the morning."

"Burned! That poor man!" Lucy's eyes filled with tears. "He didn't deserve this."

***

The trip to town was not a pleasant one, to say the least. The southwest wind blew Jeremiah's stench in their direction, permeating their clothes and the very air they breathed.

When they crossed the railroad tracks H.W. said, "Let's swing round north of town, and hitch up there. No use taking this stink in town."

"Good idea."

It was high noon by the time the two men entered Sheriff Hensley's office.

Sanford began. "Sheriff, we got something for you. Don't know quite what to do with it."

"What is it?"

"Old Jeremiah Jump. Found him out west in Doc McPeek's pasture," said H.W.

"Where is he?" The Sheriff looked out the window for their wagon. "Dealing you a fit again?"

Sanford removed his hat, took his handkerchief from his pocket and wiped his sweatband with it. "Not this time. He's much in need of a burying. We've got him in the wagon out north of town. The prairie fire got him. From the looks of things, a spark from his campfire might have been what started it."

"Well, I'll be. Wondered what caused it. No chance it was a lightening strike–not with this drought. Come to think of it, hadn't seen him around much this past month. Kinda wondered what happened to him. Burn much on your place?"

Sanford placed his hat on the back of the chair and sat down near the sheriff's desk. "Yes. Took my wheat crop."

"You and most everybody out that way," the sheriff said.

H.W. spoke up. "Come winter we're going to be in a fix, for sure."

"Looks like only thing growing is turnips. Seems everybody's planting em," Sheriff Hensley said. "What you plan to do with ole Jeremiah?"

"You know of any next of kin we can notify?"

"Nope. Been a loner, far as I know."

"Is there a public burying place round here? Don't think Doc Mc Peek would appreciate us planting him on his place. Besides, ole Jeremiah deserves more than a grave in a pasture."

"I heard Luther Peek offered a little patch of their field for a burying place a while back. It's on the road going out east of town. Up on that high knoll. Might check with them."

Sanford stood and retrieved his hat. "Much obliged. We're needing to find some place quick, Sheriff. He's pretty ripe."

They stopped at the feed store to buy a fifty-pound bag of corn for seed. It was all they could afford.

By the time the two located Mr. Peek for permission to bury Jeremiah, the sun was far into the west. They struggled to dig a hole deep enough into the dry crimson clay to bury him. After lowering him in Sanford said a prayer and they filled the grave with dirt. Sanford carved "J. Jump - 1890" on a small flat limestone rock for a headstone.

"Sure would hate to have to bury folks for a living, H.W."

H.W. nodded in agreement.

They rode home in silence, glad to have the evening breeze in their face. The smell of charred earth had begun to die down. Small sprigs of fresh grass appeared among the burnt remains, despite the drought.

They rounded the last turn before Sanford's place. Stars winked like thousands of faraway lanterns across the pitch-black sky. H.W. pulled the team to a stop in the yard and Sanford stepped down.

"See you in the morning, Sanford. We'll get started on busting sod. Can't grow anything if we don't plant."

"If we plant, maybe it'll rain." He waved H.W. on.

A gentle glow from the kerosene lamp greeted him through the two windows on the east side of the house. Sanford surveyed the quiet darkness. Despite the disappointment of a ruined crop and the uncertain future, he wondered if there was any place more beautiful in all the world than this soddy with his family waiting inside.

Lucy opened the door. "Where's my young 'uns?"

"They're already fed and bedded down. Why are you so late? I was getting worried about you. I'll dish up some cornbread and beans while you get washed up."

Sanford dipped water from a bucket into the gray metal wash basin and scrubbed with a bar of lye soap. "I had to chase down a fella by the name of Luther Peek about a mile out east of town." He grabbed a towel on the chair and dried his hands. "Sheriff Hensley said they had offered a spot for burying if the need arose. It's a pretty knoll just a little east on town on the south side of the road."

"Did the preacher say any words over him?"

"Nope. Just me and your dad. Put him a little rock for a headstone."

"You're a good man, Sanford Deering." Lucy put Sanford's dinner on the table and poured them each a cup of coffee. Lucy sat and watched him as he scooped the beans and cornbread like a hungry wolf.

"Sure wasn't a job I'd like to do again," he said between bites. "But then, we couldn't leave him out there for the coyotes."

Lucy watched Sanford slather a knife full of butter on his bread.

"You're an amazing man. You're as stubborn as all get-out, but your heart is as big as this whole Oklahoma prairie."

Finishing his second helping of beans he looked up and said, "My doe, you about ready for bed?"

Was that a gleam she saw in his eye? "Soon as I put your plate to soak. I'll finish the dishes in the morning."

They snuggled together in the straw mattress. A coyote called to his mate in the still night. Sanford kissed Lucy's neck in a warm embrace.

***

"Dag nab it Sanford! No matter how I sharpen this plow, it's not a gonna bust this sod. It's like cutting through rock."

"Let me give it a try, H.W. Haw! Get up there!" The mules pulled but the plow failed to bite into the sod. "Never saw nothing like this. Rain's the only thing that will soften this soil."

H.W. took off his hat. With his hands on his hips, he looked out over the crusted earth. "Here it is almost Easter. I thought sure by now we would have some kind of field ready to plant. I think we better give up till we see some moisture."

Slipping the knotted reins off his shoulder, Sanford wrapped them around the plow handle and wiped his brow with his red bandana. "Won't argue with you, H.W."

The two men sat down in the shade of a cottonwood tree. "What's next on our list of things to do, Sanford?"

"Well, Lucy's been after me to plaster the inside of the house. She's got it in her mind that that'll keep the snakes and bugs out. That's what our neighbor, Clementine North said."

H.W. took off his hat, scratched his head, and gave a sideward glance at Sanford. "Just because Clementine said it, does that make it so?"

"According to Lucy, whatever Clementine says is gospel truth. Guess there's no getting out of it come hell or high water."

"Well, it may be cleaner, but I doubt it'll get rid of any varmints. That daughter of mine sure has a thing about bugs and such."

Sanford stood to his feet. "Since I can't plow, guess I better give up and plaster."

"You'd do anything for that daughter of mine, wouldn't you?"

"Anything but go back to Missouri." Sanford said with a wink and a nod.

The job of plastering the soddy proved to be quite an undertaking. More water had to be hauled from town. Sanford mixed clay and cow manure in a large bucket until it was the right consistency to spread on the walls with a trowel. The walls now took on a liver color instead of brownish red.

"When this gets dry, Lucy, I'll white-wash it. That way you won't have to look at a red house anymore... from the inside, anyway. It'll be almost like a wood house."

"Even though it's still red, it looks beautiful, Sanford. I can't wait till it's done."

***

It was Easter week. Lucy busied herself with plans for Sunday.

"Sanford, if you can bag a couple of rabbits, I think I'll make rabbit stew and cornbread. I've been saving some dried apples for a pie. Turnip greens will finish out our meal."

"Sounds good to me. I'll see what I can scare up."

While Sanford was out hunting, Lucy began to feel slightly ill. *Wonder if I'm coming down with something?* She shrugged it off and picked up Albert.

"Come on. Let's go outside for a while," Lucy said to Nora. She went out and sat Albert on the ground. "Watch your brother, Nora. I'm going to feed the chickens and slop the hogs." She picked up the bucket and headed down toward the dry creek bed.

On her way back to the house, a wave of nausea hit her in a flash. She dodged behind the house and threw up her breakfast.

Oh, dear Jesus! I know this feeling. Is another little Deering on the way? How am I going to tell Sanford? He doesn't need another mouth to feed; not just now.

She looked up and saw Sanford coming over the hill in his long-legged gait. His gun was on his shoulder but there were no rabbits in his hand.

"No luck?"

"Nope. I think the fire has kind of wiped out a lot of wildlife." Propping his gun against the soddy, he turned to look at her. "You alright? Look kinda peaked."

Lucy turned her back and began to cry.

"What's wrong, my doe?" He put his big hands on her shoulders and turned her around, drawing her close. "It's okay. Maybe I can find a turkey tomorrow. Saw some down by the timber the other day."

"It's not the rabbits or the turkeys, Sanford," Lucy sobbed. "I'm afraid I'm in a family way again."

Sanford held her close but didn't say anything for a long time–just let her cry. Finally, he spoke. "We'll find a way, Lucy. We always have." She knew he was saying this just to make her feel better, but even hearing him say it relieved some of her anxiety.

Easter Sunday the family gathered at H.W. and Mary's for a worship service and dinner. Rebekah and Uriah and their children drove down from their place and joined them. They ended up having smoked ham for their dinner, thanks to Mary who had managed to save it through the winter for just such an occasion. They also had turnips. Lots of turnips. And turnip greens and one small apple pie. Nothing else was available.

While the women did the dishes after dinner Lucy remarked. "I can't believe this year has gone so fast, Mary. Just last year I spouted off to Rebekah at church that I wouldn't be going to Oklahoma, and now look at me–a genuine Oklahoma homesteader."

"Complete with a fine home, I might add," Rebekah said with a grin.

"That's not all," Lucy said. Her mouth turned up slightly at the corners.

Mary looked her square in the face. "What's that for?" Mary's squinted. "You're in a family way again, aren't you, girl?"

"Never can tell. Guess you'll just have to wait and see."

"Why Lucy Deering! I do declare!" Mary said as she gave her a big hug.

"Shhhh." She put her finger to her lips and looked around the room for Nora. "We haven't mentioned it to short stuff yet. Don't know how she'll feel about another rival for her daddy's affection."

CHAPTER 20

July 29, 1890 - Went to town for a loan.

In late April, Lucy awoke with a start. What was that sound? Rain! Glorious rain! She woke up and shook her husband. "Sanford! Wake up! Wake up! It's raining!"

Lightning lit the room, as deep rumbling thunder rolled across the sky in a deafening roar shaking the sod house. Both children woke and began to cry. Nora ran across the dirt floor from her bed to her parents.

"Daddy! Daddy! I'm scared."

He pulled her on to the bed, wrapped her in his long arms and stroked her blond curls. "It's alright short stuff. It's just the apple wagon rolling across the sky."

Lucy lit out of bed to comfort Albert. She scooped him up in her arms, held him tight and leaned her cheek against his silky hair. "You poor baby! It's been so long since it rained, you can't remember what it sounds like, can you?" She snuggled him in between her, Sanford, and Nora. They all lay there listening to the wonderful sound, grateful for a dry, warm place to be.

Before very long, the roof had all the rain it could take. The saturated sod began to drip. First in small drops here and there; then in rivulets down the walls. Before the rain finished, the roof leaked enough to make the dirt floor a sticky mud pie.

It took several days to dry out the floor. The whole place had a wet, musty smell. Some of Sanford's fine plaster job was going to have to be redone. He'd never gotten to the whitewash project yet. Just as well, Lucy reasoned. We'd have to do the whole whitewash thing all over again, anyway.

In a few days the fields dried out enough to bust the sod and plant some corn in the field just beyond the house. The prairie grass sprang to life in a luscious green; a welcome sight indeed.

"Now, with any luck, we'll have hay and corn for the animals for the winter." Sanford said with a big grin.

Sanford seemed to have a heavy weight lifted from his shoulders. It was good to hear him laugh again when he played with the children.

He turned earth for a garden in the side yard, just south of the soddy. All the families pooled what little money they could spare and bought potatoes, carrots, corn, cabbage, onions, green beans and tomatoes, along with squash and more turnips.

She straightened from planting the last row of onion sets and rubbed her lower back. "Looks like we'll have a crop after all, Sanford."

"I told you we'd get by somehow."

It was good to see the laugh lines around her husband's eyes wrinkle in a whole-hearted grin again.

Lucy wasn't as nauseated as she had been with the other children. Maybe I'm just getting used to this pregnancy thing. Lord knows, I've done it enough times these past five years. Maybe the fourth time is the charm.

***

The joy and hope the April rain afforded was short lived. It didn't rain again all through the month of May and on into June. The promising crops shriveled in the rows. The corn was reduced to dead short brown stalks rattling in the wind. Rusty dust blew up and formed blinding clouds. Sanford grew more and more withdrawn.

Albert's first birthday came. It seemed like a lifetime since that day in Walker just a year ago when she delivered that little boy by herself; something she never wanted to do again. She turned her thoughts to the future. *I wonder what things will be like a year from now? This new baby will be six months old by then. Lordy! Little Albert will be two and Nora almost four. Time's flying.*

One night in late June, Lucy awoke in the wee hours of the morning. Sanford wasn't by her side. She tried to see him in the dark room. She called softly. "Sanford. Sanford. Where are you?"

She lay back down. Perhaps he's just gone to the outhouse. She waited a while longer. No Sanford.

Finally, she crept out of bed and peered out the window into the moonlit night. There he was, sitting by the garden. Lucy slid her feet into her shoes and slipped quietly out the door.

"Sanford. What's wrong? Why are you out here? Why aren't you in bed?"

He picked up a handful of dirt and let it run through his fingers as he gazed at her with a look she had never seen before. One that struck fear into her heart.

"Lucy, these crops are good as dead. All except the turnips. Not even a toad-strangler would bring them back. I've just been out here trying to figure out what we're going to do next. I don't see any way out for us. We're pert-near out of money. Our cash is out there burning up in this cursed red dirt. I put everything we had into seed for that field and the garden. We can't go back to Missouri. We've no way to get there and no place to go."

Lucy stood in stunned silence. Suddenly, this whole thing seemed like a nightmare. She pinched herself. No, it wasn't a dream. It was real; too real. Sinking down beside him, they sat arm in arm, without saying a word until the first rays of daylight broke across the horizon in a blazing red glow.

"I'll go into town this morning and see if I can get a loan at the bank for some feed money for the animals. Doesn't look too promising. Everybody's in the same shape we're in. I'll feed Jers a little grain and milk her before I leave.

Lucy hurt for her husband for she knew how much this whole Oklahoma dream meant to him. She prayed silently, "Lord, please make a way for us where there seems to be no way. You told me this was the place for us to be. You didn't bring us all this way and carry us through this far to abandon us here. Show us what we're to do. Thank You, Lord, for Your provision for us, whatever that is."

Lucy went inside to fix Sanford some breakfast.

***

The skinny little banker sat ramrod straight; tapping a pencil in his spider-like fingers on his immaculately organized desk. With downcast eyes he spoke in a thin, condescending tone, "I'm sorry, Mr. Deering. We can't oblige your request for a loan. We are part of this farming community. As the farming goes, so go we. Loans are risky business in this drought. When times are better, do keep us in mind, however. We'd be glad to consider a loan then."

When Sanford stood, he forced his hands to stay in his pockets and resisted the almost uncontrollable urge to punch the scrawny banker in the nose. He took a deep breath and struggled to keep his voice even. "By the grace of God, sir, I'll not need to trouble you for a loan when times are better. Good day." He turned quickly, willing his feet to propel him out the door.

He felt dizzy as he stepped into the sizzling sunshine. *Keep going Sanford. Don't look back. Keep moving.* "God, if you're out there, help us!"

In a daze, he stopped by the post office and drew out a slip of paper from box number 54.

"Mr. Sanford," the postmistress said. I have a Montgomery Ward's catalog here for you also."

He reached for the catalog and tipped his hat. "Much obliged, ma'am." He read the folded paper. It was a notice he had a telegram at the rail office.

Sanford entered the train station and inquired of the man behind the telegraph cage. "Got a telegram here for Sanford Deering?"

Pulling an envelope from a coiled wire holder on his desk, the clerk said, "Here you are sir."

"Had this long?

"Came this morning," the clerk said.

Sanford sat on the wooden platform at the train station and tore open the envelope. It was from Winston, Missouri. It read:

NEED HELP STOP
SAM HAD HEART ATTACK STOP
COME RUN THE MILL STOP
NELLIE YOUTSEY

Sanford read it over and over. He tried to take all this in. Sam wasn't that old. *I'm going to have to talk this over with*

Lucy. He grabbed his catalogue and unhitched Ginger from the hitching post in front of the bank.

***

"What did Mr. Banker-man have to say?" Lucy asked as she peeled some turnips. She couldn't read the strange bewildered look on his face.

"Wasn't favorable."

Her heart sank. She opened her mouth to ask what they were going to do but before she could get a word out, he handed her the telegram. "Look at this."

Tears filled her eyes. "Oh no! How could this be? Sam always looked healthy as a horse."

He slumped in a chair and set his hat on the table. "Even horses get sick, I guess."

"What are you going to do?"

"Need time to think." He went outside to sit under the big cottonwood tree by the stream.

Albert woke up from his nap. While she changed his diaper she prayed. "Dear Jesus! Help Sanford sort all this out. Bless him with Your wisdom." Her mind raced. Nellie wouldn't ask Sanford to come unless she was desperate. "Oh Lord! Help me accept Sanford's decision, whatever that is." She started out the door, but thought better of it.

***

Meanwhile, Sanford was in a wrestling match with his own thoughts. *Is this God's answer for us or is this just a coincidence? Should we pull up stakes here and go back to Missouri? Maybe I can explain to Nellie how things are here. I'm sure she would understand if I didn't come. But how can I leave Sam in his time of need? He's been like a dad to me. If we move back, it'll be an end to all our work here; but if we stay here, we might lose it all anyway.* The longer he sat there, the more confused he became.

A voice called from beyond the yard. "Hey Sanford! What are you doing under that tree? You some kinda lazy man?" H.W. chuckled. "I stopped by to see if you wanted to ride to town with me this afternoon." He pulled the wagon to a stop. "Whoa, there!"

Sanford stood up. "Already been to town one too many times today, H.W."

"You look like the world fell on you. What happened?" H.W. climbed down off the wagon.

"Got turned down for a loan at the bank and then got word Sam Youtsey had a heart attack in Winston. Nellie wants me to come back to run the sawmill."

"You going?"

"Don't know what to do. Feel like I need to go back and help her."

"How serious is he?"

"Don't know. Must be bad or she wouldn't have telegraphed me."

"Maybe you could go up there for a look-see. Even help THem out for a spell. Lord knows they'll be no need for harvest hands round these parts this summer. We can hold things together here till you get back."

H.W.'s words were like a lantern held high on a dark, treacherous trail. A thought popped into Sanford's head. "Maybe I could help Sam at the mill and earn some money to keep this whole thing together."

Sanford jumped to his feet and slapped his hat against his thigh. "That's it! That's it, H.W!"

"What's it? What did I say?"

"Come inside. I need you to send a message at the telegraph office," he said as he ran for the house. "Lucy! Where's a pencil and paper?"

She drew out a stubby pencil and an old envelope from the pie cupboard. "Will this do?"

"Yep!" Sanford stood at the table and wrote:

Will leave tomorrow.
Sanford

"What are you doing Sanford?" Lucy asked.

"I'm going to Winston. Gotta help Nellie for a while. Here, H.W. Take this message to the telegraph office and send it right away. I've got some packing to do."

"But..."

"No 'buts' Lucy. This is the answer."

Lucy watched Sanford wave good-by to H.W. She sat at the table with her head in her hands. Sanford came back in the house.

"Lucy, don't you see? I'll go up there and help Nellie. I can earn the money we need to keep going here."

"How long will you be gone?"

"I don't know yet. Depends on Sam. How long he needs help."

"What about us?"

"Your folks can help you while I'm gone. I'll not be away long. Here I'm about as useful as tits on a boar hog." Once Sanford made up his mind to do something, nothing stopped him.

She prayed, "Is this your solution, Lord? If it is, help us all."

The next morning, Sanford kissed the children and gave Lucy a lingering hug and kiss before he and H.W. headed for town. As the wagon pulled out of the yard, he turned and called, "See you all soon. Love you."

"Bye, Sanford," Lucy whispered. "God bless." She pulled the children to herself and waved at him until he turned his face toward town. Blowing dust stuck in her throat. She coughed and gently rubbed her belly. The wagon disappeared over the ridge as she quickly brushed away a tear so Nora wouldn't see.

"When's Daddy coming back, Mama?"

Lucy forced a smile. "Don't know short stuff. Soon, I hope." She felt a desperate emptiness inside her heart.

CHAPTER 21

October 18, 1890 - Helping Sam.

Lucy and Mary sat in the sod house peeling turnips, trying to get some relief from the pounding August sun. The relentless wind moaned as it puffed fine, red dust through the cracks in the windows.

Finally Mary spoke. "If that hot south wind doesn't quit soon, everything's gonna dry up and blow away."

"Don't know that I've ever seen a drought so bad." Lucy wiped her forehead with the sleeve of her dress and continued peeling. "I used the last of the corn meal to make corn cakes this morning. Guess we'll have to feed the chickens and pigs these turnip peels. Don't have any more feed for them.

"Nothing for us either. Never been that fond of turnips but it'll have to do. Hear anything out of Sanford?"

"Not since he sent those strawberry plants. He might as well have not gone to the trouble. They dried up within a week."

"He say much about Sam's health?" Mary grabbed another turnip to peel.

Lucy shook her head. "His last letter just talked about him doctoring with some new fella in town. Says doc just keeps telling him to rest, but you know Sam. That's about the last thing in this world he wants to do."

"It should ease his mind a bit, knowing there's good help to run everything for him."

"Sanford writes Sam's pretty irritable. Course, that could just be the illness. Never knew him to be too hard to work for." Lucy sliced her turnip and dropped it in the pot.

"Maybe he's sicker than he's letting on. Poor man. Lord knows, he and Nellie sure have had their share of heartaches. Wasn't their boy about Sanford's age? When did he drown, when he was about six? It was almost like there was a curse on their family."

"Yes, their son just turned six when he was swept away. Sam kinda regards Sanford as his own." Lucy propped her elbow on the table and rested her chin in her hand as she gazed out the window at the rolling dust. "Sure hope he gets well soon so my man can come home. This has been the longest month of my life. I sure do miss him."

"This time next year, I'm sure things'll be better. With the money he makes at the mill, it'll be enough to keep you all going."

Brushing her hair out of her eyes, Lucy looked at her stepmother for a long moment. "You amaze me, Mary. You can always see the bright side of even the darkest day."

"Better than looking on the dark side," she shrugged and smiled. "Besides, most times what we worry about never happens anyway, girl. You feeling okay?"

Lucy sighed. "Just tired a lot. Guess that's just part of motherhood."

"I think you might have more energy if you had something besides these turnips to eat."

"Could be. Last night I dreamed of fresh carrots and lettuce. I did so love all the fresh stuff from the garden back in Missouri."

"Next year we'll grow all that stuff here, too." Mary stood up carefully balancing the turnip peels in her apron. "Guess I'll go feed these to the animals. Lord knows, they got to eat something."

The children woke up from their naps. "What's for supper, Mama? I'm hungry."

She put her arms around them and drew them close and smoothed Nora's blond curls away from her face. "Wish I could tell you it was a birthday cake for you, my little three-year-old princess, but it isn't. Just turnips."

***

The drought dragged on until late in September when the sky filled with heavy, black, clouds that rolled over the parched prairie from the southwest as if chased by the devil himself. There was an eerie green cast to the air.

Lucy stopped digging turnips and looked at the sky. She dropped her shovel and cried, “Nora! Albert! Come here! Quick!”

Nora grabbed Albert’s hand and ran toward her mother. “Is it night, Mama? Why is it so dark?”

Lucy scooped Albert up and stashed him on her hip and jerked Nora by the arm as she scanned the sky. Red dirt stung their face and eyes making the root cellar barely visible. She let go of Nora’s hand and jerked the wooden door open. “Get in. Quick, Nora.”

The child stumbled into the earth-covered hole, Lucy and Albert close behind. Lucy struggled in a tug-of-war with the wind to close the wooden door behind them. She secured it with a two-by-four in the iron hooks.

“Go in the back corner,” she yelled above the wind. “We’ve got to get as far from this door as we can!”

In the darkness Nora fell and began to cry. “Mama! Mama! Where are you?”

Nora scooped her up in her free arm.

“It’s okay honey. We’re safe in here.”

The children sat huddled in a corner on their mother’s lap. The wind sounded like a freight train bearing down on them. Soon it passed overhead. Flashes of lightning lit up the dark cellar through the cracks in the wooden door. The ground shook as thunder rumbled across the sky. Torrents of rain dumped on the decimated ground. After what seemed like forever, the storm slacked off.

Lucy picked up her frightened children in the damp darkness and made her way to the barred door. Exhausted from fear, they picked their way through the pitch-black night and entered the undamaged soddy. With shaking hands Lucy lit the lantern and cut them a few slices raw turnip for their supper.

While Lucy choked down a few bites of turnip, she wished for the day her man would be home again.

After a quick wash off with a rag, they all fell into bed, exhausted.

Early the next morning, Lucy awoke to a knock at the door. "Open up. You all right?"

Lucy opened the door and beheld her father's face, wrinkled and drawn. He stepped in the door, took off his hat, and gave her a big hug. It felt good to have the assurance of strong arms about her.

He drew back and looked at her. "You come out all right?"

All she could do was nod her head.

"Some folks around didn't fare so well." He grabbed a cup from the cupboard. "Got some coffee?"

Lucy set the pot of yesterday's coffee on the stove.

"Stopped by Frank's on the way over here. He told me Clementine and Charlie North's barn was damaged. Killed that one horse that ran off all the time. Did you get to the storm cellar?"

"Barely. Sure came up quick, didn't it? Charlie says there's a lot of these storms out here."

"Mary didn't come with you?"

"She's not feeling too pert this morning. Up half the night worrying about you all."

Nora woke up. "Grandpa!" She crawled onto his lap and snuggled into his lap.

Lucy poured him a cup of the black coffee.

"Did you hear the angels bowling last night, short stuff?"

She nodded at him and wrinkled up her nose. "God better tell them to quit it, Grandpa."

H.W. threw his head back and laughed. "Well, we'll have to see what we can do about that."

He hung around the rest of the morning to set the outhouse erect again and repaired the wind damage to the chicken coop. The children didn't let their grandpa out of their sight.

At one point, H.W. brought Albert into the house. "This one's a little too helpful. Mind if he stays in here a spell? He was trying to hammer my boot."

"Lucy laughed. "Maybe he's going to be a carpenter."

"Or a cobbler."

While she peeled turnips, Albert sat at her feet and played with the peels. “You poor baby. You need to have your Papa here.”

He looked up at her with questioning eyes.

“I wonder if you’ll even know him when he gets home.”

The sun was high overhead when Lucy called, “Father, bring Nora in. Dinner’s ready.”

“I was looking at your chickens, girl. They’ve not got much meat on them, for sure.”

“We might as well butcher a couple. No point in having them starve to death. It would be a real treat to have some meat. They’ve stopped laying all together.”

“I’ll butcher a couple before I leave, ” he said.

“Thanks, I don’t have the umph to go chasing those squawkers to ring their necks.”

“On second thought, why don’t you catch four. Take a couple home for dinner. I’ll set the water to boil now so I can pluck the feathers before you go.”

“Would be a nice change from turnips. Much obliged.”

After dinner, H.W. caught each hen, took hold of its head and swung it in a circle over his head. The remaining chickens ran in all directions squawking their alarm.

“Put the head down, Grandpa. I want to see it hop.”

“You always like that part, don’t you, short stuff?”

Nora and Albert squealed as they watched the heads without bodies hop in the mud.

Lucy plunged the chickens into a pot of boiling water on the woodstove. The room filled with the familiar stench like burnt hair, but this time there was an added aroma. Turnip.

“Wonder if I left a turnip in the pot?” She checked. Only chickens. “Why do you suppose they smell like turnips?” she asked.

“That’s all they’ve eaten for months. Wouldn’t surprise me if they taste like turnips too.”

The odor made her feel like she might throw up. Lucy wondered if she would ever be able to stand that stink again. She charged outside to the newly righted outhouse and lost the turnips she had just eaten for dinner.

When she went back in the house to pull the feathers off the steaming chickens, her father had already completed the job.

Butcher knife in hand, he said "It's the least I can do," while he cut the chickens into parts.

"Appreciate it," was all she could manage to choke out.

H.W. left by late afternoon when the children and Lucy went down for a rest.

Near the end of the day, she felt well enough to fry the chicken in bacon grease in her big black skillet. Even the bacon grease smelled of turnips. She forced herself to eat a chicken leg for dinner, in spite of the turnip taste.

***

Another month passed. The rain from September helped the crop grow–the only crop they had–turnips. It got to the point, even the hogs wouldn't eat them.

H.W. stopped by to see Lucy on his way home from town. He rubbed his hands together over the woodstove.

"Sure a nip in the air. Winter must be coming early. Need help digging those turnips to put in the storm cellar?"

"I dug some of them. I was kind of hoping Sanford would get home to dig the rest."

"Need to be dug before a freeze. I'll see if I can get to it in the next day or two."

Lucy hated to ask, but she didn't have the strength to do it herself. "Would it trouble you too much to cut some wood too? Wind's been kind of raw these past few days."

"Be happy to."

"If Sanford doesn't come soon, you and Frank better butcher the hogs. They're doing so poorly."

"They're not the only ones. You don't look like you're any ways near fleshy enough to have another one. Some fresh pork might fatten you up some. You feeling all right? You're looking kind of peaked."

Lucy wasn't aware it showed so much. She could hardly keep up with the children. "Awful tired. Have to rest when the children lay down in the afternoon."

"How much longer you got to go?"

"Two and a half months, more or less." Lucy tried not to notice the worried look that passed over her father's face.

"You were a lot more plump with the others at this stage. Sanford say anything about coming home?"

"His last letter said Sam was trying to go to work once in a while, but Sanford doesn't think he'll ever be able to run the mill by himself again."

"Old Sam better look for some other help. Sanford can't stay there forever."

"That's what I wrote him. He said he's trying to stay till sometime in November. Thinks by then he'll have enough money to order a mill saw from the Montgomery Ward catalogue. That way he wouldn't be so dependent on farming. He kind of hinted to Sam he needed to head home soon."

"Have you told him how bad things are down here?"

She shook her head. "I didn't want to worry him. Besides, it won't make him get the money to buy the saw any faster if I complain. He'll come soon as he can."

"What's it been now, about three months?"

"Four and a half months but it seems like years. I figured up yesterday Albert's spent more than a fourth of his life without his Papa."

"Nora say much about him?"

Lucy nodded. "She asks every day if Papa's coming home today."

Thanksgiving came and went. Still no Sanford. All the family gathered at Lucy's to help process the hogs the men butchered. H.W. and Frank built a smoke house in which to cure the hams.

"Sure glad we're doing this butchering today. I'm about out of lye soap," Mary said as she stirred the boiling hog fat in the big black pot on the fire beside the house. The warm fire felt good in the winter nip.

Anna poured the lye into the mixture. "Nothing better than lye soap for getting those stains out of Frank's clothes. I swear. I tell him he must crawl around in the dirt from the way he looks when he comes in. Don't know how one man can get so filthy."

Lucy poured wood ashes into the boiling pot. "Just wait. When you have kids, he'll look pretty clean compared to them."

She pulled her shawl tighter around her shoulders. A gust of cold wind whipped at the fire.

"I can wait. I don't know how I would fare having little ones around. They make me kinda nervous."

"You'll get over that. Nothing like a baby around to change your outlook on things," Mary said as she continued to stir the simmering soap.

"I hope you're right, Mary. Guess they'd be no sending one back, once they're here."

Lucy burst out laughing. "Now that would be quite a trick."

CHAPTER 22

December 3, 1890 - Wrote a letter to Lucy.

The newly butchered hogs tasted like turnips, just like the chickens. Lucy swore the soap made from the hog renderings had the same dreaded smell. She wondered if they would ever again enjoy the traditional taste of any meat. The occasional egg she managed to get, had a "turnip twang," as she called it.

H.W. brought Lucy a letter from Sanford on the fifth of December. It read:

My Dear Doe,

Told Sam I can't stay any longer although his health isn't much better. Know your time is coming soon. I hope to leave Winston no later than the 12th. He wants me to stay till just before Christmas, but I can't wait that long. I miss you and the children. Tell your father to check the telegraph office when he goes to town as I'll send word of the exact date.

I have enough money to buy the mill saw, but staying to make a little more for hay and feed money to winter the animals. Next year will be better.

Can't wait to see you and the children, my doe. Tell them I am coming soon.

Yours always,

Sanford

Her eyes brimmed with tears as she looked up at her father and laid the letter on the table. "He's coming home next week." She looked around the room for a long moment. A new strength surged into her spirit. Suddenly, she stood and began to spout plans like a rapid-filled river.

"Sanford never got to finish the plaster job last summer. Let's finish it. Do you think we could whitewash the walls too? He would be so surprised. Are the hams cured yet? Let's have a celebration. We'll all gather here." She clasped her hands together under her chin as she whirled around. "He's coming home! He's coming home!"

H.W. put out his hands to steady her. "Whoa there, girl. Take it easy. One step at a time. I'm no young buck, just an old geezer. I can handle about one thing a week. Sounds like you're pushing my work schedule clear into next spring. You got more ideas than Carter's got pills."

She turned and looked him in the eye and gently put her hands on his arms. "Just want everything to be perfect when he comes."

Her father rubbed his chin as he looked over the room. "Well, I suppose I can fix the plaster, but it'll have to dry some before we can whitewash it. That man of yours may be home before we get that done."

Lucy threw her arms around his neck. "Oh, Father, it's been so long since June. I'm sure he'll make it before the baby comes. It'll be such a comfort to have him here again." A joy she hadn't known for long time welled up within her and a happy little tune spilled over her lips.

H.W. went home to gather the trowels to mix more mud and cow manure for the plaster repair. Lucy busied herself with plans for her husband's return. Suddenly, in spite of all the hardships, life had a sweet savor once again.

***

H.W. showed up the following morning ready to begin his task. He plunked the tools in the corner and looked at the chore before him. "After I plaster, I'll have to go to town to get some whitewash. This is going to take a few days."

"Time's short. Have to get right to it."

"Now girl, that plaster'll have to dry for a couple days before I can start whitewashing it. I swear. You women get your bowels in such an uproar. You get something on your mind and you won't let go till it thunders. Just like an ole swamp turtle."

Lucy shut her mouth. She'd not known her father to be so short-tempered. While she watched him mix the cow manure and mud for the plaster, she observed he'd lost weight this past year. He seemed to be moving slower than usual, too. *Maybe that's what happens to you when you get to be sixty. I can't imagine being that old.*

Nora and Albert got into a tussle over an extra trowel lying on the kitchen table.

"I had it first, Albert. I wanna help Grandpa," Nora said as she jerked the tool from her brother's hand.

Albert wailed, tears streamed down his face.

H.W. turned from his plastering and shook his trowel at the children. "Quiet down, you two! You'd think the world was falling in. Get straight or I'll find a willow stick. High time your Papa got home."

Lucy picked up Albert and held him in spite of her swollen belly. She was unsuccessful in her attempt to shush him. Big tears rolled down her cheeks. Suddenly, the last few months of being without her husband crashed in on her.

She thought *I can't endure one more day of being both mother and father to these two. Weren't there some limits to how far a wife should have to go when she says yes to her man? These past six years have certainly been a severe test of the "better or worse" phrase I agreed to.* Truly, it surely did seem like more than six years since she said yes to that tall handsome man.

Nora tugged on her skirt. "Why you crying, Mama?"

Lucy turned her back and swiped her tears with a quick flick of her apron. "It's all right Nora. We're just trying to get things ready for Papa to come home."

"Is he coming today, Mama?"

"Don't know yet, Sweetheart. Maybe when Grandpa goes to town for the whitewash, we'll have a message. He'll be here soon. You two sit down and behave yourselves. That's the best way you can help Grandpa," she said as she pulled a special treat, a cracker from the tin in the cabinet.

H.W. stopped his plastering and put his gnarled hand on Nora's head. She looked up at him with a mouth full of cracker. "Short stuff, I'm sorry I was sharp with you. Grandpa's just kind of tired, that's all." He took Lucy's hand and murmured, "Sorry. Things'll be better when Sanford gets home."

She squeezed it, gave it a loving shake and smiled. "Guess we're all a little on edge."

***

The next afternoon, H.W. came by with the whitewash and dumped it behind the rocker.

"Any word from Sanford?" Lucy asked.

"Nothing yet. Sure he'll be sending us word any day now."

"At this point, yesterday wouldn't be soon enough."

"Patience, girl, patience." He rubbed the fresh plaster with his worn palm. "This'll be ready for whitewashing in a day or two. I'll come back then."

"Thanks, Dad. We appreciate all you do for us."

He took a long look at his eldest daughter sitting on the edge of the bed. "I can't believe you're going to be mamma to three little shavers. You doing all right today? Looks like your time's coming pretty soon."

"I figure I've got another couple of weeks."

He buttoned his heavy wool coat and picked up his felt hat from the table. "Do you want Mary to come stay with you? I could bring her by tomorrow morning."

Lucy struggled to get up from the edge of the bed and shook her head "No. Thanks. Surely Sanford will be home soon."

He gave her a hug, put on his hat and pulled up his coat collar. "If the weather holds, I'll go into town again tomorrow to see if there's any word."

***

The next day when he stopped on his way home, she questioned him with her eyes.

He merely shook his head and went to warm himself by the stove, trying to avoid the fact Sanford hadn't sent word for yet another day. "Bitter out. Makes my bones ache like some old man."

"You're not old." She hoped she sounded convincing.

"Wish I was twenty years younger. I guess you never feel you're given enough time."

"I think we all feel that way at times, Dad."

"Oh, by the way, Mary wanted to know if I could bring the children over to stay till I come back. She thought you might appreciate some time alone before the baby and Sanford get here."

Nora dropped her doll and came running to her grandpa.

"I wanna go, Grandpa."

Lucy thought of all the things she had to do before the baby came. She hadn't even washed the flour sack diapers and baby clothes. It might be easier if the children weren't around.

"All right," she sighed. "But only for a day or two. It'll give me a chance to get baby clothes ready."

Nora clapped her hands and jumped up and down.

"Goodie! I get to go with Grandpa!"

Lucy put her hand on her shoulder. "Not so fast, short stuff. Your brother has to come too. And you better behave yourself, or Grandpa will bring you back quick as a wink. Understood?"

"Yes, Mama. Can I take my blanket?"

"Of course. Let's pack some things to take to Grandpa's. Want to help me?"

"I'll go to the well and draw some water and bring in extra wood for you while you pack," H.W. said as he plopped his hat on his head.

In no time, Lucy packed a few things for the children into two tea towels and bundled them for the trip to Grandma and Grandpa's. Lucy gave each child a hug and a kiss and helped tuck them into the wagon with a large quilt to keep the winter wind out.

With the children gone, she boiled the baby clothes and draped them on the windowsills and over chairs and bedsteads to dry.

***

The next morning Lucy arose early. *I better get the ironing started.* She placed the heavy irons on the stove and flicked water on the clothes. She then rolled each garment in a tight bundle and wrapped each few pieces in a towel. After smoothing several tea towels on the kitchen table for her ironing board she carefully pressed the first little dress. It's so tiny. It's hard to imagine we'll have one so little again soon.

When one iron cooled, she put it back on the stove and used the other one. These irons seem heavier than usual. She sat to rest while she placed the dresses in a wooden crate at the end of the bed and went out to pump more water and started the whole wash process over again with every rag she could find.

"I should have told Dad to have Mary get her rags together. Knowing her, she's probably got her birthing box together weeks ago. Sure wish I could be that organized."

Into the second crate, Lucy placed the sewing scissors, string and the rags and a couple of washbasins. *As soon as that last batch is dried I'll be ready too,* she thought as she smiled.

She sat to have a cup of mint tea; the last in the jar she kept hoarded in the cabinet while she enjoyed the quiet. "Your Papa'll be home soon, little one," she said as she gently rubbed her belly. "This famine won't be so bad with him here. I wonder when he plans to buy the mill saw? He'll be a happy man when that day finally comes."

While she savored the tea and eyed the sack of whitewash in the corner, an idea began to form in her mind. *I wonder how much trouble it would be to mix that whitewash and start on it this afternoon? Dad would be so surprised to know he didn't have to do it all himself. It would please Sanford, too.*

In a flash, she jumped up and mixed a bucket full of whitewash and smoothed it on the brownish red wall with a wide brush her dad had left on top of the sack. *How beautiful! I'll just see how much I can get done before dark.*

Lucy was oblivious to the snowstorm gathering on the horizon.

CHAPTER 23

December 10, 1890 - Got a telegram from H.W.

By suppertime, Lucy had one whole wall whitewashed. She stopped to boil some turnips.

I'll never get used to the smell of these things. And to think I used to like turnips. Forgive me Lord for being ungrateful. If you hadn't provided these, we wouldn't have anything to eat. Nibbling at the turnips, she poured boiling water over her mint leafs again hoping to still have a hint of the mint taste in the water. While eating her meager meal, she admired the paint job. Wind moaned through the door and windows.

Better get some lamps lit before it gets too dark to see in here. She glanced out the window. Flakes of snow filled the air. Good. We need the moisture. Make for easier planting next spring. Sanford'll be pleased.

She contemplated stirring up some more whitewash, but suddenly, a wave of fatigue came over her. *Think I'll just turn in and get started at first light. Surely he'll be here in the next day or two.*

After making a final trip to the outhouse, she stoked the stove with fresh wood, put out the lamps, and snuggled under the blankets. Sleep came quickly to her fatigued body after she found a comfortable position–as comfortable as a nine-month pregnant body could be.

***

In the wee hours of the morning, she dreamed. A giant had her in his grip and wouldn't let her go, no matter how she tried to break free. When she came to consciousness she realized she was in labor.

Oh baby! You're coming early! I wonder if I could make it to Frank and Anna's.

She rolled out of bed... or at least attempted to and fell back hard against the pillow.

Guess I'm not going anywhere. This baby is coming... fast.

The wind mounted to a gale outside. Between pains, Lucy forced herself to light the lamp in the pre-dawn darkness and sat in a nearby chair. Sweat poured down her body in spite of a chill in the room. Before another pain, she managed to pour the last of the water in the house into the large teakettle and refueled the fire in the stove. Her hands shook as she shut the stove door. Snow blew in under the doorway. All she could see out the window was a mass of swirling white.

"Oh Sanford! Why couldn't you have come home earlier!" A tear rolled down her cheek as she clasped the lower part of her belly and cried out in pain. *Oh, that Mary was here. I don't want to go through this alone again.*

She made her way back to the bed before another pain hit. Gripping the footboard of the bed, she inched her way around to the edge. All strength seemed to ebb from her as she lay back to rest. The pain was almost constant now. *Thank God, the birthing box is on the floor next to the bed.*

What providence that I got this stuff together yesterday. I would be in a fix if I hadn't. Lord, help me birth this baby. I need your strength. Mine's all gone.

Before first light, she felt the urge to push; then to push again. A very blue baby boy lay between her legs. She picked out a rag from the box and began to rub him vigorously.

He was motionless. "Breathe, you little skinned rabbit!" Lucy held her breath. "Live, little one." The quiet was deafening. "Oh God. Help this baby live."

He jerked as if startled and sucked air into his lungs giving out a frail cry.

"That's it, little one! Do it again!"

Lucy heaved a grateful sigh. This one was much smaller than the others. She tied off the cord and wrapped him in a blanket.

"You look like a Freddie, to me, little one. That's what I'll call you–Freddie Sanford."

She looked at his perfect little fingers. They were still quite blue, as were his lips. He wasn't crying much–just laid there. Kind of like a sleeping angel.

He wouldn't nurse so she laid him near the foot of the bed. She felt kind-of light headed–like she was floating. Then she noticed it. Blood everywhere.

"My Lord! I didn't know I had so much blood in me! What am I going to do? How am I going to get this stopped?"

She fell back into the bed, out cold.

***

By full daylight, the snow stopped. H.W. hitched up the horses and drove to Lucy's place to start the whitewashing. He knocked on the door. No answer. Knocked again. Silence. He pounded.

"Lucy! You in there? Answer me."

Then he heard it. An infant's cry, barely audible. He burst in.

"My God! What happened?"

There was Lucy. Blood everywhere. A tiny bundle on the bed at her feet. He grabbed her limp hand and patted her ashen face. Was she dead or alive? He couldn't tell so he threw back the covers and listened for a heartbeat.

Thump... thump... thump.

"Lucy! Lucy! Wake up!"

He grabbed a rag and dipped it in the washbasin beside the bed and wrung it out. Lucy's breathing was shallow; almost undetectable. He wiped her clammy face with the rag. The nightmare of his first wife's death twelve years before replayed before his eyes. "Not again, Lord! Not again!" he said as he sat on the edge of the bed.

Lucy barely opened her eyes. "Dad," she said weakly. "His name's Freddie Sanford."

She exhaled and was gone.

"Nooooooooo!" he screamed. He gathered her in his arms and rocked her back and forth. "Come back! Come back! My precious daughter! Come back!"

Grief overwhelmed him. He cried not only for the loss of his daughter, but for Sanford. H.W. knew the long, lonely nights and empty days ahead for his son-in-law; the hardships of a father alone trying to raise three tiny children.

He held her, for how long, he didn't know. The baby began to stir.

"The baby! My God, what will we do with such a tiny one?" H.W. forced himself to stand. Mechanically, he covered her head with the quilts and wrapped little Freddie in a blanket and drove back to his place in a daze.

With his precious bundle in his arms, he came in the house. The children were in the bedroom. Their laughter made him want to scream, "Stop! There is no joy here!"

Mary looked up from the bread dough she was kneading, hands covered in flour and saw blood on his coat and overalls.

"What in the world... what do you have there? What happened to you?"

He carefully placed the tiny bundle on the table.

"Lucy?"

"She's gone. She left this little boy behind." Tears streamed down his face.

"Oh, no! Oh, no!" Mary whispered. They beheld each other. Time froze.

Nora ran into the kitchen when she heard her grandpa's voice, Albert close behind. "Why are you crying, Grandpa?"

"I brought you a present, short stuff. A baby brother. Mom says his name is Freddie Sanford."

"Oh, he looks like my dolly! Where's Mama?" Nora looked around the room and then noticed his bloody clothes. "Ohhh, Grandpa! You got blood."

No one said anything for what seemed like an eternity. How could they tell these precious children their mother was dead?

Finally, Mary sat and drew the children onto her lap. "Your Mama's gone to be with Jesus."

"Will she come here soon?" Nora asked.

"No, short stuff. You'll see her when you get to heaven."

"Am I going there?"

Mary brushed the hair out of her eyes. "Not for a long while, Lord willing."

"But I don't know how to get there."

"Jesus will show you the way."

Nora wrinkled up her nose with a puzzled look. "Oh," she said softly.

H.W. turned for the door. "I'm going to town and send Sanford a telegram."

"You better change your clothes first," Mary said. "Someone might think you murdered somebody."

"What's murdered, Grandma?"

"Never mind, child; just never you mind."

***

Sanford was working at the mill. A boy from the telegraph office brought a message.

"Sanford Deering about?" the clerk shouted above the machine.

"I'm Sanford," he said as he looked up from the saw.

They walked outside. The boy handed him the envelope.

Sanford opened it. It read:

LUCY DEAD STOP
COME HOME STOP
H W

Sanford leaned hard against the hitching post. He felt dizzy. Was this some kind of cruel joke? He read it again. Surely this can't be true. "I was going to the telegraph office myself this afternoon to send word I was coming home day after tomorrow."

"A relative?" the delivery boy asked.

Sanford choked out the words, "My wife."

The delivery boy backed off and whispered, "Sorry, sir," and turned to go.

"Wait. I need to send a message."

He scribbled H.W.'s name and town and a message on the back of the envelope.

Leaving on 5:30 train.
Sanford

He handed it to the boy along with a fifty-cent piece. "Make sure this gets out right away."

The telegraph messenger said, "Yes, sir," tipped his hat, and headed back for the telegraph office on the run.

Sanford barely made the 5:30 train. Maybe this was all just a bad dream. Maybe there was a mix-up at the telegraph office. Maybe this was for some other Sanford Deering. He knew it was crazy to make up all these maybe's, but he couldn't face the harsh reality of truth. The thought of never being with his doe again nearly crushed him. By the time he reached Mulhall the next day, he was numb from grief and lack of sleep.

They buried Lucy on that high knoll close to where he and H.W. buried Jeremiah Jump less than a year before.

He penned in his diary that night,

December 11, 1890

Went to pay my last respects to my best friend in the whole world.

CHAPTER 24

December 18, 1890 - Dreamed of Lucy.

It had been a week since Lucy's passing. Before he was fully awake, Sanford thought he smelled her scent in the bedclothes. He rolled over to put his arm around her. There was only a great emptiness that jerked him to full consciousness. Grief engulfed him like a giant avalanche. All strength drained from him and tears leaked from beneath his eyelids as he softly whispered, "My doe. My dearest doe. How can I make it without you?"

His clothes were dirty and unkempt, the straight-edged razor stayed in its case on the kitchen shelf. The baby's soft whimper barely arrested his attention. When had he fed him last? He couldn't remember. It was all a fog.

Nora and Albert got out of bed and tugged on his shirtsleeve as he lay in bed.

"Daddy, we're hungry."

"Dip some milk out of the bucket."

"There isn't any."

Had he milked the cow last night? He sat on the edge of the bed and pulled his boots on. The baby bottle lay on the table with curdled milk in the bottom.

"I'll go do the milking." Sanford pulled on his coat and went outside in the cold December morning. He couldn't remember why he was out there. Oh, yes. The cow. He went back inside and grabbed the bucket.

Nora and Albert were fighting.

"Stop it you two, before I whip you!" He sat each child forcefully in a chair on opposite sides of the table. "Don't move till I come back, hear?"

They nodded their heads eyes wide, afraid to budge.

When Sanford came back in, he set the milk on the table and dipped them each a glass. Albert reached for it and knocked it over.

Sanford exploded in a rage. Nora grabbed her brother's hand. They hid behind the white wash sack in the corner where Lucy had left it. He sat at the table, rag in hand, and sobbed. "I can't do this."

The baby began to cry louder. Sanford forced himself to clean out the baby bottle and feed him. Slowly the children ventured from the corner.

Nora gently put her hand on his arm. "I love you, Papa."

Her words struck him in the heart. He looked at his little daughter as tears welled up in his eyes. "I love you too, short stuff. He drew his children to himself. "I love you all very much." They all cried together.

***

The next morning Mary set out for Sanford's place to bring them some turnip soup. She really came to check on them. Her whole family had been sick with diarrhea since the burying.

She drove the team through the fresh snow into the yard and jumped off the wagon, pulling the pot of soup from under the seat. An eerie silence hung over the place; the kind that makes chill-bumps on your arms.

Setting her pot by the door, she knocked. There was no response. "Sanford. You in there?" she softly called.

No answer, so she opened the door a crack and peered in. The smell of dirty diapers and sour milk hit her in the face. She took a deep breath of cold air and entered. There at the table, with his head in his hands, sat Sanford, dirty dishes and diapers everywhere. Freddie was asleep. Little Nora and Albert sat transfixed in the middle of the bed, eyes wide.

"Grandma, Papa's sad."

She scooped them up and gave them a bear hug and a pat on the back. "I know, little ones. I know. It's gonna be all right. Just stay put for a while."

Mary came over and gently placed her plump hand on his shoulder.

He looked up at her and whispered, "I killed her Mary. It's all my fault. I should have been here."

Mary sat across from him. He looked ten years older than when she saw him the week before. His dark circles and swollen face alarmed her. Such pain in those eyes.

"You've gotta stop this. All the blaming yourself in the world's not going to bring her back. This grieving's only digging you a deeper hole. You got three little ones here to care for. You're the only parent they got left."

"If we'd stayed in Missouri maybe this wouldn't have happened. There we would have had decent food to eat. I should have taken them with me when I went back last summer. I should have known better."

She looked at her son-in-law for a long time. Had he eaten at all in the past week? His clothes hung on him. It was obvious he hadn't shaved for days. She wondered what she could say to him that he would hear. From the looks of things, he was beyond listening.

Choosing her words carefully, she grasped his hand and whispered, "Sanford, Lucy could have died in Missouri just as easy as here. We have no guarantees any of us will live till tomorrow. Look at little Frankie."

"I thought that was the worst day of my life, but this is worse. My doe's gone." He pulled away from her hand, walked to the window, and stared out for a long moment. With a jagged sigh he turned back to Mary. Leaning against the wall, tears streamed down his face. "How am I going to raise these three young 'uns and prove up this land? I can't even think about running a saw mill with these little shavers under foot."

"You can't just quit. This was your dream. Lucy wanted this for you as much as you did. You've got to honor her coming here by sticking it out, at least till you prove up your land."

He dug his heel into the dirt floor, thumbs hooked in his overall straps.

"What's done's, done," Mary said. "You can't take it back. You always found a way through the hard times before. We're here to help. Have you prayed about any of this?"

"No words," he said as he shook his head. "All my praying words are buried up there in the cemetery. God's forgotten me."

Mary surveyed the room. It was in shambles. Dirty dishes everywhere. Turnip peels on the floor. Unmade beds. Dirty diapers in a pile. She thought this was kind of a picture of Sanford's life right now.

She took a deep breath, almost choking on the smell. "You need some time to sort this out. I'll take the little ones home for a few days and give you a chance to get things thought through."

With his hands folded under the bib of his dirty overalls, he remained silent.

Mary scurried around and put the children's things in the wagon, including the dirty laundry. It took a high and low hunt to find one last clean diaper. She finally found one in Lucy's "birthing box" at the end of the bed. She woke the baby and changed his diaper, stifling a gasp when she saw his raw bottom.

"Got any petroleum jelly?"

"Beats me," he shrugged.

"Never mind. I got some at home."

Not only did the baby's red bottom concern her, he didn't cry when she wiped him clean. She didn't say anything. Sanford had enough on his mind, without adding another care to his burden.

Mary fed the older children some of the turnip soup she brought, dressed them quickly, and bundled them for the ride to her house.

"I'll leave the rest of this soup here. Make sure you eat some of it, hear?"

After she was gone, Sanford shuffled back to bed and stayed there for the rest of the day. Nothing mattered anymore.

"I wanted this land for my doe. Now there's no reason to stay here; no reason to go on."

That night he had a dream. At least he thought it was a dream. Or was it?

It was a warm spring day. He and Lucy sat beside their stream. Her gingham dress was pulled up to her knees as she dangled her bare feet in the water and sucked on a piece of prairie grass. A gentle breeze blew her tatted collar. He watched the sunlight through the trees play on her auburn hair. As he reached out to touch her, she turned, looked him in the eye, and said, "It's time to move on, my love."

He awoke with a start, sat up, and rubbed his eyes. He tried to focus as he looked out the window. The reflection of bright sunlight off a new blanket of snow partially blinded him. How could it be winter? The smell of lilacs filled his nostrils. Where was Lucy? She was there; but, how could she be?

Throwing some fresh wood in the stove, he struggled to remember what she said. What was it? It was a moment before he could remember. The encounter had been so vivid. Oh yes. "Time to move on, my love." That was it.

Sanford seriously wondered if he was as crazy as old Jeremiah Jump. He contemplated all this while he ground some coffee beans and threw them into a pan of water. He couldn't tell anyone. They'd think he was loony, fer sure.

He drank his cup of coffee and surveyed the room.

"Can't live like this. If Lucy saw all this she'd have a fit," he mumble as he set the teakettle on the stove to heat some dishwater, and picked up the littered house and made the bed. After he washed and dried the dishes, he placed them back in the pie cupboard. At the end of the top shelf, he noticed Lucy's Bible. He threw the tea towel across his shoulder, sat in the rocker, and opened it to a place marked by a red ribbon.

His eyes fell on Jeremiah, chapter twenty-nine. It read,

> *For I know the thoughts that I think toward you, saith the Lord, thoughts of peace, and not of evil, to give you an expected end. Then shall ye call upon me, and ye shall go and pray unto me, and I will hearken unto you. And then ye shall seek me, and find me, when ye shall search for me with all your heart.*

Could these words be for him? His heart fluttered. He read them again, and then again. An unexplainable peace began to settle over him like he had never known before. Was this the kind of peace Lucy experienced when she finally came to terms with Frankie's death? He looked at the page again. What was that penciled in the margin? He held it up to the window to get a better look. It read. "Aug. 1, 1887."

"That's right before Nora was born. She must have read that while she stayed at her folks," he whispered. Sanford felt like he had discovered a buried treasure. Perhaps God hadn't forgotten him after all.

He spent a good portion of the afternoon browsing through Psalms. Each passage seemed to have new relevance to him, personally. He even prayed as he did the chores that night. Not empty prayers. There was a very real sense Someone was listening to his heart cries; Someone who cared for him more than any person he'd ever known.

By the end of the third day alone, the fog had completely cleared in Sanford's mind and he began to miss the children. He wondered if H.W. had come to greater faith through the death of his first wife. He'd have to ask him, if the opportunity ever presented itself.

When Sanford pulled up to the hitching post at H.W.'s the next morning, he could see Albert and Nora jumping up and down in the window. They were out the door in an instant yelling "Papa's here! Papa's here!"

Their welcome warmed his heart and his spirit began to rise within him. He heard himself murmur, "I do have a reason to live. Those children need me." He scooped them up in his arms, and said "Let's get in inside. Don't want you all to catch cold."

***

Somehow they got through Christmas. The weeks blurred into the new year. Sanford spent a little portion of each day reading Lucy's Bible. He found many notations and dates she had written in the margins. Each scripture was like a golden nugget to him. His faith and trust grew as he came to understand this God who Lucy had come to know so intimately. He found himself praying often for his children, especially baby Freddie.

It was evident Freddie was not a well child. When Sanford bathed him he noticed his fingers, toes and lips had a blue cast to them; his skin was almost the color of skimmed milk. Instead of kicking in his bed like the other children used to, he just lay there, barely moving. He never laughed; he was thin and cried a lot.

Mary came one day to help out with the children. "Sanford, think you ought to take him to see Doc McPeek," she said with a frown. "He doesn't seem right, somehow." The baby refused to eat, in spite of her gentle coaxing and rocking.

"Think he might pink up some when we can get him out in the sunshine?"

"Don't know. Seems mighty puny to me."

"He reminds me of my cousin's little Rosa back in Missouri. She didn't live long enough to make old bones. Wonder if Freddie's headed down the same road?"

"Give old Doc a visit. He's seen many a babe in his time."

"Maybe he could give him some medicine to pink up those cheeks and put some flesh on his bones."

The next Saturday, the weather turned off warm and Sanford brought all the children to town. Before they headed for home, he stopped by Doc's office.

"Got time to see a little one, Doc?"

"Sure. Who we got here?"

"Freddie. Born in December. His mother died birthing him."

"Oh. You're the ones who live east of me, aren't you?"

Sanford nodded.

"Sorry for your loss. You doing all right?" Doc eyed him over the top of his glasses.

"Tolerable."

Doc nodded. "It's a terrible thing. I lost my first wife. It took a heap of getting over."

"Kind of like dragging a full wagon single-handed over the Rocky Mountains."

Doc laughed. "Well, yes. I never thought of it that way, but that's a good description."

Doc fell silent as he weighed Freddie and checked him over.

Sanford watched Doc's face to try to read any signs he might betray.

Doc's brow furrowed. "Seems pretty light for a two month old. Was he little when he was born?"

"We figure he was about two weeks early. He didn't weigh much."

"Kind of quiet, too. Does he eat good?" he asked as he prodded Freddie's abdomen.

Sanford shoved his hands in his pockets, shook his head.

Freddie looked at Doc quietly with large, hollow eyes.

"Don't imagine your wife ate much besides turnips while she was carrying him last year, did she?"

Sanford managed to squeak out a weak, "Nope." He fought back the accusing thoughts that were ever ready to bite at him.

"This last year has been hard on young ones. They don't thrive much on just turnips. You got help with these three?"

"My wife's parents help out some."

"How old are these others?"

Sanford put his hand on Nora's head. "This one's three and a half. Talks like a magpie after she gets to know you. Albert here will be two in June."

"You need to get a woman. These three'll wear their grandparents out in a hurry."

Doc handed Freddie back to him. Then looked in his cabinet and drew out a bottle marked "Cod Liver Oil." and handed it to Sanford. "You might try him on this for a few weeks. See if it helps. Some young ones just get a slow start."

"Thanks, Doc." He gathered the children and carefully placed the bottle of medicine in the breast pocket of his overalls.

On the road home, Sanford turned Doc's words over and over in his mind. Maybe he was right. Maybe Freddie was just off to a slow start. Where had the past two months gone? Wasn't it just yesterday he came back to the Oklahoma Territory? In another way it seemed like an eternity since he laid his doe to rest.

He hadn't allowed himself to visit her grave. Not even a headstone yet. Perhaps he would do that tomorrow if Mary agreed to watch the children. Suddenly, it hit him. Tomorrow would have been their sixth wedding anniversary. He knew he had to go.

Their wedding at H.W. and Mary's seemed like a far away dream now. He wondered, would he ever have another wife? He couldn't imagine sharing his life with anyone but Lucy... but then again, when he considered living the rest of his life without a wife to care for...

As he drove the team, he was aware of his prayers, as if they were just under the surface, unnoticed, yet there. He gave breath to what was in his heart.

"Lord Jesus, I know You're for me and you want the best for me, even now. Guide me. Show me Your will. My future's in Your hands."

"Who you talking to Daddy?" Nora interrupted.

"Just talking to God in heaven, short stuff."

"Grandma says that's where Mama is. Wish I could see her."

"Me too, Nora. Me too."

***

That evening Sanford located a red limestone rock that had a flat side, down by the stream. He carved,

LMD
Died
Dec. 10, '90

The next day, Sanford went alone to Lucy's hill-top grave and planted the rock for a headstone and placed four, smaller rocks at the corners of her plot. After he packed the dirt around the last rock, he stood and looked at the gently rolling hills.

How strange. He had come to this Territory to own land. After a year and a half, this was the only land he held title to; a cemetery plot to hold six people, purchased with a five dollar gold piece. Somehow, this wasn't what he had in mind in his quest for land.

As he stood there in that quiet place, there seemed to be a new release for him. Although he had loved Lucy with everything in his being, he seriously questioned if he should stay here in this territory. Her words from the dream rang in his ears, "Time to move on, my love." Did that mean he was to move on from the Oklahoma Territory, or move on to a new wife?

He felt a part of his life ended in that graveyard; it was over and gone... forever. Although he didn't know what lay in store for him, he knew he must press on to find out.

More than five years would pass before he visited this gravesite again.

CHAPTER 25

June 5, 1890 - Cleaning up after Haynes' fire.

Charlie North stopped by in mid-January. He hadn't seen Sanford since he offered to help with the chores just after Lucy died.

As he dismounted his horse he said, "You faring all right? Got enough turnips?" A slight grin played at the corner of his mouth.

Sanford looked up from splitting logs and grinned. He rested his ax on his boot and shook Charlie's hand. "Reckon so. About all we *do* have. Have enough to last till spring, if we're careful."

He rested the ax against a log, sat, and said, "What's on your mind, neighbor?"

"Saw a notice at the post office. There's going to be a town meeting over at the Victor School House on Saturday for everybody. Will you come?"

"What's it for?"

"We need to see what we can do to petition Washington for aid since we got no seed money for spring planting."

Sanford looked around at the frozen fields. "Had good snow this winter. Just might have a chance of some crops... if we could get some seed, Lord willing."

"Be by around 9:00."

"See you then." Sanford grabbed a load of split wood and headed for the house.

The next Saturday, Sanford and Charlie joined their neighbors to seek aid for their fix. Sanford spotted Uriah Miller at the back of the crowd.

"There's my friend from Missouri. He's kind of the reason we came down here. Haven't seen much of him since last fall." He waved at his friend, but failed to make eye contact.

"Why's that?" Charlie said.

"Don't know. Have to see him after the meeting."

During the gathering, they heard from several settlers as to their desperate needs. After much discussion, they elected three men to travel to Washington, D.C. to petition for "help for the sufferers." After it was over, Sanford remembered he wanted to see Uriah.

"Charlie, I need to talk to my friend a minute. Do you mind waiting?"

"I'm in no hurry. Nothing but a bunch of wood waiting to be chopped at home."

"I won't be long."

Sanford worked his way through the crowded room to the outside. The only thing he saw of Uriah was his back as he and his horse hightailed it in the direction of Uriah's place.

"Well, I wonder what kind of burr he's got under his saddle?" Sanford said, as he removed his hat and scratched his head.

Charlie came up behind him. "Find your friend yet?"

"Nope. He lit out before I could greet him. I'll have to go up there and pay him a visit. That's not like him. Hope nothing's wrong."

On the way home, Charlie said, "Hope those fellas' can do something for us."

"If they can't, a lot of folks'll probably pull up stakes and go back where they came from."

"Don't know about you, but we got no place to go back to."

The two fell silent the rest of the way home. While they bumped across the frozen prairie, Sanford wondered how many of his neighbors would pull up stakes and leave if some kind of aid didn't come through. He had the money he earned at Sam's sawmill for seed, but most others had nothing. Of course if he spent it for seed wheat, he'd have to wait till the crops were in... if there was a crop, before he could buy the mill saw. That was a chance he'd have to take. He didn't want to take a handout. It just wasn't his way.

Stepping down from Charlie's wagon he tipped his hat. "Much obliged, Charlie. Hope those fellas can do some good."

He opened the door of his lonely soddy and hung his coat and hat on the chair. Later he stoked the stove, boiled a pan of water and threw in a handful of coffee grounds. Perhaps he should pull up stakes and go back to Missouri. Maybe he could work at Sam's sawmill again, but then he wouldn't be any further ahead than when he came here. After his second cup of coffee, he finally concluded he had put too much work into this place to turn his back on it.

Later that month, Charlie rode into Sanford's place as if chased by a mountain lion. Sanford whirled around from the grinding stone with a jerk. Charile's whoops made him look beyond the thundering horse to see if they were about to be attacked by Indians.

"What's got you so fired up, Charlie?"

He jumped down off his horse. "Did you hear? Congress voted fifty thousand dollars for us sufferers? Besides that, the railroad is going to send us some summer wheat seed at cost. That's right generous of them, don't you think?"

Sanford checked the sharpness of his sickle with his thumb. "The railroads stand to lose a lot if we can't plant. If we don't grow any crops, they're going to miss out hauling a lot of freight from here to the north and east. If they scratch our back, we'll scratch theirs."

"Well, never thought of it that way. Good way to prime the pump, I guess," Charlie said, sliding his felt hat off to scratch his head. "You going to take the government money?"

"Not if I can help it. Don't want charity."

While the farmers waited for the seed wheat to arrive, Sanford kept busy; it helped to ease the pain of his loneliness. One of his projects was to hew logs to enlarge the Victor School.

Mary kept the children most of the time. Sanford's sister-in-law, Anna, helped out some, but the three little ones made her "nervous condition" worse, as she put it, even though that left Mary with three extras, besides her own two.

Sanford came over to H.W. and Mary's to see the children one morning before going to cut logs.

Nora ran out to meet him in her usual fashion.

She threw her arms around his neck as he swooped her up and spun around with her. "How's my short stuff this mornin'?"

Nora frowned. "Grandma's sick, Papa."

They met H.W. at the door.

"What seems to be the problem?" Sanford said as he followed H.W. into the kitchen.

Shaking his head he said, "She's got another one of her sick headaches."

"What's that make now? Third one this week?" Sanford put Nora down and picked up a cup.

H.W. poured coffee for him and then himself. "Yeh. Figger she better see the Doc. Mebbe he's got some headache powders of some sort."

He carried a cup of mint tea to his wife's bedside and came back shaking his head. "She don't seem right, somehow. Moody. Irritable. Tired all the time."

"Think the children are too much for her?" Sanford sipped the hot coffee.

"Don't know." H.W. sat at the table and rubbed the top of his bald head. "Think we better take Freddie along too. He's not eating much. Seems crankier than most young ones to me."

"I'll take them into town H.W., if you'll stay with the other two."

"Be glad to. How's the school coming?"

"We'll have enough logs in another couple of days, I figger. Then we'll get some folks together to raise the walls on the new section."

On the way into town, Mary took the opportunity to talk to Sanford about his plans.

"What are you planting this year?"

"Think I'll try some summer wheat. That way I'll have some time to go back to Missouri to look things over."

Mary eyed him for a long moment. "Thinking of going back for good?"

"Don't know what I'm thinking, Mary. Got a letter from Sam the other day. His health is better but he still needs some help at the mill."

"You're not taking those kids with you, are you?" Mary patted Freddie in his blanket.

"Well, I don't want to impose them on you all."

"That baby's not well enough to travel. Besides, who'd take care of them up there? Best leave them here with us."

"But your headaches..."

Mary waved, "Never mind my headaches. They probably won't disappear just because your kids are gone. Hanna's pretty good help for an eleven-year-old."

The doctor prepared some headache powders for Mary and prescribed another bottle of some kind of liquid to try to build Freddie up. He hadn't gained much weight since the last visit.

The wheat seed arrived in Mulhall the next week, just as they finished the addition on the Victor school.

Sanford bought seed and planted it as soon as the fields were dry enough for the team. At the end of May, he was bound for Missouri again.

***

The first Sunday in Winston, he accompanied Sam and Nellie to church. They got there late, which was unusual for the Youtsey's. They sat clear in the back. Sanford saw many familiar faces among those gathered for the service.

Rev. Jameson started with announcements.

"We buried Tom Haynes and his little daughter, Martha yesterday over at Tipton. Pray for sister Susan. Could I see a show of hands of who'll be there to help clean up from the fire?"

Sanford elbowed Sam and whispered, "My God! What happened?"

Sam glanced at him sideways, hesitated, then answered in a hoarse whisper. Their house burned down while Susan went to tend to her sick mother in Tipton. The mother's dying of consumption."

"Hadn't heard. How could it burn down around his ears?"

"The way I heard it, just after she left, Tom's new horse went loco and kicked him. Horse must have buggered him up pretty bad. Doc said he thought Tom's leg might be broke. He gave him some laudanum for the pain. We had a lightening storm that night. Must have struck the house and started a fire. Guess he took a might too much painkiller. They found him in the bed."

"And little Martha?" Sanford croaked.

"They found her by the door. Guess she couldn't get it open by herself." Didn't want to tell ya... after what you'd been through and all."

This news gnawed at him like a rat on cheese. What a horrible way to die. He thought his grief was bad, but Susan's must be worse. That precious little Martha; same age as his own Nora. He felt weak; his heart felt like a lead weight.

The pastor continued. "Later on we'll need some folks to help with the house raising."

Sanford hardly comprehended Rev. Jameson's words but his hand shot up like a rocket.

" . . .eight, nine, ten," the pastor counted. You all be there first thing tomorrow morning. You ladies plan on cooking for at least ten hands. We'll take a special offering today to pay for the materials. Sam Youtsey's agreed to furnish the lumber at his cost. We'll have this place rebuilt for our dear sister in no time."

The congregation sang a hymn and the pastor gave a short sermon while images rolled through Sanford's head continually. It was Tom who brought the chicken when Frankie died. Susan was so attentive to Lucy through the grieving over the death of that first child. Their daughters Martha and Nora were the same age. The pain she must be going through. Wonder if the awful truth of being alone has sunk in yet?

Sanford wasn't aware of his surroundings until everyone stood for the final benediction. When the service was over, he moved in a daze to the door.

Rev. Jameson greeted him with a warm handshake. "Thank you, kindly, for taking time out to help sister Haynes. We've been praying for you and your family since we heard of your heartache."

"The least I could do. Susan and Lucy were dear friends. Neighbors help one another, right?"

The reverend nodded. "We'll see you there tomorrow morning."

"Sam and I'll bring lumber from the mill."

"Thank you kindly. May the Lord reward you, Sanford."

He tipped his hat and was out the door. The heaviness of this burden followed him all day. Everywhere he looked, the faces of

Tom, Susan, and Martha hung before him. Hearing of Susan's misfortune tore his own grief open again. He spent most of the afternoon alone, praying and chopping wood until he was exhausted.

He and the Youtsey's were up before daybreak, loading the wagon with tools, lumber and supplies. Nellie busied herself with the preparation of cherry pies, cinnamon rolls, and a ham.

"Careful where you put these in the wagon, Sam. Don't want some shovel in the middle of one of my pies."

"Just leave it to me, woman." He winked at Sanford. "Wouldn't want to ruin your pie with my spade."

It took nearly a week for the volunteers to clean up the mess from the fire. Susan was still in Tipton caring for her mother.

"When we get finished cleaning up this place, are we going to wait until Susan comes back to start rebuilding?" Sanford asked as he took one of the last wheelbarrows full of burnt stuff to the deep hole where they dumped the burned goods and charred timbers.

"She sent word yesterday she was coming back tomorrow. Guess she'll tell us what to do next," Sam said. "We better get this hole covered up before she gets here. I don't want it to bring back more memories."

Sanford dumped the last load on to the trash pile. A swatch of something blue and white caught his eye. He reached down to pick it up. It was a piece of quilted cloth that looked strangely familiar. When he started to throw it back, it dawned on him. This was a piece of the blanket Lucy quilted for Susan's baby, Martha, before she was born. Somehow he just couldn't bring himself to throw it away.

Back at Sam's that night, he gently washed it at the pump and pulled off the pieces of burnt edge. In the fading daylight he examined the fine hand stitches his dear wife had worked–a little piece of what used to be but would never be again... in this lifetime, anyway. He carefully laid it out to dry in his room and in the morning, tucked it in his bag.

When the volunteers assembled at the site that day, nothing was left of the home but the limestone chimney; naked and alone.

Susan arrived shortly. Sanford was amazed at how good she looked, in spite of all she'd been through.

With tears in her eyes she stopped, looked at the chimney that once graced the home of her family, and turned to the workers. "Thank you all so much. It's a kindness I'll never be able to repay . . ." Her eye caught Sanford in the crowd. She drew in a quick breath and whispered, "Sanford Deering, is that you? I didn't know you were here. Have you been working on this crew?"

"Yes ma'am."

Sam broke in. "Miz Susan, we were wondering what you wanted us to do next. We've got some materials here to start a new house, but we don't know what your plans are, exactly."

"Oh. Oh, yes. Well, here's a plan I drew. It's a pretty simple house, really. I don't need much." From her small purse she drew out a folded piece of lined paper torn from a ledger and smoothed it out on a keg of nails.

Bending over the plans, Sam fished his spectacles from his shirt pocket, set them on the end of his nose, and pulled them back over his ears. "Well, let's see here now. Mmmm-huh. Looks like a good one Miz Susan. Figger we could finish this up by middle of July if the corn harvest holds off."

"That would be wonderful Mr. Youtsey. I... I don't know how to thank you all. I have to go back to Tipton to tend to Mother. I'll leave all this in your capable hands. You all are such good neighbors; don't know what I'd do without you." She turned to go, then turned back and walked over to Sanford. She touched his arm and in a barely audible tone said, "Sanford, I'm so sorry to hear of *your* loss. Lucy was a wonderful friend."

He looked down. Out of the corner of his eye he could see her tears welling up. He continued to look at the ground and nodded his head and whispered, "Thank you, ma'am. The same to you."

Sanford caught a slight scent of lilac as she walked away. It made his heart ache all over again for Lucy. *Funny. I didn't think lilacs bloomed this late in the summer,* he thought to himself.

CHAPTER 26

August 3,1890 - Planting peach trees.

Sam and Sanford didn't say anything on the way home. They stopped at the stream to water the horses and watched the clear brook gurgle over the smooth round river rocks.

Sam spoke. "Ever think about marrying again?"

"Can't see myself with anyone but Lucy."

"It's gonna take a powerful lot of raising for one person with those young ones."

"I know it; but Mary and H.W. are good helpers."

"They're not gonna live forever," Sam said as he slapped the reins on the horses backsides. "Get up, you two. You'd drink the stream dry if I let you."

***

Sam's words drifted in and out of Sanford's thoughts over the next several days. The words played across his mind while he worked on Susan's house or helped Sam at the sawmill. They even haunted him when he helped neighbors with their wheat harvest.

One night at supper Sanford asked, "Think we're going to finish Miz Susan's house on time, Sam?"

"Reckon we will." Sam shoveled in another bite of beef stew. "Maybe the neighbors can rustle up some furniture and the womenfolk could bring her some kitchen utensils. Sure hard to start from scratch again."

"I could make her a dry sink and some other pieces–table and chairs and such."

"Yeah, and Nellie could get some of the women together to make some quilts and a mattress."

"She'd appreciate it, I'm sure. Any word when she's coming back from Tipton?"

"Depends on her mother. She keeps hanging on. Susan doesn't have any family to help with her."

"Sure had her share of tough times, huh, Sam?"

"That she has, my boy."

***

In late July, Susan was still not back from Tipton although her house was ready to be occupied. Sanford got a letter from H.W.

Dear Sanford,

The wheat you planted will be ready in another week or so. Children are well, although Freddie's not eating much. Albert's growing like a weed. Mary and Hanna made him a little birthday cake the other day. Mary's having more sick headaches.

The last line of the letter grabbed Sanford's heart. It read,

Nora asked me yesterday if her papa had gone to heaven like her mama.

Let us know when you're ready to come home.

H.W.

Sanford stifled a moan. He jumped up from his chair and pretended to look out the window. Tears stung his eyes as he clutched the letter.

Nellie glanced up from her mending. "Are things all right in the Territory, Sanford?"

He swallowed hard fighting for control, slowly refolded the letter, and slid it into his shirt pocket. Drawing his hand over his moustache and down his chin, he whispered, "Time to go home."

She nodded as she drew her thread through the cloth. " We certainly appreciate the help you've been to Sam and me. Couldn't have made it without you."

He took a deep breath. "Glad to do it, Nellie."

"Sam told me one time he believed God sent you to us to replace the son we lost. I think he's right. We'll miss you. Ever think of coming back?"

"Sometimes. No clear direction yet. Too soon, I guess."

"You know you're welcome here any time, Sanford."

"Yes, ma'am. Thank you." He seriously doubted that would ever happen, but there was no use in discussing it with Nellie.

The day Sanford was to leave, Sam came to the back door holding a small twig with a burlap ball on the bottom.

"What you got there, Sam? Looks like a little twig all wrapped up."

"Old Man Mosby said he wanted you to have this for your home in the Territory. Kind of a 'thank ye kindly fer helpin'Miz Susan,' as he put it."

He took it from Sam and looked it over. "Is this from his peach orchard?"

"The same."

"Well, that was right nice of him. Old Mr. Mosby has the finest peaches around. Thank him for me, will you Sam?"

"Yep. We best be getting to the train depot. It'll take a while to get you loaded."

"I didn't bring that much, Sam."

"No, but you're going home with a load. This is only one of about fifty," Sam said, as he held up the little twig. "Wagon's full," nodding his head toward the buckboard.

"My Lord! I'll have enough to share with the whole countryside."

"Mr. Mosby said this way you folks would have something to eat besides turnips."

Sanford laughed. "Lord knows, we need it."

***

Sanford's longing for Oklahoma grew with each passing mile. He rubbed his arms and realized they actually ached to hold his children again. "I've been away from those young ones too long. Next time I go, I better take them with me."

The train pulled into Mulhall, right on time. He spotted Nora and Albert scrambling down from the wagon at the hitching rail. Before his work boot touched the wooden depot platform, the children screeched in a chorus, "PaaaaaPaaaaa!" Nora reached him first, arms wide. "You're home!" Albert brought up the rear as fast as his fat little legs would carry him.

He scooped them up and twirled them around as he buried his head in their blond locks. Finally, he reared his head back and feasted on the faces of his dear children and squeaked out the words, "Happy birthday, short stuff."

"I'm four, Daddy," she said and held up four chubby fingers. "See my new dress Grandma made me?" She ran her hands down the front of her pink printed dress. "She made it from a flour sack."

"It's beautiful, short stuff, but you're getting too big. I'll just have to put a brick on your head."

"Oh no, Papa," she said with a frown. "That'd be too heavy."

"Guess I'll just have to let you grow up then," Sanford said with a chuckle. He shook H.W.'s outstretched hand. "Where's the rest of the family? Didn't they come?"

H.W. hesitated and then said, "They all went to take Freddie down to Doc McPeek's."

Sanford set the children down. His face fell as he asked, "Something wrong?"

H.W. shook his head. "Just more of the same. He's not eating. Maybe he just misses his Papa."

Sanford doubted a eight-month old would notice, but he nodded in agreement anyway. "Oh. Almost forgot. Brought a surprise for you. Pull the wagon around. We'll unload it."

H.W. could hardly believe his eyes when Sanford opened the boxcar. "Lord in heaven! Where in the world did you get all these?"

"Old Mr. Mosby gave them to me for helping rebuild Susan Haynes' house. Said he sent them to us so we wouldn't have to eat turnips."

"That was right neighborly of him. Why did you rebuild the Hanes' house?"

"Tell you about it on the way home. Let's get these peach trees loaded."

They picked up Mary, Hanna, and Freddie at Doc McPeek's office. Mary handed Sanford the baby so she could get into the wagon. Sanford noticed he wasn't holding himself up like a normal eight month old.

"Mary, H.W. tells me he's not been eating."

"Nope. Don't know what he's living on. He's as pale as a moonflower in August. Doc gave me some new kind of liquid. He hopes it'll pep him up a bit."

Sanford gave Mary a hand into the wagon. "How's your headaches?"

"They've eased some."

"We can be grateful for that, anyway."

"Amen."

Just then Sanford caught sight of Uriah out of the corner of his eye. Uriah ducked into the harness shop and Sanford handed Freddie to Mary. "I'll be right back. Got to talk to Uriah a minute."

"Hey, Uriah! How have you been? Haven't seen you in a coon's age." He stuck out his hand for a shake, but Uriah didn't respond. Sanford continued. "I missed talking to you last January at the town meeting. Where you been keeping yourself?"

Uriah shifted from one foot to the other and tried to avoid his gaze. "I... uh, I... we... we're sorry to hear of your loss, Sanford," he said as he shot him a quick glance.

"Thank you kindly."

"I heard you went back to Missouri for a spell. Moving back there?"

"Not likely. After all it took to get here? I don't think so."

Uriah looked down and fiddled with the string tied around a brown paper package and said softly, "If I hadn't written that letter, you wouldn't have come... and Lucy wouldn't be dead. "

Sanford looked at him for a long moment while he thought about the last time he saw Uriah. "Is that why you left the town meeting in such a hurry?"

Uriah nodded.

"Well, I'll be switched." Sanford put his big hand on his friend's shoulder. "I thought you were mad at me or something, Uriah. Lucy's dying isn't *your* fault. Fact is, I'm not out to blame anybody. We were destined to be here; your letter just paved the way."

Uriah looked like a hundred pound weight had just been lifted off his shoulders. He straightened slightly and a grin spread across his face from ear to ear. "Glad you're back, Sanford. Got any crops in?"

"Yep. The summer wheat's about ready. Hey, you need some peach trees? I just brought some in from Missouri. Let me fetch some for you."

"Much obliged," he said as he tipped his hat.

***

For the next two days, Sanford, H.W., and Orris planted a grove of peach trees on Frank's, H.W.'s, and Sanford's place. When the last one was heeled in and watered, he and H.W. sat under a tree to admired their labor.

" I can almost taste those peaches now," H.W. said.

"Don't get too anxious. They've got to do some powerful growing first."

"They'll be bearing before you know it, my boy."

"Tomorrow wouldn't be soon enough."

H.W. sighed and plopped his straw hat on his knee and wiped his forehead and the back of his neck with his bandanna before he studied the cloudless sky. "Looks like it's going to stay hot and dry for the next several days."

"Reckon we better start on the wheat harvest tomorrow?"

"Might as well. We'll be shorthanded with Frank working his new blacksmith shop. Built him a right nice little shed for it, don't you think?"

"Yep. Seems to be no end to the folks wanting their horse shod or a machine part fixed. Right handy to have a blacksmith close by. Won't have to go into town anymore for our smithing needs."

"We're getting real cityfied out here."

Sanford stood and stretched. "Better, go home and turn up your toes, H.W. Dawn'll be here before you know it."

***

After Sanford paid the man to thresh his wheat, he pumped a fresh bucket of water and offered H.W. a drink from a gourd dipper and then had one himself. He wiped his mouth on his shirtsleeve and sat down on the side of the well. "You know, H.W., think I'll be looking to get me one of those threshing machines. I could hire out, just like that fella' does."

"You know, you just might be on to something. He must make a pretty good living at it, the way I figger."

"Sure could make more than just farming, for sure."

H.W. drew with a stick in the dirt. After a long silence he said, "Give up on the idea of a mill saw, Sanford?"

"Nope. Just haven't found one for sale, yet. They're pretty expensive in the catalogue."

"Well, I heard of a fella by the name of J.D. Townsend down at Crescent City. Heard he has one for sale. Want to go fer a look-see?"

"Sure. Why not? Let's go tomorrow."

CHAPTER 27

August 7, 1891 - Got my saw today at the railroad.

When they came into yard the next evening, Mary knew by the grins on the men's faces the trip must have gone well.

Nora and Albert came bounding out of the barn and headed straight for their father.

"Hey, kids."

Attacking him at the knees, he put Albert on his shoulders and then scooped up Nora in his arms.

"Whoa! Hold on there. You about knocked your papa over."

Nora looked at him and grinned. "Did you get the saw, Papa?"

"You betch'a, short stuff. She's a beauty, too."

She wrinkled up her nose. "Is it a girl saw, Papa?"

Sanford threw his head back and laughed. "I guess if you want it to be it is."

"Dinner's ready," Mary called. "Get in here and wash up."

While H.W. poured water into the basin from a bucket, Hanna wiped Albert's face; Nora seated Freddie at the table. Sanford sat in a kitchen chair to unlace his work boots.

"When you get those boots off, put them by the door, Sanford," Mary said as she pointed at him with a wooden spoon in her hand. "Your batching habits don't set well around here. I don't allow any dirty boots under *my* table."

"Yes, ma'am." Sanford couldn't really see the harm in dirty boots under the table, but then again, women had a different view on things. If Lucy were around, she'd probably say the same thing. Maybe he was turning into more of a bachelor than he thought.

Mary spooned the mashed potatoes into a bowl and set them on the table. "Get a good deal?"

"Yep." He pulled off his boots and dutifully placed them by the door. "Had her priced right, for sure."

H.W. winked at Sanford. He always admired how his son-in-law could make a good trade.

"It's a girl saw, Grandma. Papa said so," Nora said with all the certainty her four-year-old voice could muster.

"Well, I'm glad, short stuff. We need more girls around here, don't we?" Mary said as she patted Nora's shoulder. The little girl nodded.

"He's going to ship it on the rail this week," Sanford said as he washed and dried his hands.

"We better get a place leveled out for it. Where you figger on putting it?" H.W. asked as he reached for the towel.

Sanford pulled out a chair and sat. "Just beyond the garden seems to be a pretty good place. Wouldn't have to do much to level that out real nice."

"I'll be over in the morning."

Mary chuckled. "You men sound about as excited as a couple of little boys over a new hound dog."

"This dream's been a long time in coming, Mary. Just one more step in getting my plans in place."

She shook her head as she put the roast beef and carrots on the table. "Lord bless your dreams."

"Mmmm. Smells good. I'm starving. Start at first light, H.W.?"

"Unless you can figure a way to make the moon brighter so we can start tonight," he chuckled.

"Nope. In that case, guess I'll just have to wait till morning light."

When the saw arrived in Mulhall, a person would have thought the circus had come to town. People gathered around the boxcar and the men helped Sanford load it onto his wagon.

"Jes' what we needed 'round these parts," one old-timer said.

Another nodded. "I got a patch of timber to feed that thing. That'll make me some jingle for my pockets."

Sanford grinned. "Be glad to oblige you fellas. Have it up and running in a day or two."

"Real fine piece of machinery you got there, young fella."

If Sanford had just had a new son, he couldn't have been any prouder.

Charlie North stopped by Sanford's place a couple of days later. He didn't want anything, he just wanted to watch the saw run. Before long folks from all over the countryside came by to see the it.

When Sanford wasn't working at the mill, he helped H.W. and thirteen-year-old Orris harvest the corn. After that, they put up some hay.

Stopping to get a drink of water they rested against the bailer. Sanford handed a dipper full to H.W. He took a long look at the fields.

"Think next thing I better do is put a fence around my corn field. It'll help to keep the stray cows out," H.W. said and took a long drink.

"Wouldn't be a bad idea to fence the hay field either. I noticed some trampled places in it when we were haying yesterday."

The old man nodded and handed the dipper to his son-in-law. Sanford took a well-deserved drink and straightened from the bailer to admire the view. "This place is looking mighty different from when we first moved here."

H.W. fell silent then finally spoke. "Two years. Lot happened since then."

"Sure has. Lot of it I don't really want to remember. I wonder what the next two years will bring. When I get that money together for the threshing machine, I'll hire Orris to help me."

"Lordy, he'll be a man here before you know it."

"Yep. He's gonna make a fine farmer one day."

***

By the time the first really cold days of winter hit, Sanford had his garden safely put away in the root cellar and enough wood cut for a long cold spell.

He thought he was doing pretty well until the anniversary of Lucy's death, the second week of December. Everything seemed to go wrong. All three kids were sick with fever. Little Freddie couldn't stop throwing up, and he had a bad case of diarrhea.

It was too cold to work outside so Sanford did the laundry and tried to hang it out. It froze on the line so he brought it indoors. It seemed like it would take forever to dry draped over every chair and bedstead. Despite his best efforts, he burned the stew.

On his way to the door with the pot of burned stew, he tripped over a wet long john draped from the back of a chair and landed flat on his face. Part of the stew burned his arm.

Nora sat up in bed. "What happened, Papa?"

As he reached for a shovel to clean up the mess, he blurted out, "Dang it! I need a woman around this place!" His words surprised him. Until now, he had refused to admit it.

"Where you gonna get one, Papa?"

"I don't know short stuff. Suppose I could order one from the Montgomery Ward catalogue?"

She wrinkled up her nose and asked, "They got women in there?"

"Wish they did, little one. Wish they did."

Over the next few days, the thought of finding a woman played at the edges of his mind. Would he ever marry again? If he ever did, it would have to be someone who loved his kids as much as he did. Who in the world would want to take on three little ones and a new husband to boot? Not to mention that one is a sickly one-year-old. As hard as he tried to slam the door on his thoughts, they kept coming.

Finally, he prayed, "Lord, You know I can't do all this child raising by myself. Pretty soon the weather's gonna break so I can farm and work at my sawmill. I can't keep depending on my in-laws to watch them. If You know of a woman for me, please send her my way."

As soon as the prayer left his lips, he felt a release. Somehow he knew his prayer was heard. How soon, if ever, the answer came, was up to the Lord now. It was out of his hands.

Somehow, they made it through their second Christmas without Lucy. Memories of her were everywhere. Mary and

H.W. hosted a fine Christmas Day dinner for all the family. Although Sanford loved all the traditional family favorites of fried apples, ham, and some kind of fancy potatoes Mary referred to as "scalped," the season just wasn't the same without his doe. Maybe 1892 would be a better year.

In January, Sanford got a letter from his little sister, Maggie, who had moved back to Winston the year before.

Dear Sanford,

George Smith asked me to marry him. He has a claim up by Marshall in the Oklahoma Territory. I believe this is near you?

We are hoping to get married sometime in March of this year. Mama says it is high time I got married. She says at 23, folks are going to start calling me an old maid if I don't get on with it.

Could you please see if and when the Presiding Elder will be in Marshall? We plan to be married at the house George is building on his claim.

I am busy with the wedding plans. I have a lady making my wedding dress. She is such a beautiful seamstress. I think she might have been a friend of Lucy's.

Let me know when you hear from the Presiding Elder.

Your loving sister,

Maggie

The week of Maggie's wedding finally arrived. She kept Sanford busy picking up people from the train in Marshall, including the Presiding Elder who would perform the ceremony. The day before the wedding, he had to go to town to meet the last guests to arrive for the big day. He took Mary along on a last-minute shopping trip and dropped her off at the general store while he headed for the station.

When the train arrived, Sanford looked for familiar faces. There. There they were. Her dearest girlfriends... and Lucy's friend, Susan Haynes.

Removing his hat and bowing low, Sanford said, "Welcome to the Oklahoma Territory, ladies. Your coach awaits."

He showed them to his wagon and then carried their luggage from the train. Loading the last valise, he snuck a glance at Susan as she chatted with the other ladies. Her black bonnet framed her large blue eyes and slender face. She looked even better than the last time he saw her. A slight scent of lilac drifted in the early spring air.

Stopping by the general store, he picked up Mary and on the way to the hotel he asked, "Anyone smell lilacs?"

Mary answered. "Now? Don't be silly. You know the lilacs aren't blooming yet."

The wedding went as planned. Sanford couldn't believe his little sister was getting married... and in Oklahoma within twenty miles of his place. Maybe if he waited long enough, his whole family would come down here.

The next day the newlyweds held a reception, called an infare, at their home. The party lasted all day. Everyone brought food. There were mounds of fried chicken, biscuits and gravy, whole hams, mashed potatoes and more pies and cakes than you could shake a stick at.

Along towards evening, Mary and H.W. took Sanford's children home with them for the night. Charlie North brought his fiddle. Everyone enjoyed square dancing and Irish jigs. Charlie played till his fingers went numb.

At one point, Sanford ended up square dancing with Susan as his partner. He watched her as she wove her way around the square and back to him. It felt good to have a woman's hand in his again. He wondered if she felt the same.

Finally, Charlie announced, "Folks, my fingers is plumb tuckered out. They's done for the day. Sanford and Susan sat down outside for a drink of water.

"This dancing is a lot of work," Susan said as she sipped her water.

"I'm kind of glad Charlie's fingers wore out. I needed a rest."

"Nice breeze out tonight."

"Yep."

He was attracted to how the tree's shadow played across her face in the full moonlight. Was he staring at her? He took a drink and forced his eyes on the glass. Before he knew it, his eyes were on her face again. Sanford wasn't sure if it was from all that dancing or what, but he felt a little lightheaded and his hands shook slightly. He held onto his glass with both hands and rested his elbows on his knees. Hopefully, she didn't notice his shaking.

The following day, he bid Susan and the other guests good-bye at the train.

As she boarded, Sanford handed her the small bag she intended to carry with her on the train.

"Oh, thank you, Sanford. Wouldn't do to forget my sewing, now would it? I've got to have the next bride's things done in a week."

"Are you the one who made Maggie's dress?"

"Sure did. That's how I keep body and soul together these days."

"Looked nice on her. You did a good job."

"Thanks."

He wanted to ask if he could write her, but the words wouldn't come. All he could say was, "Have a good trip."

Susan smiled and said "Thank you, Sanford. Give your daughter a hug for me. She's a little sweetheart."

"Sure enough."

He watched the train pull out as he kicked himself for not asking permission to write, but then again, maybe it was too soon after Tom's death. "Don't want to appear too forward," he muttered to himself. "Wish I knew if she was ready to move on." A terrible thought struck him. What if someone had their eye on her in Winston... or even Tipton?

CHAPTER 28

April 2, 1892 - Wrote a letter to Missouri.

It took Sanford a month to decide what he wanted to say to Susan in a letter. He didn't want to appear too forward or anxious, and yet, he wanted to let her know he would sincerely like to write her. From watching others in his situation, he decided hunting a wife was a little like deer hunting. Any fast moves and they would likely take off like a shot.

Finally, one night after the children were asleep, he tore a piece of paper from his ledger book that served as his diary and wrote,

April 2, 1892
Dear Susan,
I am writing for permission to write to you. Please do not take offense, but I wondered if you might be interested in a deeper friendship.
I await your reply.
Sincerely,
Sanford Deering

He sat back and looked at it in the lantern light. There it was in black and white; penned by his own hand. His stomach turned over as he carefully folded it and slipped into an envelope.

In his best penmanship, he wrote "Susan Haynes, Winston, Missouri," on the envelope. He sealed it quickly and put it in his jacket pocket. He must remember to mail it in the morning when he went to town.

***

It was Albert's birthday, June 14. He was three years old already. It seemed like only yesterday when that little scamp was born, just before Sanford left to stake his claim on this land. On the other hand, it seemed like an eternity since Sanford held a woman in his arms. In reality, Lucy had only been gone a year and a half; actually, two years since he last held her.

Susan hadn't written back and he had about given up that she would. He thought of the nice little house she now occupied in Missouri. Maybe she was too comfortable there, or thought him too forward. Perhaps she had found another suitor.

There were some widows around in the Territory, but they probably wouldn't want to give up their homestead to marry him. A few spinsters were about, but who would be interested in taking on three children and a husband and give up their claim?

He entertained the thought of putting an ad in the Kansas City newspaper for a mail-order bride, but thought better of it. Perhaps God's answer was a flat "No" to his request for a wife.

Sanford headed into town with the children. Nora held Freddie on her lap in the back of the wagon. He was quiet... too quiet for almost two years old; too small, too. Most of the time in the bright sunlight Freddie fell asleep. The light seemed to hurt his eyes. Albert sat on the seat next to his dad.

The main mission today was to check on the price of a threshing machine. Before he and the children left town, they stopped off at the post office to check on the mail.

"You all stay in the wagon. I'll just be a minute. Albert, behave yourself, you hear?"

Albert nodded his head.

"Nora, you keep an eye on your brothers."

"Yes, Daddy."

H.W. didn't have any mail, but Sanford's box contained one letter. He pulled it out quickly. The return address had Susan's name on it. The postmistress eyed him.

"Get some mail, Mr. Deering?" she said with a smile.

He could feel a flush creeping up his neck and on to his cheeks. He shoved the letter in his overall pocket and tipped his straw hat. "Good-day, Mrs. Jones."

All the way home, he wanted to open the letter in the worst way, but didn't dare. Not much got by Nora, even though she was almost five. She was about as nosey as the postmistress.

After what seemed like an eternal ride home, he found a private spot behind the sawmill to read his letter. He opened it with shaking hands.

June 9, 1892
Dear Sanford,

Thank you for your letter. I did not feel it proper to write to you before the anniversary of Tom's death.

After careful consideration of your request, I would like to respond favorably to your invitation to correspond and look forward to your next letter.

Sincerely,
Susan Haynes

Sanford felt weak in the knees and had to sit on the edge of the steam engine. He read the letter over and over, looking for any hidden meanings, any hint of rejection. When he was sure there were none, he let out a big sigh. A wide grin spread across his face. It stuck there as if it were plastered on with cobbler's glue.

Lucy came out to the sawmill. "Papa. Where you been? Couldn't find you."

He quickly shoved the letter into his pants pocket and tried to wipe the smile off his face. "Oh? I've been here all the time. Didn't hear you call." He could feel the grin coming on again.

"What did you put in your pocket, Papa?"

He clenched his hand around the letter. "Oh, uh... uh... just a letter, short stuff."

"Who's it from?"

"A friend."

"Who, Papa?"

"Well, er... I... well," he cleared his throat and continued, "I... it's a lady friend. You probably don't know her, short stuff. A lady back in Missouri."

"Did she come to Aunt Maggie's wedding?"

"Well, yes... yes, as a matter of fact she did come to the wedding." Sanford cleared his throat again. This was worse than being drilled by his mama the time he took a potshot at the chickens with his slingshot.

Nora's eyes lit up. "Was it Susan?"

"Susan who?"

"Mama's friend." Nora climbed into his lap.

"You know Susan?" Sanford asked, trying to suppress his grin again.

"Uh, huh. I asked her if she would marry us at Aunt Maggie's wedding."

Sanford was dumbstruck. Finally he squeaked, "You what?"

"I asked her to marry us. She laughed and said she'd think about it. She has pretty eyes."

Sanford was overcome with laughter. Here he had tried to be so cautious and proceed at just the right pace, and short stuff was miles ahead of him.

"What's so funny, Papa?"

"Oh, nothing, short stuff."

He gave her a big hug.

***

Just after the 4th of July celebration in Mulhall, Sanford made a trip into town to order a J.I. Case Threshing Machine. This year, *he* would be the one to call on for wheat threshing. The steam engine he used for the sawmill would provide the power for the threshing machine, and he was in business. Letters to Susan were sporadic, at best. Writing was something Lucy always did, not Sanford.

Before threshing season began, he stayed at H.W.'s so he could see the children at supper. There was little time to correspond or run the sawmill. His daddy always said "Make hay while the sun shines," and that's exactly what he was doing.

Sanford didn't remember Nora's fifth birthday in August until a week after the fact. He worked in the harvest fields from sun up to sun down and didn't go home to sleep or eat, just camped out in the field by the machine.

After the last of the grain had been threshed, Sanford came to dinner at H.W.'s.

Mary was quieter than usual.

"You feeling all right?" Sanford asked as he washed up before dinner.

She sighed as she put the pork chops on the table. "I've felt better."

"Headaches again?"

She turned away and said, "No... yes. Well, the headaches aren't the problem." She took a deep breath, let it out slowly, and put her hands on her hips. She looked at him for a long moment. "Sanford, I don't know how to say this, but I just can't watch the children anymore. I feel I'm getting too old for keeping such small ones. Breaks my heart to not help you out. I love these little ones so."

Sanford wiped his handlebar moustache on the towel, looked out at Nora and Albert playing tag in the yard, and then back at Mary. "Is it something they did?"

"Nope. I just can't keep up with them anymore. The baby needs more care than I can give him. You need a woman." She turned and bustled out of the room.

Sanford looked over at H.W. washing his hands at the dry sink.

"You feel this way too, H.W.?"

He picked up the towel and dried each finger, one at a time. Finally, he answered, "It's coming up on two years, Sanford. A man can't raise young ones in this country without a woman's help, and my woman's about Mama'd out."

That night Sanford slept a few minutes, awoke, prayed, and fell back into a fitful sleep, over and over. At dawn, he knew what he needed to do–ask his sister-in-law, Anna if she would watch the children.

Sanford found Frank working in his blacksmith shop. He puffed the bellows to increase the heat on the horseshoe in the hot fire.

"Frank, how are things?"

"Busier than I want to be. Seems like somebody's got something broke all the time." He glanced up at Sanford. "Look like you got the weight of the world on your shoulders."

"I do, in a way. Do you think Anna could help me out some with the little ones?"

"I don't know. You'll have to ask her. You know how nervous she is."

"I'm kind of in a fix; Mary feels she can't watch them anymore."

Frank picked up a hammer, and pulled the red-hot horseshoe from the fire and gave it a few good whacks on the anvil.

Anna came into the blacksmith shop wiping her hands on her apron. She pulled her shawl more tightly around her shoulders against an unseasonal chill in the air, and moved toward the fire. “Hi, Sanford. Thought I saw your horse out there. How you been?”

“I’ve been better. I’ve come to ask if you could give me some help with my little ones some.”

Her smile melted into a frown. “Oh, I... I, don’t know that I could handle all of them.”

He whispered a quick prayer. “Help, Lord.”

Sanford jumped in quickly, “Nora’s a big help. She’s as good as a ten year old, and twice as smart.”

Anna sat on a bale of hay. After a long pause, she shrugged and said, ”I could give it a try. Lord knows, I could use some extra help in the kitchen.”

Sanford’s smile made his moustache appear as if it went ear to ear. “Thank you kindly, Anna.”

On the way home, he sang a happy little song to the Lord he made up, to the tune of “Turkey in the Straw.”

Later that week while he chopped wood, Sanford caught H.W. out of the corner of his eye.

“How you been?” Sanford asked as he put down his ax, and wiped his forehead with his shirt sleeve.”

“All right. I’m just worried about Mary.”

“Headaches?”

“Yeah. Getting worse. Some days she doesn’t even want to get out of bed.”

“That’s not like her.”

“For sure. Doc’s about give up on her. I think he’s tried about every kind of remedy he knows. Figured I’ll take her back to Missouri for a while. Maybe that’ll perk her up.”

“I’ll be glad to tend to your stock while you’re gone. Going to take Orris and Hanna out of school?”

“Think I’ll leave them here with Anna if she’ll hear of it. I don’t know if Mary’ll go along with it, but that’s my plan.”

“Be glad to help any way I can.”

“Much obliged.”

***

On the second anniversary of Lucy's death in December, Sanford accepted an invitation from his sister, Maggie, and George, who invited him and the children to stay overnight at their house near Marshall. On the way, he and the children sang Christmas songs and hymns while the wagon bounced over the miles of ice-packed snow. When they arrived, he was pleasantly surprised to discover his sister was in a family way.

"So when does the little one arrive?" Sanford asked over dinner.

"Early February." Both Maggie and George beamed.

"Guess there's no chance of one of the town gossips calling you an old maid now, is there?" Sanford winked at George.

"Not a chance," Maggie blushed and smiled.

***

Mary and H.W. took their trip to Missouri and left Orris and Hanna with their Aunt Anna. They were back by Christmas. Mary was able to have her traditional gathering for the holiday, and she actually looked better than Sanford had seen her in a long time. She reported her sick headaches "eased a heap" while she was there.

Sanford missed Lucy worse this year than the year before, if that were possible. Unable to be in the fields, he wrote Susan more frequently, in an attempt to force himself to focus on his future, rather than his past.

Rather than send the children to Anna's, he kept them at home through the winter. He would need more help in the spring and summer than now.

Finally, in February, he felt it was time to ask Susan to marry him.

He wrote:

February 10, 1893

Dear Susan,

I want to ask you this in person, but it isn't possible at this time as I cannot leave the children.

I would like to ask for your hand in marriage. I know this sod home is not as nice as the one you have in Missouri, but I would appreciate your consideration of my offer.

If you agree, I will do my best to make you a good husband.

Awaiting your reply,

Sanford

P.S. Maggie had a baby girl last week. Named her Beulah.

He didn't have long to wait. Her reply came within the week. Frankie was sick again and Sanford went to town for yet another bottle of medicine. Mary came to watch the children. She said she needed to "get some grandbaby dust on her," adding she sure missed them while she was in Missouri.

With shaking hands, he pulled the letter out of the post box. Thankfully, the postmistress was busy with a customer. Ducking in behind the post office, he ripped the envelope open in the cold winter wind while he whispered, "Please, God." He could hardly breathe as his eyes darted across her lovely penmanship.

February 15, 1893

Dear Sanford,

I would be pleased to accept your proposal of marriage. Although this is a lovely home, I am tired of living alone.

I feel it is best to sell my place here in Missouri before I come to the Territory. Then I would have no unfinished business here. I trust this is satisfactory with you.

Give Maggie a hug for me. And the children, too.

Looking forward to seeing you again.

Sincerely,

Susan

Sanford was overwhelmed. He didn't know if he should laugh or cry. "Just wait till I get home and share his news with my little matchmaker," he whispered. "As nice as Susan's place is, it shouldn't take long to find a someone to buy it."

***

The months dragged on, one into another without a suitable buyer.

One day in late August, Anna came to the field where Sanford was threshing. She got off her horse and began, "Sanford, I just can't abide your little Albert much longer. He is always into something."

Sanford cut the power to the machine. He waited for the noise to die down, took Anna's arm and walked her over to a shade tree, wiping the sweat off his forehead and neck with his bandana. "What seems to be the problem, Anna?"

"It's Albert. I just can't handle him. If he's not teasing that poor baby, he's running off somewhere. Today, he got into the cornfield and got lost. We couldn't find him for hours." She fanned herself with the hem of her apron. "I'm just not up to such. We're gonna have to do something different."

That night, Sanford wrote another letter to Susan inquiring about the progress on the sale of her place.

She responded within the week:

September 5, 1893
Dear Sanford,

I have a Mr. Pearson interested in buying my place. He wants me to finance the mortgage, rather than going through a bank. I am considering his offer. He plans to pay a down payment of $50.00 now and 1/3 of the balance due each year in October.

I think it's a good offer and am going to tell him I agree to his terms. To wait any longer seems pointless.

Sincerely,
Susan

He replied:

September 19, 1893
Dear Susan,

As anxious as I am to have you here, I don't feel this is a good idea. If the banks won't loan him the money, there must be some risk.

I would advise against it, but the final decision is up to you.

Sincerely,
Sanford

Susan answered by return mail:

September 30, 1893
Dear Sanford,

By the time I received your letter, I had already agreed to the sale. We are to sign papers on October 15. I can be down to the Territory by November first, if that meets with your approval.

Sincerely,
Susan

"So be it," he breathed. "Hope this fella works out. I'll have to contact the Presiding Elder to see when he'll be around this end of his circuit to perform a wedding."

CHAPTER 29

September 19, 1894 - Applied for a patent in Guthrie today.

Susan finished her business in Missouri, and arrived in Mulhall on the sixth of November. Sanford got her a room at the hotel. He had been reading his Bible and wanted to have "no appearance of evil" for the town gossips to use.

The Presiding Elder came in on the train on the seventh, and performed the wedding in the hotel lobby on the eighth.

When he finished the last "Amen" Nora ran to her new mother and asked, "Are we married now?"

Susan knelt down and wrapped her in a bear hug. "Yes, Sugar. We're married now." Susan drew out a small box from her blue velvet drawstring purse. "I brought you something."

Nora's sparkling eyes widened. "What is it?"

"Open it and see."

Inside was a small gold heart necklace.

"Ohhhhh. It's beautiful."

"Be very careful with it, Nora. It was given to me when I was just your age by my mama."

"Oh, I will. I will." Nora felt the locket while Susan knelt to latch it around her neck.

She turned and hugged Susan. "Thank you, Mama," she whispered.

Susan's eyes filled with tears. It had been so long since her own little girl had called her Mama. She looked up into Sanford face as he mouthed, "Thank you." Susan thought she saw his eyes misting, too.

After the guests enjoyed cookies and punch, Anna announced, "Come, children, Uncle Frank and I are taking you home for the night."

Nora protested with a flood of tears. "But Aunt Anna! We just got married. I thought we got to stay with our new mama!"

"Not tonight, my dear," she said. Before Nora could appeal to her dad, Anna took Nora's hand in a firm grip and marched her to the wagon, despite her protests.

Sanford and Susan spent their first night as man and wife in the hotel, away from the curious eyes of their too-old-for-her-britches six-year-old and her brothers, now four and almost three. They enjoyed their new marital status to the highest degree.

***

Susan had a baptism by fire that first winter in her new home. Freddie was sick from the first of December on through planting season. She hardly had the opportunity to stick her nose out the door.

Sanford was true to his word. He looked for opportunities to help her and make her feel welcome in her new home.

"Charlie tells me Clementine is having a quilting bee on Wednesday. Want to go?"

She shook her head. "Doubt Freddie should be out in this cold."

"I'll stay home and watch the children. You go. You need to have some neighbor time."

She looked up from rolling her pie dough, smiled, and wiped her hands on her apron. "Sanford, you are such a wonderful husband."

"I know that closed-in feeling with Freddie sick all the time. I wish it were different."

"Maybe one day he'll be well."

"One day..."

***

Mary and H.W. came over occasionally. Mary's headaches plagued her worse than ever. One Sunday, they came to

Sanford's for dinner. Albert took Freddie's favorite blanket, and Freddie protested with a shrill shriek.

"Mary, will you please stir this soup while I deal with those two?"

When Susan came back to the kitchen, she found Mary in tears.

"You all right?" Susan said as she put her hand on her shoulder.

Mary shook her head. "Just can't take loud noises when I'm having a sick headache."

Susan made her some tea and tried her best to keep the children quiet. After their guests left, Susan remarked, "Do you think Mary looks older than when I got here?"

"Older?" Sanford said.

"Her face seems so wrinkled... drawn. Looks like she's not as fleshy either. Think she's losing weight?"

"Now that you mention it, she does look skinnier. She looked better after they got back from Missouri last year. According to H.W., Doc doesn't think he can do any more for her."

"We need to be sure and remember her in our prayers."

"For sure."

***

During the summer of '94, Sanford was busier than ever with his threshing machine. Susan began to wonder if he had abandoned her and the children altogether.

At dusk one night Sanford came home dirty, tired, and hungry. She heated water in the large teakettle on the stove, fried some potatoes and warmed the beans. Pulling the galvanized tub off the nail outside the house, she drug it into the center of the kitchen floor. It took several buckets of water to get a few inches in the bottom. Afterward she poured one teakettle of hot water into the tub and set another on the stove to boil. Sanford ate his supper while she bedded the children.

Susan watched him take off his clothes as she poured out the second load of hot water. "Sanford, you're working too hard. You're just skin and bones."

He eased himself into the tub. "Got to get this harvest over so I can send in my papers to prove up my claim. I can't believe it's been five years."

Susan set another kettle of water on the stove. "You've put a lot of sweat and tears in this place." she said as she took the bar of lye soap and scrubbed his back.

"We ought to be sitting pretty come this fall, once I get all my collecting done from the threshing machine."

"That payment on my farm ought to be coming soon too."

She poured in another load of hot water.

Sanford sighed and closed his eyes. "You know, there were times I never thought I'd make it here. The goal seemed too far to grasp."

She took his face in her hands and smiled. "I'm so proud of you. You did what you set out to do."

For a long moment he feasted his eyes on this beautiful woman God had given him as a helper in place of Lucy. He drew her to himself. The lantern gave a soft glow to the room.

Nora turned over in bed and for a brief moment, beheld her new mother and her dad in this tender moment before her eyelids dropped in sleep again. She snuggled down in her bed. All was right with her world.

***

Later in September, Sanford and Susan took the children on the train to Guthrie to apply for a patent on their homestead. The description read:

"The South East quarter of Section eleven in Township eighteen, North of Range three West of Indian Meridian in Oklahoma Territory containing one hundred and sixty acres."

Sanford gave the clerk four silver dollars for the filing fee.

"Congratulations, sir. All the best to you."

"It was a struggle, but we made it."

Sanford turned and winked at Susan, as he put his change purse in the pocket of his overalls. "One more step and it's ours. All we need now is the President's signature on a piece of paper."

Finally, in early November, the long-awaited letter arrived. Application #4439 showed that on the 29 day of October, 1894,

President Grover Cleveland signed the patent on their application. The claim was finally theirs.

Sanford came in from town at suppertime.

"You look like a man about to bust his buttons, my love," Susan said.

He reached into his coat and pulled the letter out of his shirt pocket. "Do you suppose I could frame this and hang it on our wall?" he said as he handed it to her.

Susan opened the letter and read the contents. Her eyes shone. She looked up at Sanford and threw her arms around his neck. "Oh, Sanford! You've done it! Where shall we hang it?"

"How about beside the door?"

"Perfect!"

Sanford was not only the proud owner of 160 acres, but also a sawmill, a steam engine, and a threshing machine. The peach orchard had survived and actually produced fruit, just like Mr. Mosby's in Winston. His dream was finally a reality. Oh how Lucy would have loved to see this day!

***

The next year in early September, Freddie was sick with a low-grade fever... again. Despite the many bottles of "sure cures" from Doc McPeek, nothing seem to worked.

One day in early September, Susan took him into town for yet another doctor visit. He drew her aside and said in a low voice, "Susan, I'm at a loss to know what more to do for this little lad. The more medication we give him, the sicker he gets."

Susan agreed. "He's never had a good color to him, ever since I've known him."

"I think his mother's steady diet of turnips may have something to do with his condition. I've seen other children born that same year. None of them fared well. Ninety was just a bad year for babies around these parts."

"What can we do?"

"I'm afraid I can't do any more for him."

Susan went home that afternoon determined to find a solution for him. She prayed, "Father God, help our little Freddie. He's so pale and sickly. I don't know that he's had a well day in his life. Please send your healing for him."

Sanford came home that night, and Susan gave him the doctor's diagnosis. He went over to Freddie's bed and kissed him goodnight. He slept soundly.

The next morning, Freddie was gone. He had slipped away in the night.

Before Sanford went out to the sawmill to make him a coffin, he sat beside his bed for a long time holding his hand. Tears streamed down his face.

Nora quietly stood by her papa's arm and looked into her little brother's face. "Why'd he have to go Papa?" She put her hand on Sanford's shoulder.

He put his arm around her and drew her close. "Don't know, short stuff. There's just no forever in this life."

"I'm gonna miss him."

"Me too. We'll just have to wait till we see him in heaven."

They buried him beside Lucy in the Mulhall Cemetery. Friends and neighbors gathered at the gravesite. Sanford read Jesus' promise from the Bible out of John 14 that said Jesus left to prepare a place for us. Sanford paused and pointed out that this promise was to those who would put their faith and trust in Jesus. Then he read the 23rd Psalm and said a prayer.

A couple of the men went to the wagon and brought shovels. An unusual fall rain shower peppered the little group while the men shoveled dirt into the hole. When they finished, the storm was gone as fast as it had come.

Susan turned to get in the wagon and looked back to the east. "Look, Sanford. A double rainbow."

He nodded. "At last, this brave little soldier's at rest." It was then that Sanford realized he hadn't been to this place since he set the gravestone and marked out the corners on Lucy's grave. "He's with his Mama in heaven, now, God rest his soul."

***

In the spring of 1895, Susan's yearly payment due the previous October had still not arrived from Mr. Pearson, despite repeated letters from both her and Sanford.

In June, Sanford came from town with a letter from Sam Youtsey.

"Susan, I think we need to start foreclosure proceedings on Mr. Pearson."

"Why? I hate to do that to him. He was such a nice man. Said he was bringing his family out from back East."

Sanford tossed the letter on the table. "Sam says Mr. Pearson didn't plant a crop last year. There's no way he'll ever be able to pay you. He's just cheating you."

"Maybe he has some other kind of business."

Sanford looked at his kind-hearted woman. She trusted everyone, even the scoundrels. Finally he said, "Susan, we need to think this through. We can't just let the land lie fallow."

"I don't want to rent it out, Sanford. We're too far away to keep any oversight on it."

"I don't know what else you'll do with it."

Susan didn't say anything while she looked at her hands in her lap.

"What are you thinking about, my dear?"

She cocked her head sideways and said, "Oh, nothing."

"Come on, out with it."

"Well... its just... um... I'm trying to think of some other solution."

"Like what?"

She started to speak and then closed her mouth and looked into Sanford's eyes. How could she tell him what was in her heart?

"I can hear the wheels turning, woman. Just tell me."

Her lips struggled to say the words in her mind. They came out in a barely audible whisper. "Sometimes... I miss Missouri." She stood and quickly put her hand on his arm and drew closer to him. "I mean... I love it here with you... I... I just miss... the lush green countryside... and the big trees, that's all."

Sanford turned to look out the window. The thought of leaving his own piece of Oklahoma Territory made his heart heavy. That was the last thing in the world he wanted to do. He'd put almost six years into this place. The thought of giving it up had been his worst nightmare before he proved up his claim. Now that he had legal rights to it, he had no intention of selling it and going back to Missouri.

"I'm sorry, Sanford. I didn't mean to..."

The rest of her words were lost as his mind churned. "I've got to go think this thing out." He strode out, mounted his horse, and rode toward town.

The sun cast long shadows on the landscape, before Sanford and his mount rode up on the back side of the cemetery. He circled around and went in the front gate, slid off his horse and knelt at Lucy's grave. "I don't want to go back, Lucy. Not after all it cost me."

He thought about the day he staked his claim and the day he brought Lucy and the children to the Territory. It seemed like a hundred years ago now.

Night enfolded him. Words formed in his mind; words not of his own choosing. "Lord, is this what you want us to do? Move back to Susan's place? I don't want to be a stubborn Missouri mule. I want to be where you want us to be. Wherever that is, make it right with my heart. I've had a belly full of doing things my way." There. He'd said it out loud. God was just going to have to show him what to do.

When he rode into the yard it was dark. He could see Susan reading at the table by the light of the kerosene lamp. The children, tucked in long ago.

She studied his face when he came in the door, trying to read his thoughts.

As he put his hand on her shoulder he said, "We'll pray on it. Then we'll have a better idea of what to do."

She took Sanford's hand and put it to her cheek. "That we will, my dear husband."

CHAPTER 30

September 21, 1896 - Got a telegram from Nellie.

With each passing month, there was still no word from Susan's buyer, Mr. Pearson, even though Sanford wrote more letters of inquiry. But the whole matter was less of a priority than the sawmill and the numerous threshing jobs that came Sanford's way.

Susan had about given up on ever hearing from her buyer. Then one Saturday when she and Sanford were in town, they found a letter from him in their box. She opened it and read it aloud to Sanford.

October 16, 1895
Dear Mr. Deering,

Sorry you have not heard from me. My wife has never made it to Missouri yet. She has been gravely ill and I had to go back east to tend to her. I still wish to buy the property, but as yet have not had the opportunity to plant any crops, thus I have no money to make the payment we agreed to. Please advise.

Thank you for your indulgence in this matter.
Sincerely,
Phineas T. Pearson

"Well, isn't this a surprise." Sanford sighed. He was sad for what Mr. Pearson was going through, but also relieved. Now they wouldn't have to go back to Missouri, after all.

"Surprise indeed," Susan whispered.

"Guess this is our answer from the Lord."

She nodded slowly. "Guess so."

Sanford heard no more that winter from Mr. Pearson. No check. No correspondence. He also heard no more from Susan on the matter, although at times she did seem rather depressed when a random conversation turned to the subject of Missouri.

It was a wet winter–a good sign for spring crops. Sanford built a shed around the sawmill so he could work even in bad weather. Between the sawmill and farming, there was plenty of work to do. Seven-year-old Albert enjoyed farming like his uncle Orris. The saw frightened him so he stayed away from it whenever possible.

Another letter came from Mr. Pearson in July.

July 5, 1896

Dear Mr. Deering,

The doctor has informed me I must not try to move my wife to Missouri. He says the trip would be her undoing.

As bad as I hate to, I must break our agreement to buy the farm. I will thereby forfeit the $50.00 paid for the down payment.

Thank you for your patience in this matter.

Sincerely,

Phineas T. Pearson

Sanford put down the letter. "I don't have time to deal with this now. We'll have to make a trip up there this fall."

Susan nodded. Perhaps they could find another buyer when they were there in person.

***

In September of that year, Susan went to town to trade the eggs for flour and to buy some gingham to make a dress for Nora's birthday. She checked the mail. There was a notice to pick up a telegram. It was addressed to Sanford so she shoved it in her pocket and headed for home.

When she got there, Albert and Nora helped her with the packages. A stranger rode into the yard.

"Howdy, ma'am. Might Miz Lucy be about?"

"I'm Mrs. Deering. And you are...?"

"Thomas, ma'am." He took off his hat and scratched his head. "I'm kinda confused. See, I helped Mr. and Miz Deering build this place back in '89, but you don't look like Miz Deering."

"She died in '90. I'm Susan, Sanford's new wife."

He scrambled from his horse and crumpled his hat in his hands. "Oh, I'm sorry, ma'am. My condolences."

Nora came out of the house and eyed him curiously.

"This can't be little Nora."

She nodded her head.

"Girl, you growed up some since I saw you last. Where's Albert?"

"Inside. How do you know me?" Nora said as she stepped closer to Susan.

"I helped your papa and mama build this here sod house. Then I moved on to Texas."

Just then Sanford rode up. He squinted at the stranger and said, "Do my eyes deceive me? Is that you, Thomas?"

"The same, Mr. Sanford."

"Sanford jumped down from his horse and slapped Thomas on the back. "Well, you old tumbleweed, you. Where you been keeping yourself?"

"Down in Texas, mostly. Thought I'd mosey up this way for a spell. Oklahoma sure has changed since I left. Got downright city-fied."

"Well, we've put a little elbow grease into her here and there."

"Will you stay to supper?"

"Much obliged. Ain't 'et since Guthrie."

"You men get washed up. I'll get some supper on the table." Susan hustled Nora into the house. "Nora, you cut some bread and I'll put some ham on to fry. Albert, you feed the chickens and gather the eggs. We'll be needing some more of them for supper."

Susan almost forgot the telegram. "Oh, here Nora, run this out to your papa while I peel the potatoes. Must be something important."

She set the water on to boil and selected several potatoes to peel. Sanford shuffled into the kitchen and slumped into a chair with a blank look on his face. Thomas followed and stood in the doorway. Her husband held out the telegram to her.

"Sam," was all he said.

She wiped her hands on her apron and took the telegram.

SAM DEAD STOP
COME BUY THE SAWMILL AND FARM STOP
MOVING TO LEXINGTON STOP
NELLIE

Susan stood in stunned silence. How could they buy the sawmill? They had one here. They had land they couldn't get payment on in Missouri already. How would all this work out? She knew Sanford's thoughts about moving back. Suddenly, they had too many places to be, and not enough people to go around. What if Nellie wanted too much for her place? The questions swam in her head like a school of minnows, darting this way and that.

She glanced at Sanford. He had the strangest expression on his face. Shock. Disbelief. Utter confusion.

They ate their supper in almost total silence, except when Sanford asked for the salt. He did have the presence of mind to invite Thomas to spend the night. Rather than intrude on his hosts, he slept in the shed with the animals.

At breakfast, Thomas had a suggestion.

"Mr. Sanford, I been thinking. If you're of a mind to go back to Missouri for a spell, I could run things here for ya till you get back."

"If I go back to Missouri, it won't be alone. Last time I did that I missed my family too much. Besides, don't want to interrupt your plans, Thomas."

"I don't have no plans. I just go where my nose takes me."

Sanford sipped his coffee. "Well, I'll give it some thought. Thanks for the offer."

"I'll be around town, if ya need me."

He nodded.

Later that day, Sanford paid a visit to H.W. He always had good advice. Perhaps he could shed some light on this situation.

"What's on your mind, My boy?"

Without a word, Sanford pulled the telegram out of his pocket and handed it to H.W.

He read it and said, "Well, I'll be. What are you going to do about it?"

"Don't know. Thought maybe we could talk it out some."

They sat down on a big rock and weighed the pros and cons.

"We've been having a real set-to over here these last few weeks," H.W. finally admitted.

"About what?"

"Looks like Orris has his mind set on going further west. Hanna'll be grown and out of the house soon. She's kind of sweet on Doc McPeek's grandson. The way he looks at her wouldn't surprise me if he'll be around soon to ask for her hand. Mary's decided I'm too old to keep up this place alone. She wants to move into Mulhall."

"And leave your claim?"

"I told her I'd as soon move back to Missouri before I'd move into town. But she won't hear of that. No siree. Says she'd miss your kids too much." H.W. shifted his bony bottom on the rock.

"You all could come for visits."

"I already suggested that. She won't hear of it."

"You'd think she'd want to go to back to Missouri. She was free of her headaches when she was there."

The two sat there for a long time in silence.

Sanford rubbed his chin as he thought. Finally he said, "This news about Sam changes things."

H.W. leaned back and looked at Sanford. "How? You figgering on buying Sam's sawmill?"

"Maybe."

"Reckon we could find buyers for our places here?

"Don't see why not."

"Mary might be of a mind to go if you all went."

"You could move onto Susan's old place. I'd help you farm it. Want to put the word out and see if we have any takers?"

H.W.'s face brightened. "Let's give it a whirl. Got nothing to lose, my boy."

On the way home, Sanford watched for the landmarks so familiar to him now; over the ridge to Frank's blacksmith shop, down to the stand of trees by the stream and then up the hill to home. He would hate to leave this country, but maybe their time had run out here. Perhaps that *was* the next place to be.

When Sanford got home, he found Susan hanging clothes on the line. He told her about his conversation with H.W.

She listened intently and finished pinning a sheet on the line. "You sure you want to do this?"

Sanford looked down and kicked a clod of dirt with his work boot and shoved his hands in his pockets. "Don't know. Might be God's way of telling us to move on."

"Whatever you decide is fine with me. I know you'll make the right decision," she said as she picked a pillowcase out of the basket and pinned it to the line.

"I guess if someone offers me a fair price, I'd be a fool not to take it. I better wire Nellie and see how much she wants for her place."

***

Nellie wasted no time in sending Sanford a letter detailing the terms of the sale. She offered the sale of the land, the house, and the sawmill for a very reasonable sum. It was a deal "too good to pass up," in Sanford's words. He sent her a telegram that simply said, "Sold."

It didn't take long for the word to circulate around town that the homesteads were for sale. With all the improvements, they were considered a prize to be had.

Sanford came home from town that next Saturday with a big grin on his face. "Well, I did it Susan."

"Did what?"

"Sold this place for $600.00, cash money. Folks want to move in as soon as we can leave."

"What about H.W. and Mary?"

"I overheard two fellas talking at the feed store. They both wanted H.W.'s place. Don't know which one will get it, but they sounded pretty serious."

The next Wednesday, one of the men offered H.W. a very acceptable sum for his place. Charlie North bought the sawmill and the steam engine. H.W.'s buyer bought the threshing machine.

The drifter, Thomas, even hired on to work at the sawmill.

Within a month, the loose ends were tied up and they were at the train station, household goods and all. Frank and Anna were there to see them off. Thomas even happened by.

"Figger you'll ever come this way again, Mr. Sanford?" Thomas asked.

"Doubtful. Then again you never know." Sanford took Nora's hand. "Get up there, girl. Sit by your mama." He turned back to Thomas and shook his hand. "Maybe we'll meet again."

The train gave its final whistle and the conductor called, "Board! All aboard!"

Albert sat nearest the window, next to his grandfather. Sanford climbed the stairs of the passenger car and took one last look at his beloved Oklahoma Territory, tipped his hat to Frank and Anna, and ducked into the car.

As the train blew a last long blast on the whistle, Sanford slid into the wooden seat across from H.W. and squinted into the bright morning sun. Another train pulled in alongside theirs, filled with eager faces, ready to disembark. He nodded his head toward them, grinned at H.W. and said, "We laid the foundations. I wonder what those folks'll build on it?"

Afterword

I have written this book, dear reader, that we may look back and recall the high price paid by those who have gone before us.

These who entered the Oklahoma Territory are like the Israelites of old. Almighty God has an admonishment for us, the descendants of those pioneers.

"Then it shall come about when the Lord your God brings you into the land... to give you great and splendid cities which you did not build... and houses full of all good things... and hewn cisterns which you did not dig... and you shall eat and be satisfied, then watch yourself lest you forget the Lord who brought you.... You shall fear only the Lord your God; and you shall worship Him and swear by His name. You shall not follow other gods... otherwise the anger of the Lord your God will be kindled against you, and He will wipe you off the face of the earth" (Deuteronomy 6:10-15.)

May we never forget.

Sally Jadlow
July 27, 2006

Printed in the United States
58265LVS00008B/91-99

9 780937 66032